Heartland

Cover painting:
Robert Sinclair, *Red Roads in the Sunset*, 1976
83.8 cm tondo
Aquatec stain/raw cotton
Courtesy Wynick-Tuck Gallery
Private collection

Robert Sinclair was born in Saltcoats, Saskatchewan in 1939 and attended the University of Manitoba. He also studied at the University of Iowa where he received a Master of Fine Arts in 1967. Sinclair is well known for his water-colours of plants and landscapes (which he also paints in acrylic on canvas) as well as for his sculptures. At present he lives near Edmonton and teaches at the University of Alberta in the Department of Art and Design.

Heartland

An Anthology of Canadian Stories

EDITED BY KATHERYN MACLEAN BROUGHTON

NELSON CANADA

© Nelson Canada,
A Division of International Thomson Limited, 1983

Published in Canada in 1983 by
Nelson Canada,
A Division of International Thomson Limited
1120 Birchmount Road
Scarborough, Ontario
M1K 5G4

Design: Peggy Heath, Heath and Associates

Printed and bound in Canada

 9 10 11 12 BP 96 95 94 93

Canadian Cataloguing in Publication Data

Main entry under title: —
Heartland

ISBN 0-17-601763-1

1. Short stories, Canadian (English).*   I. Broughton,
Katheryn, 1926-

PS8321.H43   C813'.0108   C83-098034-2
PR9197.32.H43

To Jim for his patience and steadfastness

Contents

Introduction

In the last century, reading fiction was often considered such a sinful waste of time that those who enjoyed novels hid them behind inspirational books or historical volumes rather than exhibit poor taste. Nowadays, while literature is generally recognized as part of our cultural heritage, there are still those who question the value of its study.

"Of what *use* is the study of literature," these people ask. "Surely we should read magazines and newspapers if we wish to find the truth about life. Facts are what we need, not the creation of some writer's imagination."

Ernest Buckler has argued that through an imaginative use of "facts" a writer can make experience more understandable to the reader. "If you don't have facts to start with you don't get anywhere," he explains. "But when you start with a fact, I think you can transfigure it by embellishment, or twists, or perspective of one kind or another, which is *much truer* eventually than the thing as it actually happened."

How does this process work? It may be interesting to try this little exercise. Recall an incident that happened last week, one that was quite interesting but not really exceptional. Jot down the *facts* carefully. Imagine describing the situation to an acquaintance. What happens between the event and the telling of it? You probably omit certain details as irrelevant (or embarrassing); you add small items for dramatic effect; you allow yourself reactions that actually only occurred to you later. Have you noticed what has happened to your experience? It has become a story you want others to remember.

This is exactly the process that Buckler is describing. According to him, the writer takes the essence of the experience and shapes it into a narrative that has more meaning than the original source. The writer's purpose is to enlarge the experience for the reader.

There are various elements in short fiction that enable the writer to create an imaginative world for the reader.

Theme

The short story, because of its length, generally deals with one theme rather than many. It highlights one particular idea or truth about the human condition. The theme usually develops through tension or conflict within the inner being of the main character or between characters in the story. At the conclusion, there is generally a resolution of the situation, and the reader perceives the meaning of the story.

Plot

The ordering of events in the story is called the *plot*. Although the sequence may seem natural and realistic, it is the skill of the storyteller that makes this so. The events, in fact, follow a strict pattern. The plot line of every story generally includes the following elements: an introduction, an inciting event (which starts the action), rising action, climax, falling action, denouement or "unknotting," and conclusion. Sometimes stories conclude just as the reader expects; other times there is a surprise ending which forces the reader to think about the plot and perhaps re-read part of the narrative.

Characters

A skilled writer must be an acute observer of life and often uses personal experiences, friends, and even people seen fleetingly as the basis for characters in a story. This process does not faithfully recapture the original models but produces characters who resemble real people. Somerset Maugham noted why the writer proceeds in this manner:

> People are too elusive, too shadowy, to be copied; and they are also too incoherent and contradictory. The writer does not copy his originals; he takes what he wants from them, a few traits that have caught his attention, a turn of mind that has fired his imagination, and therefrom constructs his character.

The *protagonist* is the main character around whom the plot and theme revolve. He or she reacts to the actions of other characters and behaves according to the dictates of his or her inner being.

7

Sometimes the story is psychological, with the emphasis on the inner turmoil of the protagonist. Other times, a story emphasizes action and the main character's response to external events. The writer of the short story must make the main character believable by creating a situation that readers recognize as having some truth. Even fantasy and science fiction must do this in order that reader interest be sustained.

Other characters play a wide range of roles. There is usually an *antagonist*, a conflicting character or agency in opposition to the protagonist. Often there is a confidant(e), a person to whom the protagonist can reveal dreams and despairs.

Point of View, Atmosphere, Setting

The position from which events in the narrative are observed is called the *point of view*. Writers experience more freedom when they act as narrators because they can be omniscient, that is, all-knowing. When the story is told by one of its characters (the first-person narrator), there is a vivid sense of actuality. The scope, however, is limited by the knowledge of that character.

Atmosphere in a story is the emotional climate readers experience as they read. This aspect of a story develops through imagery and the choice of vocabulary used in describing character, setting, and action. Depending on the story, the reader's emotional response can range from humour to anger to fear. Characters in the story, however, may not share the same emotional reaction. A reader, for example, may experience a great deal of tension when a character unwittingly comes close to danger. The author's skill in creating an atmosphere appropriate to the story will draw the reader into it. The horror story must instil fear; the comedy must cause laughter; the detective story must arouse curiosity; the love story must evoke anxiety, bitter or sweet.

Setting involves two dimensions — time and place. Knowing when a story takes place adds to its effect. For example, if a story takes place in 1942, readers know that most of the world is at war; if the date is 2001, they are immediately aware that they are in the realms of either fantasy or science fiction. Where the story takes place also matters. For example, if the narrative opens in a manor house in England, readers immediately have some idea of what to expect.

Finally, there is the role played by the reader in the creative process — and it is a vital one. Writers need their work to be read. As W. O. Mitchell put it (to his writing students):

> Think of the reader as your creative partner. Make sure your words are triggers or cues which touch off explosions of recognition in them. Connect with them. Ask, did it bridge? did the art experience occur?

In reading a story, *you* complete the "art experience" by entering the world created for you by the writer. The "recognitions" will happen if the story contains valid human experience, and the rewards of the creative reader will be yours.

The Wedding Gift

THOMAS RADDALL

She shook the young man and he wakened with a start, clutching her convulsively.

"Sh-h-h!" she warned. "Something's moving outside."

Nova Scotia, in 1794. Winter. Snow on the ground. Two feet of it in the woods, less by the shore, except in drifts against Port Marriott's barns and fences; but enough to set sleigh bells ringing through the town, enough to require a multitude of paths and burrows from doors to streets, to carpet the wharves and the decks of the shipping, and to trim the ships' yards with tippets of ermine. Enough to require fires roaring in the town's chimneys, and blue wood smoke hanging low over the roof tops in the still December air. Enough to squeal underfoot in the trodden places and to muffle the step everywhere else. Enough for the hunters, whose snow-shoes now could overtake the floundering moose and caribou. Even enough for the always-complaining loggers, whose ox sleds now could haul their cut from every part of the woods. But not enough, not nearly enough snow for Miss Kezia Barnes, who was going to Bristol Creek to marry Mr. Hathaway.

Kezia did not want to marry Mr. Hathaway. Indeed she had told Mr. and Mrs. Barclay in a tearful voice that she didn't want to marry anybody. But Mr. Barclay had taken snuff and said "Ha! Humph!" in the severe tone he used when he was displeased; and Mrs. Barclay had sniffed and said it was a very good match for her, and revolved the cold blue eyes in her fat moon face, and said Kezia must not be a little fool.

There were two ways of going to Bristol Creek. One was by sea, in one of the fishing sloops. But the preacher objected to that. He was a pallid young man lately sent out from England by Lady Huntingdon's Connexion, and seasick five weeks on the way. He held Mr. Barclay in some awe, for Mr. Barclay had the best pew in the meetinghouse and was the chief pillar of godliness in Port

Marriott. But young Mr. Mears was firm on this point. He would go by road, he said, or not at all. Mr. Barclay had retorted "Ha! Humph!" The road was twenty miles of horse path through the woods, now deep in snow. Also the path began at Harper's Farm on the far side of the harbour, and Harper had but one horse.

"I shall walk," declared the preacher calmly, "and the young woman can ride."

Kezia had prayed for snow, storms of snow, to bury the trail and keep anyone from crossing the cape to Bristol Creek. But now they were setting out from Harper's Farm, with Harper's big brown horse, and all Kezia's prayers had gone for naught. Like any anxious lover, busy Mr. Hathaway had sent Black Sam overland on foot to find out what delayed his wedding, and now Sam's day-old tracks marked for Kezia the road to marriage.

She was a meek little thing, as became an orphan brought up as house-help in the Barclay home; but now she looked at the preacher and saw how young and helpless he looked so far from his native Yorkshire, and how ill-clad for this bitter trans-Atlantic weather, and she spoke up.

"You'd better take my shawl, sir. I don't need it. I've got Miss Julia's old riding cloak. And we'll go ride-and-tie."

"Ride and what?" murmured Mr. Mears.

"I'll ride a mile or so, then I'll get down and tie the horse to a tree and walk on. When you come up to the horse, you mount and ride a mile or so, passing me on the way, and you tie him and walk on. Like that. Ride-and-tie, ride-and-tie. The horse gets a rest between."

Young Mr. Mears nodded and took the proffered shawl absently. It was a black thing that matched his sober broadcloth coat and smallclothes, his black woollen stockings, and his round black hat. At Mr. Barclay's suggestion he had borrowed a pair of moose-hide moccasins for the journey. As he walked a prayer-book in his coat-skirts bumped the back of his legs.

At the top of the ridge above Harper's pasture, where the narrow path led off through gloomy hemlock woods, Kezia paused for a last look back across the harbour. In the morning sunlight the white roofs of the little lonely town resembled a tidal wave flung up by the sea and frozen as it broke against the dark pine forest to the west. Kezia sighed, and young Mr. Mears was surprised to see tears in her eyes.

She rode off ahead. The saddle was a man's, of course, awkward to ride modestly, woman-fashion. As soon as she was out of the preacher's sight she rucked her skirts and slid a leg over to the other stirrup. That was better. There was a pleasant sensation of freedom about it, too. For a moment she forgot that she was going to Bristol Creek, in finery second-hand from the Barclay girls, in a new linen shift and drawers that she had sewn herself in the light of the kitchen candles, in white cotton stockings and a bonnet and shoes from Mr. Barclay's store, to marry Mr. Hathaway.

The Barclays had done well for her from the time when, a skinny weeping creature of fourteen, she was taken into the Barclay household and, as Mrs. Barclay so often said, "treated more like one of my own than a bond-girl from the poorhouse." She had first choice of the clothing cast off by Miss Julia and Miss Clara. She was permitted to sit in the same room, and learn what she could, when the schoolmaster came to give private lessons to the Barclay girls. She waited on table, of course, and helped in the kitchen, and made beds, and dusted and scrubbed. But then she had been taught to spin and to sew and to knit. And she was permitted, indeed encouraged, to sit with the Barclays in the meetinghouse, at the convenient end of the pew, where she could worship the Barclays' God and assist with the Barclay wraps at the beginning and end of the service. And now, to complete her rewards, she had been granted the hand of a rejected Barclay suitor.

Mr. Hathaway was Barclay's agent at Bristol Creek, where he sold rum and gunpowder and corn meal and such things to the fishermen and hunters, and bought split cod — fresh, pickled or dry — and ran a small sawmill, and cut and shipped firewood by schooner to Port Marriott, and managed a farm, all for a salary of fifty pounds, Halifax currency, per year. Hathaway was a most capable fellow, Mr. Barclay often acknowledged. But when after fifteen capable years he came seeking a wife, and cast a sheep's eye first at Miss Julia, and then at Miss Clara, Mrs. Barclay observed with a sniff that Hathaway was looking a bit high.

So he was. The older daughter of Port Marriott's most prosperous merchant was even then receiving polite attentions from Mr. Gamage, the new collector of customs, and a connection of the Halifax Gamages, as Mrs. Barclay was fond of pointing out. And Miss Clara was going to Halifax in the spring to learn the gentle art of playing the pianoforte, and incidentally to display her charms to the naval and military young gentlemen who thronged the Halifax drawing-rooms. The dear girls laughed behind their hands whenever long solemn Mr. Hathaway came to town aboard one of the Barclay vessels and called at the big house under the elms. Mrs. Barclay bridled at Hathaway's presumption, but shrewd Mr. Barclay narrowed his little black eyes and took snuff and said "Ha! Humph!"

It was plain to Mr. Barclay that an emergency had arisen. Hathaway was a good man — in his place; and Hathaway must be kept content there, to go on making profit for Mr. Barclay at a cost of only £50 a year. 'Twas a pity Hathaway couldn't satisfy himself with one of the fishermen's girls at the Creek, but there 'twas. If Hathaway had set his mind on a town miss, then a town miss he must have; but she must be the right kind, the sort who would content herself and Hathaway at Bristol Creek and not go nagging the man to remove and try his capabilities elsewhere. At once Mr. Barclay thought of Kezia — dear little Kezzie. A colourless little creature but quiet and well-mannered and pious, and only twenty-two.

Mr. Hathaway was nearly forty and far from handsome, and he had a rather cold, seeking way about him — useful in business of course — that rubbed women the wrong way. Privately Mr. Barclay thought Hathaway lucky to get Kezia. But it was a nice match for the girl, better than anything she could have expected. He impressed that upon her and introduced the suitor from Bristol Creek. Mr. Hathaway spent two or three evenings courting Kezia in the kitchen — Kezia in a quite good gown of Miss Clara's, gazing out at the November moon on the snow, murmuring now and again in the tones of someone in a rather dismal trance, while the kitchen help listened behind one door and the Barclay girls giggled behind another.

The decision, reached mainly by the Barclays, was that Mr. Hathaway should come to Port Marriott aboard the packet schooner on December twenty-third, to be married in the Barclay parlour and then take his bride home for Christmas. But an unforeseen circumstance had changed all this. The circumstance was a ship, "from Mogador in Barbary" as Mr. Barclay wrote afterwards in the salvage claim, driven off her course by gales and wrecked at the very entrance to Bristol Creek. She was a valuable wreck, laden with such queer things as goatskins in pickle, almonds, wormseed, pomegranate skins, and gum arabic, and capable Mr. Hathaway had lost no time in salvage for the benefit of his employer.

As a result he could not come to Port Marriott for a wedding or anything else. A storm might blow up at any time and demolish this fat prize. He dispatched a note by Black Sam, urging Mr. Barclay to send Kezia and the preacher by return. It was not the orthodox note of an impatient sweetheart, but it said that he had moved into his new house by the Creek and found it "extream empty lacking a woman," and it suggested delicately that while his days were full, the nights were dull.

Kezia was no judge of distance. She rode for what she considered a reasonable time and then slid off and tied the brown horse to a maple tree beside the path. She had brought a couple of lamp wicks to tie about her shoes, to keep them from coming off in the snow, and she set out afoot in the big splayed tracks of Black Sam. The soft snow came almost to her knees in places and she lifted her skirts high. The path was no wider than the span of a man's arms, cut out with axes years before. She stumbled over a concealed stump from time to time, and the huckleberry bushes dragged at her cloak, but the effort warmed her. It had been cold, sitting on the horse with the wind blowing up her legs.

After a time the preacher overtook her, riding awkwardly and holding the reins in a nervous grip. The stirrups were too short for his long black-stockinged legs. He called out cheerfully as he passed, "Are you all right, Miss?" She nodded, standing aside with her back to a tree. When he disappeared ahead, with a last flutter of black shawl tassels in the wind, she picked up her skirts and went on. The path climbed and dropped monotonously over a succession of wooded ridges. Here and there in a hollow she heard water running, and the creak of frosty poles underfoot, and knew she was crossing a small stream, and once the trail ran across a wide swamp on half-rotten corduroy, wind-swept and bare of snow.

She found the horse tethered clumsily not far ahead, and the tracks of the preacher going on. She had to lead the horse to a stump so she could mount, and when she passed Mr. Mears again she called out, "Please, sir, next time leave the horse by a stump or a rock so I can get on." In his quaint old-country accent he murmured, "I'm very sorry," and gazed down at the snow. She forgot she was riding astride until she had passed him, and then she flushed, and gave the indignant horse a cut of the switch. Next time she remembered and swung her right leg back where it should be, and tucked the skirts modestly about her ankles; but young Mr. Mears looked down at the snow anyway, and after that she did not trouble to shift when she overtook him.

The ridges became steeper, and the streams roared under the ice and snow in the swales. They emerged upon the high tableland between Port Marriott and Bristol Creek, a gusty wilderness of young hardwood scrub struggling up amongst the grey snags of an old forest fire, and now that they were out of the gloomy softwoods they could see a stretch of sky. It was blue-grey and forbidding, and the wind whistling up from the invisible sea felt raw on the cheek. At their next meeting Kezia said, "It's going to snow."

She had no knowledge of the trail but she guessed that they were not much more than halfway across the cape. On this high barren the track was no longer straight and clear, it meandered amongst the meagre hardwood clumps where the path-makers had not bothered to cut, and only Black Sam's footprints really marked it for her unaccustomed eyes. The preacher nodded vaguely at her remark. The woods, like everything else about his chosen mission field, were new and very interesting, and he could not understand the alarm in her voice. He looked confidently at Black Sam's tracks.

Kezia tied the horse farther on and began her spell of walking. Her shoes were solid things, the kind of shoes Mr. Barclay invoiced as "a Common Strong sort, for women, Five Shillings"; but the snow worked into them and melted and saturated the leather. Her feet were numb every time she slid down from the horse and it took several minutes of stumbling through the snow to bring back an aching warmth. Beneath her arm she clutched the small bundle which contained all she had in the world – two flannel nightgowns, a shift of linen, three pairs of stout wool stockings – and of course Mr. Barclay's wedding gift for Mr. Hathaway.

Now as she plunged along she felt the first sting of snow on her face and, looking up, saw the stuff borne on the wind in small hard pellets that fell amongst the bare hardwoods and set up a whisper everywhere. When Mr. Mears rode up to her the snow was thick in their faces, like flung salt.

"It's a nor'easter!" she cried up to him. She knew the meaning of snow from the sea. She had been born in a fishing village down the coast.

"Yes," mumbled the preacher, and drew a fold of the shawl about his face. He disappeared. She struggled on, gasping, and after what seemed a tremendous journey came upon him standing alone and bewildered, looking off somewhere to the right.

"The horse!" he shouted. "I got off him, and before I could fasten the reins some snow fell off a branch – startled him, you know – and he ran off, over that way." He gestured with a mittened hand. "I must fetch him back," he added confusedly.

"No!" Kezia cried. "Don't you try. You'd only get lost. So would I. Oh, dear! This is awful. We'll have to go on, the best we can."

He was doubtful. The horse tracks looked very plain. But Kezia was looking at Black Sam's tracks, and tugging his arm. He gave in, and they struggled along for half an hour or so. Then the last trace of the old footprints vanished.

"What shall we do now?" the preacher asked, astonished.

"I don't know," whispered Kezia, and leaned against a dead pine

Clarence Gagnon, François in the Blizzard, *1928-1933*

stub in an attitude of weariness and indifference that dismayed him.

"We must keep moving, my dear, mustn't we? I mean, we can't stay here."

"Can't stay here," she echoed.

"Down there — a hollow, I think. I see some hemlock trees, or are they pines? — I'm never quite sure. Shelter, anyway."

"Shelter," muttered Kezia.

He took her by the hand and like a pair of lost children they dragged their steps into the deep snow of the hollow. The trees were tall spruces, a thick bunch in a ravine, where they had escaped the old fire. A stream thundered amongst them somewhere. There was no wind in this place, only the fine snow whirling thickly down between the trees like a sediment from the storm overhead.

"Look!" cried Mr. Mears. A hut loomed out of the whiteness before them, a small structure of moss-chinked logs with a roof of poles and birch-bark. It had an abandoned look. Long streamers of moss hung out between the logs. On the roof shreds of birch-bark wavered gently in the drifting snow. The door stood half open and a thin drift of snow lay along the split-pole floor. Instinctively Kezia went to the stone hearth. There were old ashes sodden with rain down the chimney and now frozen to a cake.

"Have you got flint and steel?" she asked. She saw in his eyes something dazed and forlorn. He shook his head, and she was filled with a sudden anger, not so much at him as at Mr. Barclay and that — Hathaway, and all the rest of mankind. They ruled the world and made such a sorry mess of it. In a small fury she began to rummage about the hut.

There was a crude bed of poles and brushwood by the fireplace — brushwood so old that only a few brown needles clung to the twigs. A rough bench whittled from a pine log, with round birch sticks for legs. A broken earthenware pot in a corner. In another some ash-wood frames such as trappers used for stretching skins. Nothing else. The single window was covered with a stretched moose-bladder, cracked and dry rotten, but it still let in some daylight while keeping out the snow.

She scooped up the snow from the floor with her mittened hands, throwing it outside, and closed the door carefully, dropping the bar into place, as if she could shut out and bar the cold in such a fashion. The air inside was frigid. Their breath hung visible in the dim light from the window. Young Mr. Mears dropped on his wet knees and began to pray in a loud voice. His face was pinched with cold and his teeth rattled as he prayed. He was a pitiable object.

"Prayers won't keep you warm," said Kezia crossly.

17

He looked up, amazed at the change in her. She had seemed such a meek little thing. Kezia was surprised at herself, and surprisingly she went on, "You'd far better take off those wet moccasins and stockings and shake the snow out of your clothes." She set the example, vigorously shaking out her skirts and Miss Julia's cloak, and she turned her small back on him and took off her own shoes and stockings, and pulled on dry stockings from her bundle. She threw him a pair.

"Put those on."

He looked at them and at his large feet, hopelessly.

"I'm afraid they wouldn't go on."

She tossed him one of her flannel nightgowns. "Then take off your stockings and wrap your feet and legs in that."

He obeyed, in an embarrassed silence. She rolled her eyes upward, for his modesty's sake, and saw a bundle on one of the low rafters — the late owner's bedding, stowed away from mice. She stood on the bench and pulled down three bearskins, marred with bullet holes. A rank and musty smell arose in the cold. She considered the find gravely.

"You take them," Mr. Mears said gallantly. "I shall be quite all right."

"You'll be dead by morning, and so shall I," she answered vigorously, "if you don't do what I say. We've got to roll up in these."

"Together?" he cried in horror.

"Of course! To keep each other warm. It's the only way."

She spread the skins on the floor, hair uppermost, one overlapping another, and dragged the flustered young man down beside her, clutched him in her arms, and rolled with him, over, and over again, so that they became a single shapeless heap in the corner farthest from the draft between door and chimney.

"Put your arms around me," commanded the new Kezia, and he obeyed.

"Now," she said, "you can pray. God helps those that help themselves."

He prayed aloud for a long time, and privately called upon heaven to witness the purity of his thoughts in this strange and shocking situation. He said "Amen" at last; and "Amen," echoed Kezia, piously.

They lay silent a long time, breathing on each other's necks and hearing their own hearts — poor Mr. Mears' fluttering in an agitated way, Kezia's as steady as a clock. A delicious warmth crept over them. They relaxed in each other's arms. Outside, the storm hissed in the spruce tops and set up an occasional cold moan in the cracked clay chimney. The down-swirling snow brushed softly against the bladder pane.

"I'm warm now," murmured Kezia. "Are you?"

"Yes. How long must we stay here like this?"

"Till the storm's over, of course. Tomorrow, probably. Nor'easters usually blow themselves out in a day and a night, 'specially when they come up sharp, like this one. Are you hungry?"

"No."

"Abigail — that's the black cook at Barclay's — gave me bread and cheese in a handkerchief. I've got it in my bundle. Mr. Barclay thought we ought to reach Bristol Creek by supper time, but Nabby said I must have a bite to eat on the road. She's a good kind thing, old Nabby. Sure you're not hungry?"

"Quite. I feel somewhat fatigued but not hungry."

"Then we'll eat the bread and cheese for breakfast. Have you got a watch?"

"No, I'm sorry. They cost such a lot of money. In Lady Huntingdon's Connexion we — "

"Oh well, it doesn't matter. It must be about four o'clock — the light's getting dim. Of course, the dark comes very quick in a snowstorm."

"Dark," echoed young Mr. Mears drowsily. Kezia's hair, washed last night for the wedding journey, smelled pleasant so close to his face. It reminded him of something. He went to sleep dreaming of his mother, with his face snug in the curve of Kezia's neck and shoulder, and smiling, and muttering words that Kezia could not catch. After a time she kissed his cheek. It seemed a very natural thing to do.

Soon she was dozing herself, and dreaming, too; but her dreams were full of forbidding faces — Mr. Barclay's, Mrs. Barclay's, Mr. Hathaway's; especially Mr. Hathaway's. Out of a confused darkness Mr. Hathaway's hard acquisitive gaze searched her shrinking flesh like a cold wind. Then she was shuddering by the kitchen fire at Barclays', accepting Mr. Hathaway's courtship and wishing she was dead. In the midst of that sickening wooing she wakened sharply.

It was quite dark in the hut. Mr. Mears was breathing quietly against her throat. But there was a sound of heavy steps outside, muffled in the snow and somehow felt rather than heard. She shook the young man and he wakened with a start, clutching her convulsively.

"Sh-h-h!" she warned. "Something's moving outside." She felt him stiffen.

"Bears?" he whispered.

Silly! thought Kezia. People from the old country could think of nothing but bears in the woods. Besides, bears holed up in winter. A caribou, perhaps. More likely a moose. Caribou moved inland before this, to the wide mossy bogs up the river, away from the coastal storms. Again the sound.

"There!" hissed the preacher. Their hearts beat rapidly together.

"The door — you fastened it, didn't you?"

"Yes," she said. Suddenly she knew.

"Unroll, quick!" she cried... "No, not this way — your way."

They unrolled, ludicrously, and the girl scrambled up and ran across the floor in her stockinged feet, and fumbled with the rotten door-bar. Mr. Mears attempted to follow but he tripped over the nightgown still wound around his feet, and fell with a crash. He was up again in a moment, catching up the clumsy wooden bench for a weapon, his bare feet slapping on the icy floor. He tried to shoulder her aside, crying "Stand back! Leave it to me!" and waving the bench uncertainly in the darkness.

She laughed excitedly. "Silly!" she said. "It's the horse." She flung the door open. In the queer ghostly murk of a night filled with snow they beheld a large dark shape. The shape whinnied softly and thrust a long face into the doorway. Mr. Mears dropped the bench, astonished.

"He got over his fright and followed us here somehow," Kezia said, and laughed again. She put her arms about the snowy head and laid her face against it.

"Good horse! Oh, good, good horse!"

"What are you going to do?" the preacher murmured over her shoulder. After the warmth of their nest in the furs they were shivering in this icy atmosphere.

"Bring him in, of course. We can't leave him out in the storm." She caught the bridle and urged the horse inside with expert clucking sounds. The animal hesitated, but fear of the storm and a desire for shelter and company decided him. In he came, tramping ponderously on the split-pole floor. The preacher closed and barred the door.

"And now?" he asked.

"Back to the furs. Quick! It's awful cold."

Rolled in the furs once more, their arms went about each other instinctively, and the young man's face found the comfortable nook against Kezia's soft throat. But sleep was difficult after that. The

20

horse whinnied gently from time to time, and stamped about the floor. The decayed poles crackled dangerously under his hoofs whenever he moved, and Kezia trembled, thinking he might break through and frighten himself, and flounder about till he tumbled the crazy hut about their heads. She called out to him "Steady, boy! Steady!"

It was a long night. The pole floor made its irregularities felt through the thickness of fur; and because there seemed nowhere to put their arms but about each other the flesh became cramped, and spread its protest along the bones. They were stiff and sore when the first light of morning stained the window. They unrolled and stood up thankfully, and tramped up and down the floor, threshing their arms in an effort to fight off the gripping cold. Kezia undid her bundle in a corner and brought forth Nabby's bread and cheese, and they ate it sitting together on the edge of the brushwood bed with the skins about their shoulders. Outside the snow had ceased.

"We must set off at once," the preacher said. "Mr. Hathaway will be anxious."

Kezia was silent. She did not move, and he looked at her curiously. She appeared very fresh, considering the hardships of the previous day and the night. He passed a hand over his cheeks and thought how unclean he must appear in her eyes with this stubble on his pale face.

"Mr. Hathaway — " he began again.

"I'm not going to Mr. Hathaway," Kezia said quietly.

"But — the wedding!"

"There'll be no wedding. I don't want to marry Mr. Hathaway. 'Twas Mr. Hathaway's idea, and Mr. and Mrs. Barclay's. They wanted me to marry him."

"What will the Barclays say, my dear?"

She shrugged. "I've been their bond-girl ever since I was fourteen, but I'm not a slave like poor black Nabby, to be handed over, body and soul, whenever it suits."

"Your soul belongs to God," said Mr. Mears devoutly.

"And my body belongs to me."

He was a little shocked at this outspokenness but he said gently, "Of course. To give oneself in marriage without true affection would be an offence in the sight of Heaven. But what will Mr. Hathaway say?"

"Well, to begin with, he'll ask where I spent the night, and I'll have to tell the truth. I'll have to say I bundled with you in a hut in the woods."

"Bundled?"

"A custom the people brought with them from Connecticut when they came to settle in Nova Scotia. Poor folk still do it. Sweethearts, I mean. It saves fire and candles when you're courting on a winter evening. It's harmless — they keep their clothes on, you see, like you and me — but Mr. Barclay and the other Methody people are terrible set against it. Mr. Barclay got old Mr. Mings — he's the Methody preacher that died last year — to make a sermon against it. Mr. Mings said bundling was an invention of the devil."

"Then if you go back to Mr. Barclay — "

"He'll ask me the same question and I'll have to give him the same answer. I couldn't tell a lie, could I?" She turned a pair of round blue eyes and met his embarrassed gaze.

"No! No, you mustn't lie. Whatever shall we do?" he murmured in a dazed voice. Again she was silent, looking modestly down her small nose.

"It's so very strange," he floundered. "This country — there are so many things I don't know, so many things to learn. You — I — we shall have to tell the truth, of course. Doubtless I can find a place in the Lord's service somewhere else, but what about you, poor girl?"

"I heard say the people at Scrod Harbour want a preacher."

"But — the tale would follow me, wouldn't it, my dear? This — er — bundling with a young woman?"

"'Twouldn't matter if the young woman was your wife."

"Eh?" His mouth fell open. He was like an astonished child, for all his preacher's clothes and the new beard on his jaws.

"I'm a good girl," Kezia said, inspecting her foot. "I can read and write, and know all the tunes in the psalter. And — and you need someone to look after you."

He considered the truth of that. Then he murmured uncertainly, "We'd be very poor, my dear. The Connexion gives some support, but of course — "

"I've always been poor," Kezia said. She sat very still but her cold fingers writhed in her lap.

He did something then that made her want to cry. He took hold of her hands and bowed his head and kissed them.

"It's strange — I don't even know your name, my dear."

"It's Kezia — Kezia Barnes."

He said quietly, "You're a brave girl, Kezia Barnes, and I shall try to be a good husband to you. Shall we go?"

"Hadn't you better kiss me, first?" Kezia said faintly.

He put his lips awkwardly to hers; and then, as if the taste of her clean mouth itself provided strength and purpose, he kissed her again, and firmly. She threw her arms about his neck.

"Oh, Mr. Mears!"

How little he knew about everything! He hadn't even known enough to wear two or three pairs of stockings inside those roomy moccasins, nor to carry a pair of dry ones. Yesterday's wet stockings were lying like sticks on the frosty floor. She showed him how to knead the hard-frozen moccasins into softness, and while he worked at the stiff leather she tore up one of her wedding bed-shirts and wound the flannel strips about his legs and feet. It looked very queer when she had finished, and they both laughed.

They were chilled to the bone when they set off, Kezia on the horse and the preacher walking ahead, holding the reins. When they regained the slope where they had lost the path, Kezia said, "The sun rises somewhere between east and southeast, this time of year. Keep it on your left shoulder a while. That will take us back towards Port Marriott."

When they came to the green timber she told him to shift the sun to his left eye.

"Have you changed your mind?" he asked cheerfully. The exercise had warmed him.

"No, but the sun moves across the sky."

"Ah! What a wise little head it is!"

They came over a ridge of mixed hemlock and hardwood and looked upon a long swale full of bare hackmatacks.

"Look!" the girl cried. The white slot of the axe path showed clearly in the trees at the foot of the swale, and again where it entered the dark mass of the pines beyond.

"Praise the Lord!" said Mr. Mears.

When at last they stood in the trail, Kezia slid down from the horse.

"No!" Mr. Mears protested.

"Ride-and-tie," she said firmly. "That's the way we came, and that's the way we'll go. Besides, I want to get warm."

He climbed up clumsily and smiled down at her.

"What shall we do when we get to Port Marriott, my dear?"

"Get the New Light preacher to marry us, and catch the packet for Scrod Harbour."

He nodded and gave a pull at his broad hat brim. She thought of everything. A splendid helpmeet for the world's wilderness. He saw it all very humbly now as a dispensation of Providence.

Kezia watched him out of sight. Then, swiftly, she undid her bundle and took out the thing that had lain there (and on her conscience) through the night — the tinderbox — Mr. Barclay's wedding gift to Mr. Hathaway. She flung it into the woods and walked on, skirts lifted, in the track of the horse, humming a psalm tune to the silent trees and the snow.

Author's Commentary

After a few years of sea wandering I settled in a small Nova Scotian seaport whose original inhabitants had migrated there from New England before the American Revolution. Many of the present people, including my wife, could trace their ancestry back to the Pilgrims. So I heard many tales and legends from the past. Also I found a diary giving details of everyday life in "Oldport" from 1766 to 1812.

Out of all this came a series of short stories written originally for magazines and later issued in book form. In the case of "The Wedding Gift", the personalities of Mr. Barclay, the poor little bond-girl, the greenhorn parson and the wife-seeking Hathaway all emerged to form an association in my mind that demanded to be written.

There had to be what the French call a *clou* ("nail"), and the tinderbox sprang into mind.

I think "The Wedding Gift" is a good example of the way a writer's mind works. Given these people and this time and place, what might have happened?

Thomas H. Raddall (1903 —   )

Born in England, Thomas Raddall came to Halifax with his parents in 1913; he still makes his home in Nova Scotia. At the age of fifteen, he became a radio operator serving on ships and at coastguard stations along the Nova Scotia coast. In 1922 he was hired as a bookkeeper. He worked for a paper mill until 1938, when he decided to try the life of a full-time writer. He has a strong interest in history and won the Governor General's Award in 1948 for a local history, *Halifax: Warden of the North*. He has written a number of collections of short stories; his novels include some with historic settings and several that are contemporary. *The Nymph and the Lamp* (1950), set on Sable Island, is the best known in the latter category. His autobiography, *In My Time*, appeared in 1976.

What Language Do Bears Speak?

ROCH CARRIER

The hour had come: we were going to see the greatest circus attraction in the Americas, we were going to see with our own eyes the famous Dr. Schultz, our friend, wrestle a giant black bear.

Following our own morning ritual, to which we submitted with more conviction than to the one of saying our prayers when we jumped out of bed, we ran to the windows and lingered there, silent and contemplative, for long moments. Meanwhile, in the kitchen, our mother was becoming impatient, for we were late. She was always afraid we'd be late ... Life was there all around us and above us, vibrant and luminous, filled with trees; it offered us fields of daisies and it led to hills that concealed great mysteries.

The story of that morning begins with some posters. During the night, posters had been put up on the wooden poles that supported the hydro wires.

"Posters! They've put up posters!"

Did they announce that hairy wrestlers were coming? Far West singers? Strong men who could carry horses on their shoulders? Comic artists who had "made all America collapse with laughter"? An international tap-dance champion? A sword swallower? Posters! Perhaps we'd be allowed to go and see a play on the stage of the parish hall — if the curé declared from the pulpit that the play wasn't immoral and if we were resourceful enough to earn the money for a ticket. Posters! The artists in the photographs would gradually come down from the posters until they inhabited our dreams, haunted our games and accompanied us, invisible, on our expeditions.

"There's posters up!"

We weren't allowed to run to the posters and, trembling, read their marvellous messages; it was contrary to maternal law to set foot outside before we had washed and combed our hair. After submitting to this painful obligation we were able to learn that we would see, in flesh and blood, the unsurpassable Dr. Schultz, former hunter in Africa, former director of zoos in the countries of Europe, former lion-tamer, former elephant-hunter and former free-style wrestling champion in Germany, Austria and the United Kingdom, in an unbelievable, unsurpassable show — "almost unimaginable." Dr. Schultz would present dogs that could balance on balls, rabbit-clowns, educated monkeys, hens that could add and subtract; in addition, Dr. Schultz would brave a savage bear in an uneven wrestling match "between the fierce forces of nature and the cunning of human intelligence, of which the outcome might be fatal for one of the protagonists."

We had seen bears before, but dead ones, with mouths bleeding, teeth gleaming. Hunters liked to tell how their victims had appeared to them: " ... standing up, practically walking like a man, but a big man, hairy like a bear; and then it came to me roaring like thunder when it's far away behind the sky, with claws like knives at the end of its paws, and then when I fired it didn't move any more than if a mosquito'd got into its fur. Wasn't till the tenth bullet that I saw it fall down ..." Loggers, too, had spotted bears and some, so they said, had been so frightened their hair had turned white.

Dr. Schultz was going to risk his life before our eyes by pitting himself against this merciless beast. We would see with our own eyes, alive before us, not only a bear but a man fighting a bear. We'd see all of that!

A voice that reached the entire village, a voice that was magnified by loudspeakers, announced that the great day had arrived: "At last you can see, in person, the unsurpassable Dr. Schultz, the man with the most scars in the world, and his bear — a bear that gets fiercer and fiercer as the season for love comes closer!"

We saw an old yellow bus drive up, covered with stars painted in red, pulling a trailer on whose sides we could read: DR. SCHULTZ AND ASSOCIATES UNIVERSAL WONDER CIRCUS LTD. The whole thing was covered with iron bars that were tangled and crossed and knotted and padlocked. A net of clinking chains added to the security. Between messages, crackling music made curtains open at the windows and drew the children outdoors. Then the magical procession entered the lot where we played ball in the summer. The motor growled, the bus moved forward, back, hesitated. At last it found its place and the motor was silent. A man got out of the bus. He stood on the running-board; twenty or thirty children had followed the circus. He considered us with a smile.

"Hi, kids," he said.

He added something else, words in the same language, which we'd never heard before.

"Either he's talking bear", said my friend Lapin, "or he's talking English."

"If we can't understand him", I concluded, "it must be English."

The man on the running-board was still talking; in his strange language he seemed to be asking questions. Not understanding, we listened, stupefied to see Dr. Schultz in person, alive, come down from the posters.

"We talk French here," one of us shouted.

Smiling again, Dr. Schultz said something else we didn't understand.

"We should go get Monsieur Rancourt," I suggested.

Monsieur Rancourt had gone to Europe to fight in the First World War and he'd had to learn English so he could follow the soldiers in his army. I ran to get Monsieur Rancourt. Panting behind his big belly, he hurried as fast as he could. He was looking forward to speaking this language. He hadn't spoken it for so many years he wasn't sure, he told me, that he could remember it. As soon as he saw the man from the circus he told me: "I'm gonna try to tell him hello in English."

"Good day sir! How you like it here today?" ("I remember!" Monsieur Rancourt rejoiced, shouting with delight. "I didn't forget!")

Dr. Schultz moved towards Monsieur Rancourt, holding out his hand. A hand wearing a leather glove, in the middle of summer.

"It's because of the bear bites," my friend Lapin explained to me.

"Apparently the *Anglais* can't take the cold," said one of our friends whose mother's sister had a cousin who worked in an *Anglais* house in Ontario.

The man from the circus and Monsieur Rancourt were talking like two old friends meeting after a number of years. They even laughed. In English, Monsieur Rancourt laughed in a special way, "a real English laugh," we judged, whispering. In French, Monsieur Rancourt never laughed; he was surly. We listened to them, mouths agape. This English language which we'd heard on the radio, in the spaces between the French stations when we turned the tuning knob, we were hearing now for real, in life, in our village, spoken by two men standing in the sun. I made an observation: instead of speaking normally, as in French, instead of spitting the words outside their lips, the two men were swallowing them. My friend Lapin had noticed the same thing, for he said:

"Sounds like they're choking."

Suddenly something was overturned in the trailer; we could hear chains clinking, a bump swelled out the canvas covering and we saw a black ball burst out — the head of a bear.

Dr. Schultz and Monsieur Rancourt had rolled up their shirtsleeves and they were comparing tattoos.

"The bear's loose!"

The animal ran out of the canvas, came down from the roof of the bus and jumped to the ground. How could we tell that to Dr. Schultz who didn't understand our language, whose back was turned to the trailer and who was completely absorbed in his conversation?

"Monsieur Rancourt!" I shouted. "The bear's running away!"

There was no need to translate. The man from the circus had understood. Waving a revolver, he sped towards the bear, which was fleeing into a neighbouring field. He shouted, pleaded, threatened.

"What's he saying?" we asked Monsieur Rancourt.

"Words that English children don't learn till they're men."

"He must be saying the same words my father says when a cow jumps over the fence. They aren't nice."

Dr. Schultz, whom we had seen disappear into the oats, came back after a long moment and spoke to Monsieur Rancourt, who ran to the village. The men who were gathered at the general store rushed off to find other men; they took out traps, rifles, ropes. While the mothers gathered up their children who were scattered over the village, the men set out, directed by fat Monsieur Rancourt. Because of his experience in the war, he took charge of the round-up. Dr. Schultz had confided to him, we learned later:

"That bear's more important than my own wife."

They mustn't kill it, then, but bring it back alive.

The show was to begin in the early afternoon. Dr. Schultz, who had gone with the men into the forest, came back muttering; we guessed that he was unhappy. At his trailer he opened the padlock, unfastened the crossed iron bars, pulled out the pegs and undid the chains. We saw him transform his trailer into a stage, with the help of a system of pulleys, ropes and tripods. Suddenly we were working with the circus man: we carried boxes, held out ropes, unrolled canvas, stuck pickets in the ground, lined up chairs. Dr. Schultz directed our labours. Small, over-excited men that we were, we had forgotten he was speaking a language we didn't understand.

A piece of unrolled canvas suspended from a rope, which was

28

William Kurelek, Grizzly Sliding Down Glacier, *1974*
The Pagurian Corporation Limited

held in place by stakes, formed a circular enclosure. It resembled a tent without a roof; we had built it. We were proud; would we, as long as we lived, ever have another day as beautiful as this one? From now on we were part of the circus.

At last it was time for the show. The music cried out as far as the horizon. In the stands there were mostly women; the men were still pursuing the lost bear.

In gleaming leather boots, in a costume sparkling with gilt braid, Dr. Schultz walked out on the stage. He said a few words and the crowd applauded fervently; the spectators no doubt considered it a mark of prowess to speak with such ease a language of which they couldn't utter a single word.

He opened a cage and a dozen rabbits came out. On the back of each he hung a number. At the other end of the platform was a board with holes cut out of it. Above each hole, a number. The man from the circus gave an order and the rabbits ran to the holes that bore their numbers. Unbelievable, wasn't it? We all raised rabbits, but our animals had never learned anything more intelligent than how to chew clover. Our hands were burning, so much had we applauded our friend Dr. Schultz. Next came the trained dogs' act: one danced a waltz; another rode around a track on a bicycle while his twin played a drum. We applauded our great friend hard enough to break our metacarpals.

The acrobatic chimpanzee's act had scarcely begun when a great uproar drowned the music from the loudspeakers. The canvas wall shook, it opened, and we saw the captured bear come in. The men from the village were returning it to its master, roaring, furious, screaming, clawing, kicking, gasping, famished. The men from the village, accustomed to recalcitrant bulls and horses, were leading it with strong authority; they had passed ropes around its neck and paws so the furious animal had to obey. Monsieur Rancourt was speaking French and English all at once.

When he saw his bear, Dr. Schultz let out a cry that Monsieur Rancourt didn't translate. The men's hands dropped the ropes; the bear was free. He didn't notice immediately. We heard his harsh breathing, and his master's too. The hour had come: we were going to see the greatest circus attraction in the Americas, we were going to see with our own eyes the famous Dr. Schultz, our friend, wrestle a giant black bear.

No longer feeling the ropes burning its neck, no longer submitting to the strength of the men who were tearing it apart, the bear stood up, spread its arms and shot forward with a roar. The bear struck Dr. Schultz like a mountain that might have rolled onto him. The bear and our friend tumbled off the stage. There was a ripple of applause; all the men together would never have succeeded in mustering half the daring of Dr. Schultz. The bear got up again, trampled on the great tamer of wild beasts and dived into the canvas enclosure, tearing it with one swipe of its claws before disappearing.

Dr. Schultz had lost his jacket and trousers. His body was streaked with red scratches. He was weeping.

"If I understand right," said Monsieur Rancourt, "he's telling us that the bear wasn't *his* bear..."

"It isn't *his* bear..."

The men shook and spluttered with laughter as they did at the general store when one of them told a funny story.

The men laughed so hard that Monsieur Rancourt could no longer hear Dr. Schultz's moans as he lay bleeding on the platform. The undertaker apologized for the misunderstanding.

"That bear was a bear that talked English, though, because I didn't understand a single word he said."

Author's Commentary

I have written both novels and short stories.

Each time I start a novel, I begin an adventure that will usually last some months, and even years. At the outset, I do not know my characters. I do not know their lifestyles, I do not know what the novel will say. Writing a novel is a voyage into the unknown which, once completed, is as exhausting for me as any hockey game. My writing creates individuals that would not otherwise have existed. This voyage within reveals an unknown part of myself. I can better understand my relationship with my universe. Through the development of my creations, my readers will be able to follow, by reading, the same road as I have taken in writing.

A short story is a collection of words that may only last a few days, sometimes only a few hours. It is for me, however, a wonderful means of reproducing in colour and motion, and with sound and smell, the people, activities, and a reality that I know well, at one point in time. I am not satisfied with simply recording a story; mine must have a deeper meaning and not just represent a lock-step movement of characters and events. In recounting my story, I want to awaken in the reader the recollection of a familiar experience. I also try to add a moral or symbolic dimension to the story, within which the reader will meet characters that are a little naive, or credulous, or pitiful, or grotesque, or admirable.

To tell you the truth, I never think of all that while I am writing my novels or short stories! It's not until some time after when I am questioned on the subject, that I am able to say that I wanted this or that.

I am then forced to be serious, to lend substance to this great writing game. Real authors, writing in literary handbooks, are so serious; I am frankly unable to assume their intellectual facade to speak about my writing. Nevertheless, writing is, for me, still magic.

Basically, I only try to tell the best possible story, which may be the simplest, in the best possible way.

When I was a child, television had not yet come to the homes in my little village. Every evening, everyone would gather together to reminisce. People would tell stories that would last all evening, and sometimes would go on for several days. I remember a man who continued a story begun by his father, who had died. No storyteller had the right to continue after his story had ceased to be interesting, but the story would always end before it became tiresome. These men used many tricks to maintain interest in their stories. Listening to the simple tales of these men, who had never had the benefit of formal schooling, taught me what I now know to be the most basic truths about the art of storytelling. I think of them each time I begin to tell a story.

Roch Carrier (1937 –   )

Born in rural Quebec, Roch Carrier was educated at the Université de Montréal and at the Sorbonne in Paris. He has been the resident dramatist at Montreal's Théâtre du Nouveau Monde and has taught at the Université de Montréal and the College Militaire Royal de St. Jean. His works include: *La Guerre, Yes Sir!* (1968); *Floralie, Where Are You?* (1969); *Is It the Sun, Philibert?* (1970) – linked novels; and *They Won't Demolish Me!* (1974). The first two named were adapted by Carrier for the stage and have been performed in Montreal, in Europe, and at the Stratford Festival. Carrier's works have been translated into English by Sheila Fischman.

The Loons

MARGARET LAURENCE

Her long hair hung black and straight around her shoulders, and her broad coarse-featured face bore no expression—it was blank, as though she no longer dwelt within her own skull, as though she had gone elsewhere. I approached her very hesitantly.

Just below Manawaka, where the Wachakwa River ran brown and noisy over the pebbles, the scrub oak and grey-green willow and chokecherry bushes grew in a dense thicket. In a clearing at the centre of the thicket stood the Tonnerre family's shack. The basis of this dwelling was a small square cabin made of poplar poles and chinked with mud, which had been built by Jules Tonnerre some fifty years before, when he came back from Batoche with a bullet in his thigh, the year that Riel was hung and the voices of the Metis entered their long silence. Jules had only intended to stay the winter in the Wachakwa Valley, but the family was still there in the thirties, when I was a child. As the Tonnerres had increased, their settlement had been added to, until the clearing at the foot of the town hill was a chaos of lean-tos, wooden packing cases, warped lumber, discarded car tires, ramshackle chicken coops, tangled strands of barbed wire and rusty tin cans.

The Tonnerres were French halfbreeds, and among themselves they spoke a *patois* that was neither Cree nor French. Their English was broken and full of obscenities. They did not belong among the Cree of the Galloping Mountain reservation, further north, and they did not belong among the Scots-Irish and Ukrainians of Manawaka, either. They were, as my Grandmother MacLeod would have put it, neither flesh, fowl, nor good salt herring. When their men were not working at odd jobs or as section hands on the C.P.R., they lived on relief. In the summers, one of the Tonnerre youngsters, with a face that seemed totally unfamiliar with laughter, would knock at the doors of the town's brick houses and offer for sale a lard-pail full of bruised wild strawberries, and if he got as much as a quarter he would grab the coin and run before the customer had time to change her mind. Sometimes old Jules, or his son Lazarus, would get mixed up in a Saturday-night brawl, and would hit out at whoever was nearest, or howl drunkenly among the offended shoppers on Main Street, and then the Mountie would put them for the night in the barred cell underneath the Court House, and the next morning they would be quiet again.

Piquette Tonnerre, the daughter of Lazarus, was in my class at school. She was older than I, but she had failed several grades, perhaps because her attendance had always been sporadic and her interest in schoolwork negligible. Part of the reason she had missed a lot of school was that she had had tuberculosis of the bone, and had once spent many months in hospital. I knew this because my father was the doctor who had looked after her. Her sickness was almost the only thing I knew about her, however. Otherwise, she existed for me only as a vaguely embarrassing presence, with her hoarse voice and her clumsy limping walk and her grimy cotton dresses that were always miles too long. I was neither friendly nor unfriendly towards her. She dwelt and moved somewhere within my scope of vision, but I did not actually notice her very much until that peculiar summer when I was eleven.

"I don't know what to do about that kid," my father said at dinner one evening. "Piquette Tonnerre, I mean. The damn bone's flared up again. I've had her in hospital for quite a while now, and it's under control all right, but I hate like the dickens to send her home again."

"Couldn't you explain to her mother that she has to rest a lot?" my mother said.

"The mother's not there," my father replied. "She took off a few years back. Can't say I blame her. Piquette cooks for them, and she says Lazarus would never do anything for himself as long as she's there. Anyway, I don't think she'd take much care of herself, once she got back. She's only thirteen, after all. Beth, I was thinking — what about taking her up to Diamond Lake with us this summer? A couple of months rest would give that bone a much better chance."

My mother looked stunned.

"But Ewen — what about Roddie and Vanessa?"

"She's not contagious," my father said. "And it would be company for Vanessa."

"Oh dear," my mother said in distress, "I'll bet anything she has nits in her hair."

"For Pete's sake," my father said crossly, "do you think Matron would let her stay in the hospital for all this time like that? Don't be silly, Beth."

Grandmother MacLeod, her delicately featured face as rigid as a cameo, now brought her mauve-veined hands together as though she were about to begin a prayer.

"Ewen, if that halfbreed youngster comes along to Diamond Lake, I'm not going," she announced. "I'll go to Morag's for the summer."

I had trouble in stifling my urge to laugh, for my mother brightened visibly and quickly tried to hide it. If it came to a choice between Grandmother MacLeod and Piquette, Piquette would win hands down, nits or not.

"It might be quite nice for you, at that," she mused. "You haven't seen Morag for over a year, and you might enjoy being in the city for a while. Well, Ewen dear, you do what you think best. If you think it would do Piquette some good, then we'll be glad to have her, as long as she behaves herself."

So it happened that several weeks later, when we all piled into my father's old Nash, surrounded by suitcases and boxes of provisions and toys for my ten-month-old brother, Piquette was with us and Grandmother MacLeod, miraculously, was not. My father would only be staying at the cottage for a couple of weeks, for he had to get back to his practice, but the rest of us would stay at Diamond Lake until the end of August.

Our cottage was not named, as many were, "Dew Drop Inn" or "Bide-a-Wee," or "Bonnie Doon." The sign on the roadway bore in austere letters only our name, MacLeod. It was not a large cottage, but it was on the lakefront. You could look out the windows and see, through the filigree of the spruce trees, the water glistening greenly as the sun caught it. All around the cottage were ferns, and sharp-branched raspberry bushes, and moss that had grown over fallen tree trunks. If you looked carefully among the weeds and grass, you could find wild strawberry plants which were in white flower now and in another month would bear fruit, the fragrant globes hanging like miniature scarlet lanterns on the thin hairy stems. The two grey squirrels were still there, gossiping at us from the tall spruce beside the cottage, and by the end of the summer they would again be tame enough to take pieces of crust from my hands. The broad moose antlers that hung above the back door were a little more bleached and fissured after the winter, but otherwise everything was the same. I raced joyfully around my kingdom, greeting all the places I had not seen for a year. My brother, Roderick, who had not been born when we were here last summer, sat on the car rug in the sunshine and examined a brown spruce cone, meticulously turning it round and round in his small and curious hands. My mother and father toted the luggage from car to cottage, exclaiming over how well the place had wintered, no broken windows, thank goodness, no apparent damage from storm-felled branches or snow.

Only after I had finished looking around did I notice Piquette. She was sitting on the swing, her lame leg held stiffly out, and her other foot scuffing the ground as she swung slowly back and forth. Her long hair hung black and straight around her shoulders, and her broad coarse-featured face bore no expression — it was blank, as though she no longer dwelt within her own skull, as though she had gone elsewhere. I approached her very hesitantly.

"Want to come and play?"

Piquette looked at me with a sudden flash of scorn.

"I ain't a kid," she said.

Wounded, I stamped angrily away, swearing I would not speak to her for the rest of the summer. In the days that followed, however, Piquette began to interest me, and I began to want to interest her. My reasons did not appear bizarre to me. Unlikely as it may seem. I had only just realized that the Tonnerre family, whom I had always heard called halfbreeds, were actually Indians, or as near as made no difference. My acquaintance with Indians was not extensive. I did not remember ever having seen a real Indian, and my new awareness that Piquette sprang from the people of Big Bear and Poundmaker, of Tecumseh, of the Iroquois who had eaten Father Brebeuf's heart — all this gave her an instant attraction in my eyes. I was a devoted reader of Pauline Johnson at this age, and sometimes would orate aloud and in an exalted voice, *West Wind, blow from your prairie nest; Blow from the mountains, blow from the west* — and so on. It seemed to me that Piquette must be in some way a daughter of the forest, a kind of junior prophetess of the wilds, who might impart to me, if I took the right approach, some of the secrets which she undoubtedly knew — where the whippoorwill made her nest, how the coyote reared her young, or whatever it was that it said in Hiawatha.

I set about gaining Piquette's trust. She was not allowed to go swimming, with her bad leg, but I managed to lure her down to the beach — or rather, she came because there was nothing else to do. The water was always icy, for the lake was fed by springs, but I swam like a dog, thrashing my arms and legs around at such speed and with such an output of energy that I never grew cold. Finally, when I had had enough, I came out and sat beside Piquette on the sand. When she saw me approaching, her hand squashed flat the sand castle she had been building, and she looked at me sullenly, without speaking.

Yvonne McKague Housser, Margeurite Pilot of Deep River (Girl with Mulleins),
  c. 1932

"Do you like this place?" I asked, after a while, intending to lead on from there into the question of forest lore.

Piquette shrugged. "It's okay. Good as anywhere."

"I love it," I said. "We come here every summer."

"So what?" Her voice was distant, and I glanced at her uncertainly, wondering what I could have said wrong.

"Do you want to come for a walk?" I asked her. "We wouldn't need to go far. If you walk just around the point there, you come to a bay where great big reeds grow in the water, and all kinds of fish hang around there. Want to? Come on."

She shook her head.

"Your dad said I ain't supposed to do no more walking than I got to."

I tried another line.

"I bet you know a lot about the woods and all that, eh?" I began respectfully.

Piquette looked at me from her large dark unsmiling eyes.

"I don't know what in hell you're talkin' about," she replied. "You nuts or somethin'? If you mean where my old man, and me, and all them live, you better shut up, by Jesus, you hear?"

I was startled and my feelings were hurt, but I had a kind of dogged perseverance. I ignored her rebuff.

"You know something, Piquette? There's loons here, on this lake. You can see their nests just up the shore there, behind those logs. At night, you can hear them even from the cottage, but it's better to listen from the beach. My dad says we should listen and try to remember how they sound, because a few years when more cottages are built at Diamond Lake and more people come in, the loons will go away."

Piquette was picking up stones and snail shells and then dropping them again.

"Who gives a good goddamn?" she said.

It became increasingly obvious that, as an Indian, Piquette was a dead loss. That evening I went out by myself, scrambling through the bushes that overhung the steep path, my feet slipping on the fallen spruce needles that covered the ground. When I reached the shore, I walked along the firm damp sand to the small pier that my father had built, and sat down there. I heard someone else crashing through the undergrowth and the bracken, and for a moment I thought Piquette had changed her mind, but it turned out to be my father. He sat beside me on the pier and we waited, without speaking.

At night the lake was like black glass with a streak of amber which was the path of the moon. All around, the spruce trees grew tall and close-set, branches blackly sharp against the sky, which was lightened by a cold flickering of stars. Then the loons began their calling. They rose like phantom birds from the nests on the shore, and flew out onto the dark still surface of the water.

No one can ever describe the ululating sound, the crying of the loons, and no one who has heard it can ever forget it. Plaintive, and yet with a quality of chilling mockery, those voices belonged to a world separated by aeons from our neat world of summer cottages and the lighted lamps of home.

"They must have sounded just like that," my father remarked, "before any person ever set foot here."

Then he laughed. "You could say the same, of course, about sparrows, or chipmunks, but somehow it only strikes you that way with the loons."

"I know," I said.

Neither of us suspected that this would be the last time we would ever sit here together on the shore, listening. We stayed for perhaps half an hour, and then we went back to the cottage. My mother was reading beside the fireplace. Piquette was looking at the burning birch log, and not doing anything.

"You should have come along," I said, although in fact I was glad she had not.

"Not me," Piquette said. "You wouldn' catch me walkin' way down there jus' for a bunch of squawkin' birds."

Piquette and I remained ill at ease with one another. I felt I had somehow failed my father, but I did not know what was the matter, nor why she would not or could not respond when I suggested exploring the woods or playing house. I thought it was probably her slow and difficult walking that held her back. She stayed most of the time in the cottage with my mother, helping her with the dishes or with Roddie, but hardly ever talking. Then the Duncans arrived at their cottage, and I spent my days with Mavis, who was my best friend. I could not reach Piquette at all, and I soon lost interest in trying. But all that summer she remained as both a reproach and a mystery to me.

That winter my father died of pneumonia, after less than a week's illness. For some time I saw nothing around me, being completely immersed in my own pain and my mother's. When I looked outward once more, I scarcely noticed that Piquette Tonnerre was no longer at school. I do not remember seeing her at all until four years later, one Saturday night when Mavis and I were having Cokes in the Regal Café. The jukebox was booming like tuneful thunder, and beside it, leaning lightly on its chrome and its rainbow glass, was a girl.

Piquette must have been seventeen then, although she looked about twenty. I stared at her, astounded that anyone could have changed so much. Her face, so stolid and expressionless before, was animated now with a gaiety that was almost violent. She laughed and talked very loudly with the boys around her. Her lipstick was bright carmine, and her hair was cut short, and frizzily permed. She had not been pretty as a child, and she was not pretty now, for her features were still heavy and blunt. But her dark and slightly slanted eyes were beautiful, and her skin-tight skirt and orange sweater displayed to enviable advantage a soft and slender body.

She saw me, and walked over. She teetered a little, but it was not due to her once-tubercular leg, for her limp was almost gone.

"Hi, Vanessa." Her voice still had the same hoarseness. "Long time no see, eh?"

"Hi," I said. "Where've you been keeping yourself, Piquette?"

"Oh, I been around," she said. "I been away almost two years now. Been all over the place — Winnipeg, Regina, Saskatoon. Jesus, what I could tell you! I come back this summer, but I ain't stayin'. You kids goin' to the dance?"

"No," I said abruptly, for this was a sore point with me. I was fifteen, and thought I was old enough to go to the Saturday-night dances at the Flamingo. My mother, however, thought otherwise.

"Y'oughta come," Piquette said. "I never miss one. It's just about the on'y thing in this jerkwater town that's any fun. Boy, you couldn' catch me stayin' here. I don' give a shit about this place. It stinks."

She sat down beside me, and I caught the harsh over-sweetness of her perfume.

"Listen, you wanna know something, Vanessa?" she confided, her voice only slightly blurred. "Your dad was the only person in Manawaka that ever done anything good for me."

I nodded speechlessly. I was certain she was speaking the truth. I knew a little more than I had that summer at Diamond Lake, but I could not reach her now any more than I had then. I was ashamed, ashamed of my own timidity, the frightened tendency to look the other way. Yet I felt no real warmth towards her — I only felt that I ought to, because of that distant summer and because my father had hoped she would be company for me, or perhaps that I would be for her, but it had not happened that way. At this moment, meeting her again, I had to admit that she repelled and embarrassed me, and I could not help despising the self-pity in her voice. I wished she would go away. I did not want to see her. I did not know what to say to her. It seemed that we had nothing to say to one another.

"I'll tell you something else," Piquette went on. "All the old bitches an' biddies in this town will sure be surprised. I'm gettin' married this fall — my boyfriend, he's an English fella, works in the stockyards in the city there, a very tall guy, got blond wavy hair. Gee, is he ever handsome. Got this real classy name. Alvin Gerald Cummings — some handle, eh? They call him Al."

For the merest instant, then, I saw her. I really did see her, for the first and only time in all the years we had both lived in the same town. Her defiant face, momentarily, became unguarded and unmasked, and in her eyes there was a terrifying hope.

"Gee, Piquette — " I burst out awkwardly, "that's swell. That's really wonderful. Congratulations — good luck — I hope you'll be happy —"

As I mouthed the conventional phrases, I could only guess how great her need must have been, that she had been forced to seek the very things she so bitterly rejected.

When I was eighteen, I left Manawaka and went away to college. At the end of my first year, I came back home for the summer. I spent the first few days in talking non-stop with my mother, as we exchanged all the news that somehow had not found its way into letters — what had happened in my life and what had happened here in Manawaka while I was away. My mother searched her memory for events that concerned people I knew.

"Did I ever write you about Piquette Tonnerre, Vanessa?" she asked one morning.

"No, I don't think so," I replied. "Last I heard of her, she was going to marry some guy in the city. Is she still there?"

My mother looked perturbed, and it was a moment before she spoke, as though she did not know how to express what she had to tell and wished she did not need to try.

"She's dead," she said at last. Then, as I stared at her, "Oh, Vanessa, when it happened, I couldn't help thinking of her as she was that summer — so sullen and gauche and badly dressed. I couldn't help wondering if we could have done something more at that time — but what could we do? She used to be around in the cottage there with me all day, and honestly, it was all I could do to get a word out of her. She didn't even talk to your father very much, although I think she liked him, in her way."

"What happened?" I asked.

"Either her husband left her, or she left him," my mother said, "I don't know which. Anyway, she came back here with two youngsters, both only babies — they must have been born very close together. She kept house, I guess, for Lazarus and her brothers, down in the valley there, in the old Tonnerre place. I used to see her on the street sometimes, but she never spoke to me. She'd put on an awful lot of weight, and she looked a mess, to tell you the truth, a real slattern, dressed any old how. She was up in court a couple of times — drunk and disorderly, of course. One Saturday night last winter, during the coldest weather, Piquette was alone in the shack with the children. The Tonnerres made home brew all the time, so I've heard, and Lazarus said later she'd been drinking most of the day when he and the boys went out that evening. They had an old woodstove there — you know the kind, with exposed pipes. The shack caught fire. Piquette didn't get out, and neither did the children.

I did not say anything. As so often with Piquette, there did not seem to be anything to say. There was a kind of silence around the image in my mind of the fire and the snow, and I wished I could put from my memory the look I had seen once in Piquette's eyes.

I went up to Diamond Lake for a few days that summer, with Mavis and her family. The MacLeod cottage had been sold after my father's death, and I did not even go to look at it, not wanting to witness my long-ago kingdom possessed now by strangers. But one evening I went down to the shore by myself.

The small pier which my father had built was gone, and in its place there was a large and solid pier built by the government, for Galloping Mountain was now a national park, and Diamond Lake had been re-named Lake Wapakata, for it was felt that an Indian name would have a greater appeal to tourists. The one store had become several dozen, and the settlement had all the attributes of a flourishing resort — hotels, a dance-hall, cafés with neon signs, the penetrating odours of potato chips and hot dogs.

I sat on the government pier and looked out across the water. At night the lake at least was the same as it had always been, darkly shining and bearing within its black glass the streak of amber that was the path of the moon. There was no wind that evening, and everything was quiet all around me. It seemed too quiet, and then I realized that the loons were no longer here. I listened for some time, to make sure, but never once did I hear that long-drawn call, half mocking and half plaintive, spearing through the stillness across the lake.

I did not know what had happened to the birds. Perhaps they had gone away to some far place of belonging. Perhaps they had been unable to find such a place, and had simply died out, having ceased to care any longer whether they lived or not.

I remembered how Piquette had scorned to come along, when my father and I sat there and listened to the lake birds. It seemed to me now that in some unconscious and totally unrecognized way, Piquette might have been the only one, after all, who had heard the crying of the loons.

Author's Commentary

Short stories and novels seem to begin in very different ways in my mind. With a novel, the main characters come first; they grow slowly in the imagination until I feel I know them well; what happens to them arises out of what they *are*. Most short stories I've written seem to be triggered off by some event, either in my own life or something I've observed or read about. The characters in a short story seem just as real to me as the characters in a novel, but I have not seen them, in my mind, in as many situations – they arc visualized more in relation to one main situation. Perhaps this points up some of the differences between a novel and a short story. One form is not better than the other. They simply do not serve the same function. I see a novel as a fictional form containing many themes, and when I am writing a novel, I feel rather like a juggler trying to keep a dozen plates spinning up there in the air. In my stories, on the other hand, there tends to be one central theme, although of course it may have ramifications. As with a novel, one hopes to set up echoes in the reader's mind, which will lead them beyond anything on the printed page.

Why does a writer put some things in novel form and others in short story form? Every writer might give a different answer to this question, and my answer probably sounds vague, but the closest I can come to an explanation is that some situations and characters are naturally meant for a novel, and others for a short story, depending upon the variety of themes and the emphasis one wants to give these. Actually, I don't decide by doing a long analysis or even by flipping a coin. It is a decision which seems to be taken partly at a subconscious level, perhaps for reasons related to what I've said about stories and novels.

Margaret Laurence (1926 –   )

Margaret Laurence was born in Neepawa, Manitoba, and attended United College in Winnipeg. She married in 1947 and accompanied her engineer husband to Somaliland and Ghana where she lived for several years. She spent five years in Vancouver, followed by a number of years in England. She now resides in Ontario. Her publications include: *This Side Jordan* (1960); *The Tomorrow-Tamer* (1963); and *The Prophet's Camel Bell* (1963) – all written with African settings. Five linked novels followed, all with settings in Canada: *The Stone Angel* (1964); *A Jest of God* (1966) (filmed as *Rachel, Rachel*); *The Fire-Dwellers* (1969); *A Bird in the House* (1970); and *The Diviners* (1974). *A Jest of God* and *The Diviners* are both winners of the Governor General's Award. The author has also written a collection of essays, *Heart of a Stranger*, and several children's books.

Dead to the World

H. A. HARGREAVES

The machine retained his card for what seemed an agonizing length of time. Finally, with a kind of hiccough, the card was released, and from a special slot at the side there issued an instruction sheet.

In the murmuring voice of a thousand quiet sounds, the great machine sang softly to itself; a never-ceasing, contented sort of song, sentient, and somehow self contained. It sprawled beneath innumerable acres just on the outskirts of the once-small city of Rugby, North Dakota. Through its myriad channels, like blood through a human body, two hundred and fifty million cards moved swiftly, surely, momentarily caught here to receive an electronic notation, passing elsewhere to be relieved of that notation. In a hospital in Indianapolis a baby was born, placed before a scanner, touched briefly by tendrils at head, chest, wrist and ankle. A new card appeared in the smaller machine beneath that great city, to be duplicated an instant later at Rugby. IN97246-IND38452 had been incorporated into the population of Americanada, had received her permanent ID card, and no matter what name she might be given by her parents, no matter what her friends might call her, no matter what husband she might choose, she would remain to the machines, those recorders, masters and manipulators of vital statistics, all sixty-five of them if required, as IN97246-IND38452.

In Saskatoon, Saskatchewan, a police robot picked up one male, adult, from the prone position into which he had fallen, carried him through the crowd to the cruiser at the curb, and after a cursory examination fished an ID card from the body's pocket, passed it through a scanner, and made a report. In machine number fifty-eight, about fifty miles north of that metropolis, card SA537SAS8442 was flicked into a side channel, passed beneath several recorders, and dropped at last into a receptacle marked Deceased, stilled for the first time in several years. Again, an

45

Christopher Pratt, Exit, *1978-79*

instant later, card SA537SAS8442 was sidetracked in the machine at Rugby, to drop eventually into a similar receptacle. This time, however, the one-in-a-hundred-million possibility discounted by technicians and authorities came to pass. As the card was flicked into the side channel a minute variation in current caused an "echo", and the card behind was flicked in too. So it happened that LA96647ONT374699 came to rest, and shortly thereafter at London, Ontario, the duplicate did likewise – Deceased.

In Lambeth, Ontario, it was one of a lifetime of identical days for everyone, including Joe Schultz. Having finished his work at the antique furniture plant, Joe had decided that he wanted the company of an autoteria rather than the drab silence of his bachelor roomette. Prices being the same whether you slipped your ID card into the slot at home or at the autoteria, the main difference was that you could see the actual rows of offerings rather than mere pictures, and there was life, such as it might be, around you. Moreover, there were opportunities for an enterprising man like Joe. He had punched his choices, picked them up at the robo-cashier's desk, and noted with some discomfort that his receipt was blue, though it was still nearly a week till "pay day" rolled around. Well, he thought, often enough he was on the red by this time, and had once or twice even had to go through the lengthy routine of securing extra credit to be placed against his account a few days before pay day. And he was one of the fortunate ones: he actually performed physical work of a certain specialty, thereby gaining a little higher credit in his account. (Let no one ask how he had got the job.) He wondered how others could survive as mere button pushers.

Joe looked carefully at the diners, finally choosing one some-what overweight, middle-aged woman who sat alone with her tray of calorie-rich foods. Slipping deftly between tables, he came to a firm stop, flashed a brief smile, said "May I?" and sat solidly opposite her. For the first moment or so he concentrated on the fairly meagre contents of his own tray, ignoring the faint but insidious background music which was psychologically designed to speed up the act of eating, to move more people through the place each hour. Then he began to size up his table companion, the "target", in order to plan his brief campaign. She was obviously unaffected by the music. A tough case for his purpose, but this made it more of a challenge. As an opening gambit, he deliber-ately pushed aside some of his greasy french-fried potatoes, clucking softly to himself. He caught a flicker of interest in the woman's eye, a hint of surprise, and it was all too easy after that.

"Keelosterole," he said to his companion, stabbing with his fork at a pale-green snap bean. "You know," he added, as the woman's brow furrowed with concentration, "gets the insides of your arteries." He went back to worrying the contents of his plate for a moment. Then, just as her attention was about to shift away from him, he flashed a rueful grin at the woman. "Had a buddy go that way last year, so I'm touchy on the subject. Nice guy he was, though. Big, happy, healthy, he looked, until the day he . . . went. Hardened up arteries, the Doc said. Yes, sir. Heart couldn't take it, you know. Doc warned him. He said leave those calories alone, and those fat foods . . . they're poison. Nothin' but poison. Old Art wouldn't listen, though. Nice guy, he was."

Joe subsided, just barely watching out of the corner of his eye as the woman's mouth went hard and straight. Then she shrugged her shoulders and picked up her fork. Joe shoved his half-empty plate away and lit up a cigarette, watching the news-fax as its words crawled across the far wall. The woman paused, fork halfway to her mouth. She took a mouthful of food. Slowly her fork came down, dropped to her plate as she sighed, pushed back her chair and heaved herself up. Only after she had left the restaurant did Joe slip her dessert onto his tray, finish his own meal in leisurely fashion and savour his prize. It had been easy after all.

Feeling as much at peace with the world as he ever did, Joe decided that his little victory warranted an extra cup of coffee, sidled over to the beverage area in a mood of self-congratulation, and slid his ID card into the slot. For a fraction of a second it failed to register on him that his cup remained empty, that in fact the machine had rejected his card. Puzzled, he looked at card, cup and machine, then tried again. Again the machine dropped his card into the rejection tray. Joe stood in complete amazement, trying to think out what might be wrong, only moving away when the line behind him began to grow restive. Such a thing had only happened to him once before, and then he had been given sufficient warning from his red receipts but had chosen not to ask for advance credit until he actually ran out. But he knew the simple meal he had bought just now could not have run him completely through the blue and onto the red.

Shaking his head, he moved down to the end of the service spaces, to a slot with a malevolent red light over it, and a sign which read Official Enquiries. After a moment of hesitation he slipped his card into the slot and waited. The hum of scanning equipment stopped, but the machine retained his card for what seemed an agonizing length of time. Finally, with a kind of hiccough, the card was released, and from a special slot at the side there issued an instruction sheet. Joe pulled the sheet free and read with mounting incredulity:

NOTICE: The card you have found belonged to a person now deceased. Please deposit it in the nearest Government Incinerator chute, labelled Official Documents.

WARNING: It is legal offence to retain the ID card of any person deceased. A record of this enquiry has been preserved, and action will be initiated if the accompanying ID card is not destroyed within 48 hours.

Aware now that something had gone drastically wrong with his "records", Joe was quite uneasy, but still, his mind told him, it must be relatively easy to straighten this out. He knew that occasionally something went wrong, and he had heard of people who had run into problems larger than mere overspending. There was the legend of the guy who had been billed for something like one hundred times his expected life earnings, though. Seems, Joe mused, that he was made president of something so he could pay it off. That's right — he was made president of the foreign country whose loan had been placed against his account. Well, at least his own next step was clear. He would have to find a written enquiry booth, fill out a form and get this straightened out quick. Suiting action to thought, he left the autoteria and headed for the local government building.

Half an hour later, Joe Schultz, deceased, was on the walkway again, shaking his head in utter disbelief. He had tried three different forms, none of which seemed precisely to fit his case, each one being returned by the machine with the identical notice and warning he had first received. Finally, in desperation, he had filled out a form requesting information on persons deceased and received a sheet directing him to his nearest Coroner's Office or an accredited spiritual advisor. With this sheet still clutched in his hand, he returned slowly towards his apartment block, painfully attempting to make some sense out of the situation. But more complications were still to come. On arriving at his own door, he found a pair of robo-movers meticulously cleaning up after having removed all his personal belongings and the one or two pieces of furniture that he had purchased over the past few years.

It was too much. In a burst of anger, Joe stepped in front of one of the movers and wrenched the polishing cloth out of its grasp. "Whatta you tryin' to do?" he shouted at the machine. It simply stood still, waiting, humming to itself, while the second machine, obviously more complex, turned and moved swiftly up to him. Scanners moved up and down briefly, another sheet of paper was ejected at Joe, and both machines went back to work. Helplessly, he stood and read the directions for "Next-of-kin", which advised him that his goods had been removed under seal to a government warehouse, pending issue of redirection orders, and warning him that it was a felony to attempt to remove any article, or to impede, obstruct, or in any way to interfere with the work of the robo-mover. Now totally confused, Joe wandered aimlessly from the building and down the walkway trying to understand what had happened to him in so brief a time, and to think of something, anything, he could do next.

The Coroner's Office, his first sheet had said. But it would be closed now, he realized, and moreover if it was like the few offices he had been in there would be a robo-clerk anyway. He watched the faces of the few people moving purposefully along the walkway, wondering idly if any of them had ever run into such a problem. It would do no more good to ask for help from any of them than it would to drop onto one of the motorways far beneath him, with its unceasing flow of muted thunder. You lived your own life, these days, and the fewer questions asked the better. Stop that burly guy there, for example, and ask him for help, he thought. Looks like the kind who would set you up for the hospital first, and find out later if you were trying to heist him.

"The hospital," Joe said aloud. That might be the answer. At least temporarily. He had been in hospital twice in his life, and each time it had been a very pleasant experience. Lots of rest, good food, even some nice-looking girls around, though they didn't have time to talk to ordinary patients. He could stand that, all right, at least for the night. Of course, if they stuck him in the analyzer he might get thrown out, but the second time he'd been admitted they hadn't examined him till the next morning. He remembered being pretty riled up over that, thinking at the time that he might die before they got around to finding out what was wrong with him. And he'd felt pretty foolish the next day when they told him he'd just had too much of a bad batch of Alkade down at the Lambeth Auto-Bar. At least it was worth the chance that they would admit him tonight, before they found out he was faking. "Nineteen-hundred right now," he mused. "Can't take a flipper anyway, if I can't pay the fare, so if I walk it will be 19:30 when I get there. I'll wait till 20:00 and then try to get in." He felt a bit better now that his mind was functioning again, though he still wasn't sure what he'd do next day. He set out towards the hospital, mulling over possibilities.

The little park in front of the hospital was pleasant, one of the newer models ingeniously designed to provide an illusion of isolation almost immediately one entered it. It took a sharp eye to determine which of the shrubs, trees and flowers were synthetics at this time of year, when everything was determined to grow, no matter what the odds. Joe noticed that the grass had recently been replaced: there was one spot where the manufacturer hadn't got enough green into it. In all, though, the effect came through, and he began to relax a bit for the first time since his card had been rejected. It was almost dusk when the robo-watchman arrived and the concealed air rejuvenators had begun to hum, before he decided to try his luck at the admittance entrance.

Taking a deep breath, he stepped slowly through the doors and up to the desk, where a slim and decidedly junior staff member was busily stacking punched cards. In a hoarse and, he hoped, sick-sounding voice, he gave his name and asked to be admitted. The girl straightened up, faced him, and asked, "Could you give me some idea of what the, uh, nature of your complaint is?"

Joe had already thought this out in the park, and now he looked down at the floor, shuffled a little, looked at the back wall of the office and muttered, "Well, Miss, I'd rather tell a doctor. But it hurts a lot, a lot, you understand. If I have to...I could wait a little..." He let his voice trail off and shuddered slightly.

"I'll let you go to one of the emergency stalls," the girl said quickly, "and send an intern as soon as possible."

"Thanks," Joe said between gritted teeth. "Which way is it?"

"Down this hall to your left," the girl answered, and as he turned to leave she continued, "You have your ID card with you, of course."

"Sure," Joe said, fishing it out and holding it up in front of the desk while she rose as if to glance at it. Then, faster than he could have anticipated, she reached out and took it from him, held it between trim thumb and forefinger, and slipped it into the admissions machine. Numbly, Joe stood waiting, not sure of what might happen next, but certain that something would. It did.

While the girl watched, horrified, two light-green robo-attendants moved swiftly and silently to a stop, wheeled stretcher between them. Before she could do anything to prevent it, they had picked up a submissive Joe, slipped him onto the stretcher, strapped him down and headed back down the hall. Joe had no idea of where he was going, but he was fairly sure it wasn't to an emergency stall. He was deftly wheeled into an elevator, plummeted into the depths of the building, and just as deftly wheeled out into a subterranean corridor.

In front of a door labelled *Morgue* they stopped for a brief second, and as it opened soundlessly Joe suddenly realized what had happened. He was paralyzed with fear as the robo-attendants lined him up with toes pointing towards a bank of overlarge drawers. One of the machines opened the drawer as the other efficiently loosened the straps. Without really thinking, Joe sat bolt upright, slipped around the attendant, and made for the end of the bank of drawers. Looking back over his shoulder, he caught a glimpse of the two robo-attendants moving in futile circles, searching the floor for their missing body. Then the door opened in front of him and he was through it, into the corridor, and leaning weakly against the wall.

Summoning up his strength, Joe headed back to the elevator, punched the button and glanced feverishly over the floor list beside it. "Walkway Admissions − 35", he read, and as the elevator door slid back he whipped in and punched 35. Breathing deeply as the car ascended, he tried to slow his racing pulse. Then, moving quickly without actually running, he retraced his path. Ahead, the little girl, as white now as her uniform, was explaining to a full-fledged nurse, waving his ID card to give emphasis. Breaking into a run, Joe passed between them, grabbing his card on the way. Only when he was across the walkway and into the park did he stop, slumping down onto a bench to seek for calmness after his narrow escape.

The robo-watchman had passed twice, and was standing unobtrusively but warily in the shadows of a Manchurian elm down the path, before Joe had collected his wits sufficiently to consider his next move. Hospitals were out. The Coroner's Office was closed. His "accredited spiritual advisor" seemed like the only remaining hope, and here there was a small problem. He had never had even a nodding acquaintance with a spiritual advisor, though he knew they existed in some sort of continental association to whose advertising he had been exposed.

Trying hard to remember the name of the association, he went quickly back across the street, down the express escalator till he came to a visitor's entrance, and cautiously moved through the hospital lobby to a seetalk booth. Thumbing the scanner for the Yellow P., he watched racing capitals until *S* appeared, then hit the mid-speed until *Sp* came up, and switched to slow until *Spiritual Advisors* showed. "Christian Unitarian Spiritual Society" was second in a short list that began with "Buddhist Friends Society". Scanner reversed, he moved at high speed back to the C range, stopping at CUSS. It took a short time to find the address of his nearest advisor, the list again containing fewer names than he had expected. He was about to place his call when he realized that he could no longer do so, since one had to present his ID card even for a collect call. Instead, he memorized the address and took to the walkway yet again, happy to be doing something to keep his mind from being paralyzed by creeping hysteria. Within fifteen minutes he was standing before the sub-level apartment door of Benjamin Scroop, B.A., M.A., B.D., Ph.D., D.D., Spiritual Advisor.

Scroop, Joe quickly learned, was a man who clearly gave far more attention to the needs of the spirit than the body. He stood about six-five, weighed about one-sixty, and had huge, wistful brown eyes that looked from a distance like chocolate mints adrift in a bowl of instant milk. Eager to be of help, he invited Joe to step in and unburden himself, and Joe accepted. It was incredible, Joe thought, as he squeezed onto a thinly-upholstered bench at one side of a fold-down table, how much could be recessed into the walls of an Efficiency Living Space. He had read about the ELS in passing, but this was his first experience with one. Here were three rooms, counting bathroom, in a space smaller than his one-and-a-half. No door, of course, between this and the bedroom, where he could see three triple-tiered bunks folded up to the wall. Scroop answered his casual question with a rueful "Seven. Seven children, my wife and myself. The children seem to spend every waking minute at the House Centre, and my wife works. It's only crowded for breakfast, supper and sleeping."

Joe made an inane comment about not needing an office with such an arrangement, thinking all the while that in these surroundings a well-fed soul *would* be much more comfortable than a well-fed body. But it was time to get down to his problem, since he figured the rest of the family would be back pretty soon. Briefly he sketched out what had happened to him, and filled in details in response to precise questions from the extremely sharp Scroop. This character, Joe thought, might be a spiritual advisor, but he certainly seemed to know the shape of the hard world outside his door. He allowed himself a bit of hope.

But any optimism he might have generated was soon squelched by Scroop, who said quite frankly that in his dealings with the Coroner's Office he had gone through more foul-ups than straight-forward situations. No more than two months ago they had, on the same day, cremated a Fleshly Resurrectionist, and mummified a Fiery Purger, both with relatives seeking Scroop's counsel. If anything, the robo-clerks were more to be trusted than the occasional human clerk, who invariably fed the wrong data into the larger machines. As for the chief coroner, he was in London Proper and Scroop had suspicions that he wasn't human either, since his decisions were arbitrary and calculated to inflict spiritual suffering on the living, if they could merely subject the dead to indignities. Joe commented that from his own knowledge of the world it sounded as if the chief coroner were all too human. However, he saw there would be little help in that direction, and asked if there were any other way Scroop could think of to get him out of his now-desperate situation.

Scroop could think of little more that might be done, and they were slowly discarding possibilities when, in quick succession, the rest of the Scroops arrived home for sleep. A few of the youngest wanted milk, and Joe, after much urging, accepted the cup of coffee he had tried to get so long ago. Well, it seemed ages ago, even if it was only five hours. Scroop used his Householder's ID Card, and Joe couldn't help but notice in such close quarters that the family was on the red. He felt an unaccustomed flush of guilt, as he realized how hard it must be to feed and clothe this mob. Scroop had seen his discomfort, however, and laughed a bit ruefully, trying to make Joe more at ease. "Don't worry about it," he said. "In this house it's the children who feed the rest of us, anyway."

Joe wasn't used to family life, but he knew that children didn't get all that much government allowance so he raised an eyebrow. Scroop explained. "You see, all the money that people donate to our society is deducted from their accounts by the government. It's used first to cover land taxes and rent, next mission expenses, then operating expenses, and finally the rest is evenly distributed in salaries. I make about half as much in a month as one of my children gets in subsidy. But the children, bless them, believe in the work I do, so they have all, at age six, given up their personal allowance entirely to our household account. It's a rare display of faith in their parents on the part of youth, especially for these days." Joe was forced to agree. Things hadn't been so totally controlled by government until after he had left home, and he wondered if he would have consented to such a thing when he was a kid, considering the tough times his family had seen in the Soaring Sixties.

After the children and Mrs. Scroop had gone to bed, Joe and

Scroop sat talking for a short time, but it was clear that there would be no solution here. Scroop promised to make out as many forms as he could think of that would be remotely related to Joe's case, but he did not hold out much hope for quick relief. He offered to put Joe up and feed him, and he was sincere, but he and Joe knew it was next to impossible under the circumstances. Without seeming to rush, Joe brought the talk to an end. "If I don't mosey along," he finally said, "my friend Max will've gone to bed. And he doesn't like to be woke up late at night. He gets real ugly. So thanks for everything, and I'll be dropping around sometime. I might even take in one of your services." After a firm handshake and a look of real compassion from Scroop, Joe found himself outside, heading for the blessed walkway, this time presumably to see the mythical Max, who, Joe decided, lived under a bench in the park across from the hospital.

Back in the park, with the time nearly a murky 24:00, Joe carefully chose a secluded nook surrounded by thick shrubs and overhung by an original Canadian maple. He had not realized how tired he was until he stretched out with his jacket under this head. Then, despite the turmoil of his thoughts as he tried to find some way out of his dilemma, he dropped into a deep, uneasy sleep. He dreamed of running down long, twisting corridors whose walls pulsed rhythmically, threatening to close on him. Paradoxically, it seemed that he could always see a dark abyss at the end, no matter what direction he tried. Then, dimly, he became aware of an insistent, toneless voice, and slowly roused to find the robo-watchman standing over him in the darkness of the park.

"It is forbidden to remain off the pathways after dark," the watchman repeated. Joe was stiff, incredibly tired and totally discouraged. He could think of nothing more to do, so he lay there in complete resignation.

"I will be forced to call for the police if you do not leave at once," said the watchman, and Joe thought, well, it had to come to this sooner or later. Then he brightened. Why not? Why not go to jail? At least he would have a place to sleep in peace, and maybe someone would straighten the whole thing out when his case came up. Of course, loitering must be a minor offence and he would be dealt with by machine again, but at worst he would merely stay in jail. He put his hands behind his head, relaxed and waited.

It couldn't have been more than three minutes later when the robo-cop arrived, moving swiftly and competently across the grass while his companion remained behind, at the cruiser. Joe had obligingly placed his ID card on his chest, and now he waited with grim satisfaction to be apprehended. But it didn't happen quite that way. After a quick glance, the robo-cop's tentacle flicked down and took his ID card, shoved it into its scanner, and transmitted the information. Joe watched with bewilderment as his card was placed back in his shirt pocket and the robo-cop stood still, obviously waiting. Then with a soft swoosh a "black hack" settled on the grass close by, two attendants got out with wheeled stretcher, placed him on it and wrapped him in a sheet, put him in the back of the vehicle and took off.

This time it was the District Morgue, but the procedure was precisely the same. As the sheet was unwrapped, Joe slipped off his stretcher and made for the door. Glancing back, he saw the attendants making those same futile searching movements in widening circles around the floor. It was somehow ludicrous now, as Joe made his way in leisurely fashion through the sub-basement area, not really caring where his wandering took him. It was almost pleasant down here, the warm, dim passage inviting him to find a little nook or cranny, curl up and finish his sleep. He had to make a real effort to keep going, realizing that this was no solution either: that he had to make his way to the outside, if only to eat. And now that the thought had occurred, he was acutely hungry. It must be early morning, at least.

O-five-thirty, said the clock over the back entrance to this level of the mammoth civic building. He knew he shouldn't really be so hungry, but Joe had been through a lot since supper the night before, and it definitely wasn't all psychological. He would have to find some way to get breakfast, and if it required desperate measures, well, it was a desperate situation. One or two meals he might go without, but he wasn't going to starve, even if it seemed that the "machine" was intent on having him dead to make the records accurate. He set out for an autoteria, still not quite sure of what his next move would be.

There was a big one only a block down, and Joe stood across from it watching the early-morning crowd scurry in and out. There was no use going in until he knew what he would do. He could try to force the serving doors, but he couldn't guarantee that they would pry open easily, and besides, there would be loads of people watching him. Not that it mattered much now, but he still wasn't ready to commit an open theft. No, there had to be a better way. What about a back entrance, he thought. It has to have a service area. He began to search, and before long found a neutral grey door marked *Food Services*. Gently, he tried the door, opening it slowly until it stood wide, revealing a small room with three more doors. One said *Accounts*, one said *Maintenance* and the third said *Unauthorized Persons Not Permitted.* Like the old stories on Kid-vid, he thought, in a flash of wild humour. Obviously it was the last that he wanted, and without further delay he opened it and passed through.

To his left a scanner blinked officiously at him, demanding that he present his ID card, but he was interested in the magnificent view that stretched in front of him. Racks of prepared plates lined one side, coming up on a conveyor belt from an escalator at the far end, while smaller belts moved endless amounts of food to the pigeon-holes where customers made their purchases. Entranced, Joe watched toast and jam, eggs, bacon and eggs, ham and eggs, pancakes, muffins, buns—enough for an orgy. Then, shaking his head as if hypnotized, he loaded himself down with pancakes, bacon and coffee. He reached across a belt and picked up knife and fork, seated himself on a stack of waiting trays, and began wolfing his meal. Halfway through the coffee, the robo-cop came. Joe stood still, licking syrup off his fingers, as the cop moved warily into the room blocking his escape. "Please do not move," said the cop, "or I will have to detain you by force." Joe reached for his coffee cup, and almost too fast to be seen the robo-cop pinned his arms to his sides. Another tentacle snaked out and checked his pockets, removing his ID card and inserting it in the scanner. At the same time, Joe felt himself being touched at head, chest, wrists and ankles; a procedure that had familiarity somewhere beyond the fringes of memory.

The robo-cop hummed as time spun out, and Joe began to sense that something was not going quite right. Gradually the hum increased, the robo-cop's visual sensors began to glow brighter, and it even seemed to Joe that the tentacle that held him grew tighter. Soon he could smell the odour of scorched insulation, and see tiny wisps of smoke issuing from minute fissures in the robo-cop's shell. At last, with a belch of smoke and a drunken lurch, the robo-cop disgorged his card, unrolled limp tentacles, and went dead. Amazed, Joe could only watch for a moment or so. He had never seen any piece of automated equipment do this before, particularly none with any degree of independent decision-making abilities. It was almost like watching a person die. He picked up his card half-expecting the cop to come to life and seize him again, but nothing happened. Regaining some composure, Joe moved cautiously to the belts, picked a slab of apple pie, and with studied disdain held it between thumb and fingers as he swaggered by the silent, burnt-out robo-cop. Only when he reached the outer room did he hurry.

It was 10:00, and Joe Schultz, deceased, was reclining in a luxurious bed, in one of the most luxurious hotels in the Greater London area. He had got there by the simple expedient of reaching across the end of the desk, behind the recepto-clerk, and taking one of the two keys in a slot nearest him. Check-out time was 14:00, European style, he knew from the high-priced ads following the newsfax. He might have seven hours of uninterrupted sleep, he figured, but if he were interrupted, so what? For Joe Schultz had found the solution to his problem. It had been right there in front of him all the time, if he had only stopped thinking like a good, law-abiding citizen. The real tip-off had come when the robo-cop, efficient law-enforcement officer that it was, had broken down under the onslaught of conflicting information. When it apprehended a moving, living law-breaker, it seized and identified both ID card and offender. Joe knew little about the information patterns of such machines, but he lay there in delight, imagining what had gone on. Offender carried card of Joe Schultz. Joe Schultz was deceased. Offender was identified therefore as...Joe Schultz. Joe Schultz was deceased. Offender was alive. Offender's card there identified him as...Joe Schultz Pluooi! And if he preferred, he could always stay absolutely still, to be carted off to the morgue. He squirmed and stretched into a more comfortable position, drifting off into sleep as he envisioned the clothes he would secure, the foods he would eat, the places he would sleep. In the immense peace of the truly free, Joe Schultz lay, dead to the world.

Author's Commentary

Everything contributes in a short story: word choices, transitions, even pauses. Whatever the prime objective — suspense, action, characterization, thematic revelation — the author must strenuously control his writing from conception to manuscript. He plans incident, device, characters, atmosphere, imagery, even nuance, for that prime objective, then shapes, revises, reduces, in several drafts. Nothing stays that doesn't contribute in at least one way. Preferably everything contributes in several ways, for short story writing is *distillation*, not simplification.

The germ of this story came when I was shuffling some unsolicited credit cards and they disappeared behind my Social Insurance and Chargex cards. Suddenly the question rose — What if *all* transactions and vital statistics were controlled by a super computer? The focus narrowed with the question — What if the computer made a mistake? The objective came clear when I decided what mistake would be absolutely crucial. It would declare some individual dead. How could he survive?

H.A. Hargreaves (1928-   )

Born in New York state, H.A. Hargreaves studied electronics in the U.S. Navy, then theology at Mount Allison University in Nova Scotia. He changed direction again, received his doctorate in English literature, and is at present a professor of English at the University of Alberta. He has published a collection of short stories *(North by 2000)*, articles in academic journals, and some poetry in literary magazines.

D.P. Brown, Young Canadian, *1968*

Skald

W. D. VALGARDSON

Not having seen anyone for so long she watched the three brothers with the intense interest of someone who, having been whisked into civilization, has been over-awed by it.

"It was my money," Alma said. She had set a cardboard box on the floor. Inside it was the grey blanket in which she had wrapped the pup to bring him home. The pup, ignoring his bed, was dragging a piece of hardfish around. He had the fillet by the tail and, every so often, he would stop, growl deep in his throat as if to intimidate an invisible enemy, and give the fillet a shake.

"You should have asked," Junior Boys said. "I've had lots of dogs. There isn't anything I don't know about them."

Although she was nearly twenty-one, Alma still had the long thin shape characteristic of eleven- and twelve-year-old girls. She had small hips and a small bust, so that she gave the impression of being fragile and light. Her bones were so delicately made that they might have been fashioned from hollow glass. The two prettiest things about her were her eyes and her hair. Her eyes were a deep brown and exceptionally large, so that they dominated her face. Her hair had the luminous sheen that hazelnut shells retain for only the briefest time just after the green hull has been removed.

"I didn't think five dollars was such a lot," she protested. She had wanted a dog badly enough to walk five miles in the cold and didn't think it was fair that Junior Boys found fault with the cost. She was pleased with her purchase. The pup was thick-bodied and sturdy, with its white coat broken only by a black splash across one cheek.

Junior Boys — in spite of their having been married for over a year and a half, she still thought of him by his full name as though, somehow, neither name by itself defined him accurately — sighed and rolled his eyes at the ceiling. It was the same hopeless expression he assumed when students proved too dumb or too lazy to understand their lessons.

"I'm calling him Skald," Alma informed him. Junior Boys' face was pressed close to his plate as he mopped up spaghetti sauce with a crust of bread. When he pushed the bread into his mouth, sauce ran down his fingers. "If that's okay with you, that is," she added.

"Call him what you want." He licked his fingers, then wiped them on a paper serviette. "It's your dog."

Without his platform shoes, Junior Boys was two inches shorter than Alma. He had a bullshaped body and so little neck that when he tried to wear a turtle-neck sweater, the collar spread out under his chin and rose up the back of his head like a cannibalistic flower.

Althought he was twenty-eight, he was in his first year of teaching. He was very proud of having become a teacher, even if it was only a teacher of mechanics and industrial arts, and he did not like to be reminded that he had ever been anything else. In Arkansas, the state from which he had emigrated because of his conscience and the implacable stupidity of his local draft board, he had been a man of many talents. At one time or another, he had sold pianos, women's underclothes, tractors, patent medicines, prophylactics, and coffins. Just before he headed north, he had worked as a welder and blacksmith. What he had revealed to Alma was that, secretly, he aspired to write songs for the Grand Old Opry.

"Har y'all," he had said when he came into the admissions office. At first, Alma thought he had a speech impediment. She had treated him as kindly as possible.

He was fiercely competitive and once he decided on wanting something, no matter how big or how small, he wouldn't stop pursuing it until it was his. He had courted Alma the way he approached life, with dogged persistence and a sure knowledge that he would eventually succeed. At the conclusion of their first date he proposed and, when she rejected him, he had begun to haunt the office, waiting to walk her home, help her shop, carry her parcels. He asked her for sixty dates, telling her that it was like buying futures on the commodity market. When she did go out with someone else, he followed half a block behind like a jealous husband, and, if his competitor had a car — Junior Boys did not have one — he waited forlornly beside Alma's doorstep.

Jenny, Alma's roommate, had advised her, during the second month of his siege of their apartment, that his persistence revealed his terrible burning desire. Jenny knew the lyrics of the top one hundred songs on the hit parade. Junior Boys, she declared, was a tragic lover.

For Alma, the dog's company was a godsend. When she had

agreed to marry Junior Boys, they had decided he would continue with his studies while she worked. Then, when he graduated, he would try to obtain a position in the city so that she could keep her position at the teacher's college. Instead, without consulting her, he had accepted the first job he was offered. When she had reminded him of their agreement, he told her that because of his accent and his age there was a prejudice against him. That meant he had to take whatever he could get. They had left Winnipeg and moved into a winterized cottage around the middle of August.

Although Alma's grandparents had lived in the area around Bifrost, they had moved from it to live in an old folks' home at Eddyville. All she remembered of them were Sunday visits in which they had ridden silently in the back seat of the car. She knew no one in the town or in the surrounding countryside. Her isolation was increased by the fact that Bifrost was not a proper town. It had a school only because it was central to a large farming area. The winter homes were scattered along the lakeshore, each house or cluster of houses surrounded by cottages that were empty for ten months of the year.

Snow had fallen Hallowe'en day. Since then, the land lay locked beneath ever-growing drifts. Everything that rose above the snow — fences, trees, telephone poles — was grey and black. The sky, heavy with cloud for weeks at a time, filtered snow over them with a slow steadiness that seemed determined to cover them over. Alma did not mind the snow or the silence but Junior Boys, when she suggested curling or skating or going to hockey games, merely glared. He complained that he couldn't make head nor tail out of curling or hockey. Skating he would not attempt for fear of humiliating himself.

On the Saturday after Alma bought the dog, there was a steady wind from the north, but it lay close to the ground and was not particularly strong. The sky was as clear as first ice cut from a pond and held to the sun. From the front window of the cottage, the drifting snow lay over the lakes like smoke.

Alma had tried to settle but was so restless that she couldn't stay in one place long enough to read more than a page in a magazine. Finally, she put on a parka and twice walked back and forth in front of Junior Boys. He was writing a song about the Civil War and was desperately trying to find a rhyme for cicada. All he could think of was dada and it didn't seem serious enough for his purpose.

"Where are you going?" he asked.

"Walking."

He gaped at her. "In this!" He would have got up to look out the window but he was in his slippers and she was in boots that increased her height by another inch and a half. His chair was on casters so he satisfied himself by leaning forward, digging in his heels and dragging the chair along.

"I'll take Skald with me."

He was still looking at the drifting snow. "I'd better come," he said.

She promptly sat down so that he could go and put on his thick-soled boots and his outer clothes. Having been raised in a warmer climate, he felt the cold more than she did. Every time he went outside, he wore long underwear, two pairs of trousers, a shirt, a sweater, a nylon jacket, and over top of everything, a quilted skidoo outfit. The skidoo outfit was bright blue and zippered up the front.

Outside, powdered snow drifted as high as their knees. Junior Boys took the lead, breaking a trail to the beach. Foundering through the drifts, he looked like an overgrown child in a snow-suit.

The beach, a narrow, wavering line of dark sand, curved like a dying moon plucked from the frozen sky and laid flat to separate land and water. The prevailing wind swept it clear. On the one side, ice formed an endless plain darkened only by pressure ridges. On the other side, the drifting snow broke upon black breakwaters of concrete and tarred poles. Behind the breakwaters, shuttered cottages lay nearly buried in snow. Spruce trees were compressed by ice.

Skald followed close on Alma's heels. When the pup finally became tired, Alma picked him up and carried him.

"You spoil him worse than a kid," Junior Boys said. "I've had lots of dogs. It won't hurt him to walk."

Alma was used to giving in to his suggestions but this time she only said, "It won't hurt him to be carried either," and kept on her way.

They saw no one. All that moved were three ravens. One sat in a bare tree while the other two pecked at the carcass of a maria that was frozen to the sand.

Alma stopped, finally, where half a dozen poplars, their brittle branches amputated yearly by the fall storms, stood in a line like the spines of some prehistoric fish. At the lake's edge, leading away from the trees, a row of granite boulders rose above the ice like an exposed and weathered backbone.

The cottages and breakwater had stopped some time before, the land flattening away to snow-covered fields. As they crossed over to a road that led back the way they had come, they saw a farmhouse set on the edge of the beach. It was two storeys high. Its metal-sheathed roof gleamed with a cold light. Topped with a black iron widow's walk, enclosed on two sides by a spindled verandah, it rose above the drifting snow like the superstructure of some great ship.

"Who lives there?" Alma asked.

Junior Boys hunched against the wind. "We'd better go back," he said.

Smoke from the chimney streamed toward the south, making the house appear to be rushing northward across the icy wastes. Although it was still early in the day, there were lights in the windows and Alma could see people moving about. A man in a blue-checked shirt appeared on the porch and waved for them to come to him.

The surface of the driveway was uneven and slippery beneath the loose snow. They picked their way along it until they reached the verandah. The man who waited for them seemed as large as a giant and, in spite of his being without a jacket, he was as casual as if it were a summer day. Icicles hung from the entire length of the eaves.

"I'm Valdi Bjarnason," he said. "We saw you standing there and thought you might like coffee." He had a sharp widow's peak of red hair and a large, friendly face.

Alma didn't wait for Junior Boys to reply but scrambled up the ice-covered stairs.

"Aren't you cold?" Alma asked.

Valdi gave a short, sharp laugh. "You should work on the lake all winter."

He held the door open for them. The kitchen was large and had a high ceiling. A net was strung through the door that led to the rest of the house. Two men, both very similar in appearance to Valdi except that one was obviously older and the other younger, were standing on either side of the net, seaming the mesh to the two lines. With a steady rhythmic movement of their hands, they worked the flat plastic needles over and under the narrow cord.

"My brothers, Axel and Helgi," Valdi said. "This is the teacher and his wife."

Junior Boys gave them a curt nod and remained on the carpet beside the door. Alma put Skald down. Then she took off her parka and boots.

"C'mon, Junior Boys," she said as she sat down at the table.

Unable to remain standing at the door, Junior Boys wiped his feet and accepted a chair. He sat cautiously on the edge of the seat as though he expected he might have to flee at any moment.

"You'll get pretty hot in that outfit," Valdi said. "It's no good to get overheated."

"I'll just unzipper it." Junior Boys pulled the zipper down as far as his waist.

Valdi brought them coffee, then poured a saucer of milk for Skald. The pup drank without stopping. When the milk was gone, he began to pounce on the jiggling net.

"Get back here," Junior Boys ordered.

"It's okay," Valdi said. "We're used to dogs."

A large wood stove was set against one wall. Blue-and-white cupboards took up one end of the kitchen. Large, red net trays with sloping sides were stacked beside a floor radio. The two white ropes that divided the kitchen in half were attached to two spikes driven into the back door.

"You're pretty isolated here," Alma said. Not having seen anyone for so long she watched the three brothers with the intense interest of someone who has been lost a long time and who, having been whisked into civilization, has been over-awed by it.

"We've got friends." Valdi had a natural shyness about him that caused him to not look directly at her but to one side as if she were made of a double image that didn't quite overlap. "And we've got lots to do. I heard," he added, "that your people come from around here."

Alma nodded. Beside her, enclosed by his quilted outfit with an American flag sewn onto the left shoulder, Junior Boys was tugging discreetly at the neck of his sweater, holding it out so the heat could escape.

"Who was your father?" Valdi asked.

"Gunnar Loftson."

"And his father?"

"Triggvi."

"Talid pér islenzku?"

"Nei," Alma replied, the word feeling at once awkward and familiar on her tongue. "I learned but I've forgotten."

Helgi and Axel had worked their way into the livingroom. Helgi's head appeared around the corner of the doorway. He was the eldest of the three brothers and had only a few scattered hairs left. His face and forehead were windburnt but his scalp was white. He looked as though someone had begun to apply stain to his head but had stopped when only half finished.

"I knew your grandfather," Helgi said. "He had a grey horse and he got drunk every Friday."

"I think we'd better be going" Junior Boys said. His face was bright pink.

66

"Do you like riddles?" Valdi asked. "Axel loves riddles."

Without any preliminary, Axel said, "A golden princess sits in a silken room with walls of ivory." It was obvious that he had been waiting for an opportunity to speak.

"Are you Icelandic?" Helgi asked Junior Boys.

"I come from the city," he replied. He stared hard at Axel. "Are those all the clues?"

"An egg," Alma said.

Axel looked crestfallen. "You've heard it before."

Helgi squatted and caught a wooden chair by one leg. He lifted the chair from the floor. His arm was as stiff as the shaft of an oar. He lowered the chair. "You try it," he said to Junior Boys.

"A cherry without a stone," Alma said.

"I'm out of shape." Junior Boys' face was as red as an over-ripe pincherry. He pulled one arm loose from his outfit, then the other. Heat rose from him in waves.

"The flower," Axel said, grinning with pleasure.

"Do you live alone?" Alma asked.

The three brothers clustered about her like children eager to please a favoured guest. They glanced at each other out of the corners of their eyes, then Valdi said, "Would you like to see our mother?"

Without waiting for a reply, Valdi started through the door. Alma bounded up and Junior Boys, not wanting her going off with Valdi by herself, flopped along behind in his unzipped boots, clutching the top half of his outfit to keep it from falling.

The livingroom was long and narrow. Furnished with an overstuffed chesterfield, two china cabinets with curved glass fronts, a faded Axminster, and a dark wood dining-table with thick, clumsy legs, it looked like a stage set or a period room for a museum. The china cabinets were full of delicate teacups in dark colours and stuffed songbirds perched on centrepieces made of branches and moss. The songbirds were so faded that they seemed less real than if they had been made of porcelain or glass. They looked like bits of coloured fluff that, if touched, would crumble to dust.

The bedroom walls were covered with wallpaper. Like the birds, it was faded. In the centre of the room there was a four-poster bed. Each post was nearly five feet high and was topped with a delicately carved pineapple. On the one post, there was a blue lace hat with a wide brim. If it had not been for the cobwebs that tied it to the post, it would have seemed to have been carelessly put down only a moment before. On a bedside table, a row of books sat between two bookends.

A woman lay in the middle of the bed. She was stretched out on her back, her arms under the covers. She made a thin, brittle ridge that barely disturbed the blankets. Her still face, devoid of expression, might, like the bed posts, have been carved from dark wood. Her cropped hair was soft as fluff.

"She's sleeping," Alma whispered. The stillness of the woman frightened her.

"She wakes in her own time and when she does, we feed and wash her." He indicated the books. "Sometimes, I read to her in Icelandic."

They crept out, easing the door shut behind them. Junior Boys stopped to study the birds in the china cabinets but Alma went to watch Axel and Helgi seam on.

"She doesn't know us," Valdi told her and his voice was full of pain. "Sometimes she remembers who we are but mostly she thinks we're her brothers and that she's back home in Akureyri."

Skald was running about under Axel and Helgi's feet. Junior Boys, after he had zippered himself up, went to catch the pup. Skald hid under the table. Alma grabbed him by the collar and dragged him out.

The wind had risen. Snow still drifted over the land. As the day waned, the temperature had fallen. They walked quickly through the gathering darkness. On either side, cottages, boarded and shuttered, their roofs covered with snow that trailed into the sky like spume, seemed to have grown heavy and sunk mysteriously into the ground like ancient stones.

"It must be wonderful to love someone that much," Alma said. She leaned into the wind, turning to one side to protect her cheek. "They try to keep everything as she wanted it."

"They like to show off," Junior Boys complained, "but I like their birds." He kicked a road apple, sending it over a fence. "I knew it was an egg," he said.

During April and May, with the security provided by Skald and with the excuse that he needed exercise, Alma went for frequent walks. Before she had bought the dog, because she was normally a timid person, she had had to wait for Junior Boys to go with her. Now, he constantly warned her against talking to strangers and against wandering about the lonely countryside by herself, but she ignored him. She started by making brief forays among the cottages while he was at school. Then, emboldened by her growing knowledge of the area and Skald's increasing size, she started hiking farther and farther afield. She and the white dog became a common sight.

On the days Junior Boys was not coming home for lunch, she

stuffed her pockets full of sandwiches for herself and the dog, and started out on all-day hikes. In the back of a closet, she had found, hidden beneath a stack of old *Reader's Digests* and *Saturday Evening Posts,* a group of small paperback books. One was about mushrooms, one about weeds and wildflowers, another about trees, still another about birds. The illustrations were not very good and the descriptions were incomplete but the books all were about the immediate area so she always took one with her. On each trip, she identified one or more objects, teaching herself to recognize highbush cranberry, birch, willow, red-winged blackbirds. She also stopped to talk to whomever she met on the road and plied them with questions about themselves.

Once June started, the fields dried enough that she was able to leave the roads. With Skald beside her, she began a restless crisscrossing of railway tracks and highway, ploughed fields and meadows. Always, however, she stayed on the edges of the swamps and forests, never going so deep into them that she lost sight of the open area she had left.

What finally drew her deep into a swampy area was her search for pink lady-slippers. She had searched for two weeks without finding any. Then Junior Boys had suggested that she try the corner two miles northwest of town. She had been surprised at his offering any assistance. He had been so opposed to her hiking all over by herself that they had hardly been speaking.

She had found pink lady-slippers by the dozen but as she was picking enough for a bouquet, Skald began to bark and make short, sharp rushes at a cluster of cranberry bushes. Finally, he retreated to where Alma was crouched over three of the slipper-shaped orchids.

As Alma tried to make out what Skald was barking at, a woman in a long black dress and a black headscarf appeared. She was carrying a pail in one hand and a cane in the other. They stared at each other in silence until the woman said, "I know you." She had a square jaw and a grey moustache that was nearly as thick as a man's.

Alma had a dozen pink lady-slippers nestled in the crook of one arm. Around her, the land was low and swampy, the bush so tangled that except for animal paths that ran confusingly in every direction, the forest might have been a vast, impenetrable bramble thicket. The light was dim and shadows fell over everything.

"I've been picking flowers," she said. The trees were in new leaf but the ground, kept from the sun, gave off the dank smell of rot and mould. Unsure of her right to be where she was, Alma said, "I'm sorry if I've been trespassing."

"That a stray?" the woman demanded. When she spoke she

raised her cane and pointed at Skald. One half of her mouth moved but the other half stayed stiff as though it had been frozen. Skald's fur bristled along the back of his neck until it stood out stiff as quills. "I need a new one."

"No," Alma replied, shocked. "He's mine."

"Mine's no good anymore." The woman tried to whistle but the sound was no more than a high-pitched squeal. She rested on her stick and glared so fiercely at Alma that she might have been going to accuse her of having done some terrible wrong. In a minute, a German shepherd staggered into view. His feet were as unsure as those of a drunk. His head shook constantly and his body was twisted like a piece of warped wood. "He can't fetch the cows. He can't earn his keep."

"What's the matter with him?"

"I can't keep them. They get sick." The woman swung her head back and forth, scowling and muttering, her stick poking the bushes.

Alma watched the dog twist its way past its mistress. "Can't you do anything to help it?"

"Costs money," the woman cried. The German shepherd staggered forward to sniff at Skald who sank back on his haunches and bared his teeth.

"I've got to be going," Alma said. She retreated along a narrow path through the tangled trees. Skald retreated with her.

The woman looked up and as if for the first time seeing the flowers in Alma's arms, called, "Pick all you want," in a harsh, slurred voice. "They're no good for nothing anyway."

It was a week later that Alma noticed drops of pus staining the corners of Skald's eyes. She swabbed it away and kept a nervous watch over him, but his appetite grew less and less until his food sat untouched from one day to the next. Normally eager to go out, he lay unmoving beside the stove. Alma tried to tempt him with bits of fresh hamburger but it did no good. A few days later, he began to have fits of trembling and he drooled until his chin and chest were soaked.

The closest veterinarian was fifty miles away. They had no car and, even if they had, she wouldn't have asked Junior Boys to drive. During her talks with farmers she had met, she had found out that when their animals fell sick, they called the school caretaker.

Alma waited until Junior Boys was gone for the day to supervise a baseball team he had started, then wrapped Skald in a blanket and put him into a long cardboard box. The box she tied onto a wagon she had discovered in the tool-shed.

The school was an old two-storey brick building worn by wind and rain and children until the outside seemed fashioned from a single piece of dark stone. The roof was faded green and the high concrete steps had been climbed so often that, like those of European religious shrines that falsely promised miracles, the centres were worn until they curved lower than the edges.

At the bottom of the stairs, she bent down and wrestled the box up to two heavy white doors. She forced open one door and dragged the box inside.

When she straightened up, she was on a small landing. To her left there were two more doors and through the windows she could see wide, worn steps leading up toward the classrooms. The woodwork was painted a dark brown and there were no decorations except for a row of portraits set in narrow frames. Before each picture there was a name in large block letters — Tennyson, Yeats, Coleridge, Eliot, Hemingway. The pictures stopped for a doorway but then continued on the far wall and followed the stairway to the floor above. Below her, she heard a noise. To her right, a single door stood open, revealing a narrow set of steep stairs that led to the basement.

All she knew about the caretaker were bits and pieces of gossip she had picked up from local people and Junior Boys. He was called Eyolfur and he lived in a three-room suite in the basement of the school. He was seldom seen because he had a violent allergy to the sun, which made his skin break out in weeping sores. He cleaned the school after sunset and, at dawn, retreated to his rooms. Often, during the day, Junior Boys had heard him banging and hammering as he worked in his machine-shop repairing and rebuilding school equipment.

"Is anyone down there?" Alma called. The first time, her throat was so tight and dry that her voice was a hoarse whisper. There was some shuffling, then a series of thumps. She raised her voice and called again.

There was a silence, then the slow scuffing of slippers on cement. A small, dark-haired man with one shoulder set slightly higher than the other and a long thin nose, squinted up the stairs. She remembered that someone had told her he was part Indian.

"What is it?" he demanded. He had lived in the basement of the school so long that he only bothered to learn a teacher's name after the teacher had stayed five years.

"My dog's sick."

"I can't come out now," he said in a high, irritable voice.

"I've got him right here," Alma said. "I brought him with me."

He twisted his head about, shielding his eyes with his hand. "All right," he snapped. "Bring it here."

She eased the box down one step at a time. The caretaker waited until she was nearly at the bottom, then he brushed her away with a quick motion of his hand. He thrust his face close to the box, scrutinizing Skald's head.

When he finally turned to look at Alma, she saw that his eyes were covered in a net of blood vessels and that the flesh along the edges was a fierce, inflamed red.

"It's the temper," he said. "Couldn't you be bothered to get him his shots?"

Alma cringed at the accusation. "I didn't know, I've never had a dog before. Can't you do something now?"

"The time's past for helping" Eyolfur replied. "His brain's affected. You'll have to do away with him"

She sat down on the lowest step.

"Wait here," he told her. He was gone only a minute. When he reappeared, he was wearing sunglasses in which Alma saw herself reflected in miniature. Between them, they carried the box to the landing.

As she rested before taking the box outside, Eyolfur said, "Done's done. Wait six weeks. Scrub your house with disinfectant. Get another pup but bring it to me first for its shots."

When she got home, she pulled the wagon up against the wall. Then she took a garden fork and began to dig. It was slow, heavy work. The ground was hard and blisters formed on the insides of her thumbs and on the palms of her hands. She didn't stop. The blisters broke and tore and new blisters formed before she had made the hole wide enough and deep enough.

She sank the fork into the ground and walked to the Bjarnasons'. Junior Boys had refused to make a second visit there, but she had stopped frequently for coffee. Every time she got a chance, she pried bits and pieces about her grandfather from Helgi's memory. One of the brothers was always at home because they were afraid to leave their mother alone in case a fire should break out. Valdi answered her knock.

"I want to borrow a rifle," she said. "My dog is sick."

"I'll do that for you," he quickly offered.

Her face was like white painted wood. "I'll do it myself but you've got to show me how."

He went into the house. He brought out a rifle so small that in his hands it looked like a toy. He led her down the steps to the yard.

"You pull back the bolt like this," he said, showing her as he spoke. He pushed a tiny brass cartridge into the chamber and slid the bolt into place. He held the tip of the barrel up to a green whisky bottle and pulled the trigger. There was a sharp bang and the bottle cracked in many directions. When he moved the rifle, there was a small, ragged hole that was white around the edge.

"You do it," he said, handing her the rifle and one cartridge. "Keep your eyes open," he ordered as she pressed the muzzle against the bottle.

After she pulled the trigger, he made her do it twice more. Only then did he count out six cartridges.

"Shoot him," he said, "right behind the ear and point the gun so the bullet will go forward." She nodded stiffly. "He'll twitch and kick but that's just muscles." Then with a quiet ferocity, he added, "You shouldn't have to do it."

"It's my dog." Her lips seemed to barely move and her body was so heavy that it took all her effort to keep from falling down.

She hurried back, afraid that Junior Boys would be there ahead of her but everything was as she had left it.

Skald still lay in the box, his eyes nearly shut with pus, his skin as loose and dirty as a cast-off rug. She stood, thinking about what he should have become and her face, already tight, drew even closer together. She would, she promised herself, get another dog and name him the same name. She would see that she got him whatever protection he needed against disease and then, if he were run over or killed by other dogs or shot for any one of the hundreds of reasons that people have for killing, she would get another, and, if necessary, another and another.

She pulled the wagon to the edge of the lot, lifted the box from the wagon and set it gently into the hole. Farther inland, the trees were already softened by leaves but, here, the chill from the lake retarded summer. The elms and ash and poplar rose starkly against the white sun.

Alma fitted the shell into the chamber. Steeling herself, her eyes open, she fired the first shot. Skald scrabbled at the box and lifted his shoulder. Her hands were distant, as awkward as blocks of wood, but she forced the second cartridge into place and fired again.

"What are you doing?" Junior Boys yelled as he came around the corner of the house. He was dressed in a bright green baseball uniform. He had his peaked cap on backwards. He jogged over to where she was standing and looked down. When he looked up, his eyes were shocked clear as window glass. "I'd 've done that," he said. "You had no need."

"It was my dog," she replied.

Author's Commentary

The art of the short story writer is, I believe, to create a new insight or emotion, or to stir an old insight or emotion, in the reader. No matter how well crafted a short story is, if it does not make the reader care, then it fails.

How does the writer make some distant stranger care about what is nothing more than a fantasy? How does the writer overcome the reader's indifference, the separation between them caused by different backgrounds, education, temperaments, cultures?

First of all it must be recognized that the art of the short story writer is created within severe limitations. He has only three major devices with which to work. He has words, the order in which he arranges the words, and punctuation. There is nothing else. This means that he must become a master of the language. With these three simple things, he must not only create but share his internal fantasies.

Furthermore, he must learn craft. He must know the effects of every possible point of view. He must learn where to begin and where to end a story, how to develop character, render description and relate narration, control pacing. He must learn all there is to know about possible dramatic structures so that he can decide to organize a story around a plot, epiphany, theme, mood. He must master not just the structure of scenes but of any possible dramatic unit.

But all of the above are as nothing if he does not have the ability to do two things: think and feel.

There can be no story unless the author has something to say. The author must be intelligent, sensitive, perceptive. Only then can his stories be intelligent, sensitive, perceptive. The art of the stories will be limited precisely as the author is limited.

Perhaps even more importantly, the author must be able to feel. If he cannot feel, his stories will have no feeling. Then the stories will either be abstract philosophy or flat, stale narrations of event.

All these individual bits and pieces must exist within the author to exist within the story. Craft, passion, intelligence must combine ultimately for one purpose, to make the reader care, even if it is only for one brief moment.

William D. Valgardson (1939 –   )

William Valgardson was born in Winnipeg and grew up in Gimli, an Icelandic community in northern Manitoba. He was educated at United College (B.A.), the University of Manitoba (B.Ed.), and the University of Iowa (M.F.A.). He has taught high school and creative writing at the University of Calgary. His three collections of short stories include: *Bloodflowers* (1973); *God is not a Fish Inspector* (1975); and *Red Dust* (1978). His first novel, *Gentle Sinners*, was published in the spring of 1980.

The First Born Son

ERNEST BUCKLER

He had kept this place, the best thing he had, till he could give it to his own son, and now when he offered it to David he saw it meant nothing. That he despised it.

The pale cast of fatigue smudged Martin's skin and little grooves of it emptied into the corners of his mouth. But this land was his own, and a son of his own flesh was holding the plough that broke it. His thoughts were tired half-thoughts but they did not ache.

He felt the wine of the fall day and for a minute his feet wandered, inattentive, from the furrow. The dogged, slow-eyed oxen followed him, straining nose-down at his heels. The plough ran out wide in the sod. David tried to flip over the furrow with a sudden wrench of the handles, but the chocolate-curling lip of earth broke and the share came clear.

"Whoa!" David yelled.

"Whoa!" Martin roared at the oxen.

"For God's sake, Dad, can't you watch where you're going? It's hard enough to hold this damn thing when you keep 'em straight."

"Now don't get high," Martin said. But there was no echo of David's temper in his voice. He knew David was tired. And David could not learn to handle his weariness. He fought it. It was no use to do that. If you let it come and go, quietly, after supper it made a lazy song in your muscles and was good to think about. Martin remembered the night David was born. They had thought Ellen would die. It was Christmas Eve. There was not a breath of wind in the moonlit, Christmas-kindled air. Snow lay in kind folds on the ground, shadowed in the dead-still moonlight like the wrinkles of a white cloak. On the brook Martin could watch the gay, meaningless movements of the children skating. And sometimes a fragment of their heartless laughter would break away and fall inside the room. Ellen's pain-tight face stared at her pale hands outside the quilt. The kind-smelling Christmas tree was a cruel mockery. Now and then Martin would go outside and listen, bare-headed, for the doctor's sleighbells, trying to separate their faint, far-off tinkle from the frost-crackle of the spruces. He would think he heard them. Then there would be nothing. Runner tracks shone like ising-glass in the moonlight. He heard nothing but the heartless laughter of the children.

It seemed hours later, when he was not listening at all, that he looked out and all at once the dark body of the horse turned in the gate, by the corner of the house. His heart gave a great leap. The helplessness left him. This man could hold Ellen back from death. The moonlight seemed to turn warm. After the doctor went in with Ellen the laughing of the children did not seem so far-off and strange.

The quick white grip of fear came again when he heard the doctor's hand on the door again ... but Martin looked up and the doctor was *smiling*. Suddenly the whole night was a great, neighbourly, tear-starting friend. He had a son now. He knew it would be a son.

Martin felt shy to kiss Ellen in front of the doctor, but there was a new peace and a strange swagger in his soul. When he got the doctor's horse for him, it seemed like the best horse in all the world; and half-ashamed and half-afraid not to, but somehow wanting desperately to thank *someone,* he knelt down for a minute on the hay and prayed. Outside the barn, the voices of the children laughing were a glad song in his ears, now. In the bedroom, Ellen murmured "My own Little Jesus" ... and the thick spruce-cosy smell of the Christmas tree and the shining moonlight outside and the soft peace after danger past clothed the minutes in a sweet armour. . . . A son. . . . A son. . . . And Ellen well. . . . Martin couldn't believe how good it was. He would never die now. He had a son, now ... when he was too old to break up the land he loved, any more, this son would come in at night and they would plan together, just the same. This son's sons. . . .

"Well, maybe you think it's *easy* to hold this damn thing," David said. It *must* be that he's tired, Martin thought. He can't mean that ... this same David... my own son cannot find it hard to plough this land of our own. I never found it so, when I was young. Ploughed land was always the prettiest sight in the world to me. It was always good at the end of the day, to stand and look over the brown waves of earth and know that I had opened my land to the sun and the air and the rain. I don't like to hear this son of mine talk that way. He says too many things like that. I don't like to hear my son talk that way. The ploughed land was here before us and it will last after us and our hands should be proud to work in it.

"Haw," Martin called, and the lip of the earth curled back and buried the grass again.

In the city, David thought, their bodies are not dead-tired now. They have not walked all day in their own tracks ... back and forth, back and forth, in their own damn tracks. There is movement and lights and laughing. Every day there is something *new* ... something to keep alive for. The same people here ... the same talk ... the same eternal drudgery ... your nose in the ground all day long, from morning till night, like a damned ox ... cooped up in that damned circle of trees.

The last brown beech leaves on the hardwood hill drifted down to the ground, dreamily, a little sad to die. A flock of partridges made their heavy headlong flight into an apple tree and began to bud. In the fields, the potato stalks lay in blackened heaps. The earth was grey and brown. All the colour was in the sky or hung in the thin air. Only the stray pumpkins, left to ripen on the withered vines, gave back any of it. They were like bubbles of the sad October sunshine. Martin loved these quick chill dusks, and then later the kind eye of lamplight in the window, and the friendly, wood-warmed, table-set kitchen.

They came to the end of the furrow. Martin split the rest of the acre with his eye.

"Will we finish her before supper, son?" he asked.

"Do you want to work all night too!"

Martin stopped the oxen.

"What's wrong with you today, Dave?" he said. "If you planned to go after the partridges. ..."

"Partridges, hell!"

'Well then, what's. ..."

David hesitated.

"I'm so damn sick of this place I. ..."

"Is *that* so!" Martin said slowly. "What's wrong with this place?" He kicked over a sod with the toe of his shabby boot. An old man looked out of his face for the first time. It was true, then. ... It had never been because David was tired or lonely or weak or young. ... It was because David had always *hated* this land ... the land that would be his own some day. A sick little cloud settled on his heart. He *had* no son, then.

"What's *wrong* with it?" David said. "The same damn thing over and over from morning till night ... every day and every day ...

78

Thoreau MacDonald, Hawk at Evening, *1937*

what future is there for anyone here?" David kept his back bent to the plough handles. He felt a little mean and ashamed when he heard the sound of his own words.

"What future is there here?" The question sounded meaningless to Martin. He had the truth, to contradict it. There is the first day in April when the fields stir again and it is good all day just to feel your breathing. ... There is the sky-blue August day when the whole green wind is full of leaves and growing, and Sunday morning you walk in the waving growth-full garden rows and wish you could keep this day forever, hold it back from going. ... It is good, too, when the snow whistles cold and mournful because it can never get inside the pane to warm itself. ... It is *all* good, all of it. ... Men live here as long as their sons live, to see the clearings their axes have made and the living grass that sprang from their tracks in the first furrow and the green things their hands gave life to. ... "The same thing over and over. ..." Martin did not speak. Only his sick thoughts pleaded, patiently, silently, incredulously. We did not plough yesterday, David. We took the day off and last night this time we sat at the edge of the woods and waited for the shy-eyed deer to come out into the old back field.

I thought it was good to sit there and smoke with my son after we boiled the supper kettle, not talking much but not feeling the silence either, and watch the dead leaves drifting down past the rocks, in the cool-talking brook. The fire itself felt good, in spite of the sun, and it was good to hear the nervous twitter of the partridges in the apple trees just before it got too dark to pick out their heads along the sights of the gun. ... Or is this like the day last spring we nodded at each other across the pool with the foam on it each time we held a broken-neck trout throbbing in the tight of our palms? Or the day we cursed the heat in the alder-circled meadow and our shirts stuck to our backs like broken blisters? The hay smelt good that night, just the same, and it was good to hear the wagon wheels groan on the sill just before the dark thunder-frown of the sky burst and the barn roof beat back the rain. I remember the night we ate our first supper in the house I had built with my own hands. That night the neighbours came in, and we danced half the night to the fiddles. It was easy with everyone, like with brothers, and we loved them all ... and it was good that night to lie in bed and let sleep's drowsy wind blow out the candles of thought. The day they brought your brother Peter home loose in their arms before it was dinner time, his dead body so broken your mother could not hold it, that day was different. ... And the next day. ... And the next day. ...

"Well what kind of a place suits *you*?" Martin said at last. David straightened.

"The city, of course! Who'd want to live in this God-forsaken hole when you can get a job in the city?"

"Did you say the *city*?"

"Yeah. The city," he said laconically.

Martin listened with sick wonder to this stranger who had been his son. The city. . . . It's *there* the days are the same. I thought it was very lonely in the city, the time I was there. The stone things move, but they do not change. My feet were always on stone. I could not walk on the ground and look over it and know it was my own. They never looked at the sky there, or listened for the rain.

When I looked at the sky there, the sun I saw was a strange one . . . it did not make friends with the stone. The stone houses were alike, and the days were alike, and never till they died could the people lie in bed at night and listen to rain on the corn after a long heat. They had nothing to breathe but their own tired breaths. I remember their faces. There was stone in them, too. They were all alike. They looked as if they never awoke from their tired dreams of the night. Their minds kept turning in their own tracks, like the weary wheels that could find no rest on the pavements. The soft-fingered women-faced men lived in houses, and the house-smell clung to everything they said or did when they went outside. When they talked, it was empty, because their eyes saw nothing but the stone things that their hands had not built . . . and none of them had anything to say that could not be said with words. It was very lonely there. They laughed too much. But not even love or death could melt their aloneness. Even when they laughed, their eyes did not change. And when they died, no one remembered, and there was nothing left of them.

I liked it in the city, now, this time, David thought. The street lights began to come on, a little before it was dark, and excitement seemed to stir in the busy pavements. The wind was not strong enough to lift itself above the street, but the women's skirts clung to their bodies as they passed. So many different women's bodies! What if they *didn't* speak? The bright, metallic faces of always-rich women seemed to shine in the shop-window light, and you knew you would feel clumsy and ashamed with them, but it was good to think of having their soft flesh alone somewhere in the dark. There was so much light there, then . . . and life. Like when you took off your work-clothes and shaved and felt smoother and brighter and ready for things. There was life, not death, at the end of the day. Here, my God . . . the same old bare maples weaving back and forth against a sky that made your lips blue just to look at it, and never the sound of a strange voice, and later the snow sifting lonely through the spokes of the wagon wheels. . . . What a God-forsaken place to be *young* in. Maybe his father didn't mind, they didn't seem to mind *missing* things when they got old. Old people didn't seem to dread being quiet and letting things slip like this. They thought it was because they were wise ... it was because they were half-dead already. If he thought he'd ever get like that about things when he got old. ... He'd never get old. He swore a desperate promise to himself that he'd never, never, never get that awful patience like his father ... standing there now, with that stupid look on his face, like one of the oxen. ...

"But Dave," Martin said slowly, "this place will be *yours* some day, you know that."

"What do *I* want of this old *place*?"

A whiteness came into Martin's face that was different from the whiteness of the cold or the weariness. He remembered the day his father had said the same thing to him. They had both felt shy and awkward, and he could say nothing, but as soon as he was alone, he had looked over this land, the tight tears of pride came warm into his eyes. He had kept this place, the best·thing he had, till he could give it to his own son, and now when he offered it to David he saw it meant nothing. That he despised it. He had known through and through how his own father felt.

"It was always good enough here for *me*," Martin said.

"All right, but what did you ever *amount* to?"

Martin was stung into a sudden anger. "As much as *you* ever will, you. ..."

Then he looked over the fields, slowly, and a break came into his anger. Why today, only a few hours ago, starting to plough, it had been, without a thought, so sweet, so safe, so sure ... he and his son ploughing and him trying to show David how to turn the furrow better and David trying his best. Things just didn't come handy for David, it must be that. He had half felt Ellen working quiet and happy in the house and the smoke went straight from the chimney into the clear, sun-filled air and there had been no hurry or fret in the fields or the slow oxen or his thoughts. Now ... it could never be the same again between him and David, now. Every time they said a sharp word to each other now, these sick things would all come back. ... What if David was right? What *had* he ever amounted to? Well, he had been young here, and youth was very fresh and full here in the fields and the sun and very long, some of it never died, it grew green again with each April sun. He had had a wife of his own kind, and everything they had, they had got with their own hands, his hands and hers. There had been a lot of tiredness but there was always the quiet night afterwards and the slow kindly talk. There had never been an end of work, but you could always stop to talk across the fields to your neighbour, and you got along just the same. There had not been much money, but there had always been the sweet smell of bread in the kitchen and the soft song of wood in the kitchen stove. There had been no strangers among them, and when you died these men you had lived your whole life with would not work that day, even if there was clover to be hauled in and rain in the wind ... and you would lie in the land that your hands and your feet knew best, and the same breezes you had breathed would always blow over you. Surely that was enough for a man. If your son. ... If David. ... It was hard to believe that your own son was not like you wanted him to be. But, Martin thought sadly, you couldn't make him see, if he didn't feel that way. You wished ... but if he felt that way, there was no way to make him see.

"Well Dave," Martin said slowly, "if you're *bound* to go away, I suppose. ..."

"Oh," David said impatiently, "let it go, let it go ... I'll stay," he added sullenly.

He is almost afraid of me, Martin thought. He won't even talk it over with me. He has no use for my talk. He wants to keep me away from him. He don't think I can understand him at all. I try. ...

He walked around to the oxen's heads and picked the whip.

"Haw," he said quietly. "Just cut her light here, son."

David put his hands back on the handles but he didn't speak. He threw the plough around when they turned the furrows, so the chain jerked taut in the yoke. "Easy now, boys," Martin cajoled the oxen.

A bare little wind started in the bare maples. The sun burned cold and lonesome in the blind windows of the church across the road and the long withered grass bent over the cold grey sand in the middle of the built-up graves. Peter's grave. ... Peter would coax to hold the whip. He could hardly make his small voice loud enough to stir the oxen, but they obeyed him. Martin could see the crazy nostrils of the running horses and then Peter's small crumpled body on the rock heap where the wheel had struck. ...

The cows came up from the pasture, calling hollowly to be let in. The sky looked away from its own darkening face in the mud-bottomed puddles of the road. The blood in Martin's face came blue to the skin, and his blue eyes, a little faded with weariness, looked like frozen spots holding up the weight of his face. He walked back-to, guiding the oxen by the horns to help David keep the furrow straight, but David did not straighten his back, even when Martin stopped for a rock. Martin would come around and kick out the rock himself.

Martin blew on his hands and tried to start a smile in the corners of his tired, cold-thin, lips.

"Time for mittens, I guess. *Your* hands cold?"

"No," David said.

A shaft of the sun broke for a minute through the blue, wind-cold clouds. Long bands of it searchlit the grey rocks, without warming them.

"Snow comin'," Martin said.

The sun went down, and the sky made a few cold-pink patterns at the horizon. It would not be as sad again until April.

Martin turned the oxen for one more furrow. He could not stop, until he was *sure* how David. . . . Maybe if he kept on, David would say something himself about stopping, and he could show him then how ready he was to listen to him and take the oxen off the tongue.

"*I'll* never ask him to stop if he ploughs all night. . . ." David was so tired the muscles of his legs felt like a frayed rope and a tight cord drew his temples together. The blood seemed to drain from his face and throb heavy in his neck. The ashes of weariness sifted through the bright surface of his thoughts. The oxen lifted their heavy feet and deposited them carefully on the ground. The plough dug its slow way through the earth.

"I guess we're just gettin' her done in time," Martin said.

David said nothing.

"I guess this clears things up, about, for winter. You'll have a little more time to hunt, now, Dave."

Ellen came to the corner of the house, holding down her apron with one hand against the tug of the wind, and called supper.

"All right," Martin called back.

"Hungry, Dave?" he said.

"No."

Dave glanced at his father's face. For the first time he noticed how tired it looked. He felt sorry for his father, for a minute, and a little ashamed. He'd *have* to stay as long as his father was alive, he supposed.

They came to the end of the furrow. Martin hesitated.

"Well, I guess we'll let her go at that for tonight," he said. "We can wind her up in the morning, easy." He hesitated again.

"David," he said, "if you really *want* to go away. . . ."

David's impatience flared again. He forgot his father's face.

"Oh, for God's sake," he said, "can't you let that *drop*? I said I'd stay, didn't I? What more do you want? I'll stay here as long as *you're* here, anyway. So you need not worry."

So it is that way. A small coal touched suddenly against Martin's heart. He will wait, but he will be glad . . . so he can go away. If he was waiting for it, so the place would be all his own then, it would be . . . but he will be waiting, so he can go away. There will be a stranger here, and nothing will be done the same. There will be a strange name in my house, and maybe they will let the alders creep back over the acre field because they did not clear it for the first time and plough it with their own hands . . . and the grass will grow tall and strange over the graves.

He pulled the bolt from the tongue. It was true. It was true, then. He *had* no son. David took his hands from the plough. Martin waited for a minute to see if he would line the plough up for the next furrow in the morning. David did not move. Martin walked around to the plough. David went to the oxen's head, took up the whip and started with them to the barn. Martin pulled the plough around and lay the chain straight out along the next furrow. Ellen came to the corner of the house and called supper again, but Martin did not answer. He watched David take the oxen past the house. He saw Ellen say something to him, but David did not reply.

He bent down and dug the mud from the ploughshare. It shone underneath, where the earth had polished it, like a sword. The earth smelled cold and silent. He moved a few stones, absently, with his foot and stood for a minute with his eyes on the ground. Like the night they buried Peter. He felt lost in the long, dead day.

In the porch, he listened to see if David might be talking to the oxen. There was no sound but the bells, as David jerked the yoke-straps. Martin caught his breath quickly. He *had* no son. Peter was dead. He *had* no son, now. He scraped the dirt from his heels with a stick from the chipyard and went inside the house.

"Well, what in the *world* have you two been doing?" Ellen said, moving across the scrubbed soft-wood floor from the stove to the table. The warm breath of food rose sweet in the oil-lamplight. She held the dipper of water for Martin's hands over the basin in the sink. "Are you goin' to do a coupla more acres after supper?" she joked.

"Yeah, I was kinda thinkin' we might," Martin laughed.

But his laughter was heavy and grey, like a hawk rising.

Author's Commentary

There was a time, not long ago, when the short story was an endangered species, trading notes of commiseration with the whooping crane. Now this is gradually changing; as if feeling were coming back into a dead limb.

Much of this, of course, is a legacy from the three great innovators. Hemingway, who sang a song of simplicity and the telling detail, bidding us to strip off the little window boxes of adjectives and adverbs from our prose and go straight to the verbs where the action is. T.S. Eliot who, despite a lifestyle that of a titmouse, charted the Wasteland for us. And the teeming Joyce, who indexed the whole stream-of-consciousness. ... Until quite suddenly the underlying truth of the whole universe dawns on us: everything is everything else. (Right you were, Miss Stein!)

The heart of loneliness is the winter dusk when the iron sky burns colder than ice with savage light...is the pewter afternoon when someone is playing the piano badly by ear ... is the old lady in the institution whispering, "There's no ice cream today." ...

And the brook as clear as the brook in a Psalm...

And the hush of freshness walks on the air like Christ ...

I myself have discovered a blazing literary genius of tender years. Herewith his work entire: "She was beautiful and young and rich and good-looking and she had diamonds and perls and opals and she used to eat succulent dinners at a canteen." At first, I found that "succulent" a mite suspect; but on second reading, perfect. For the ten-year-old's idea of heaven *is* a canteen, isn't it? God! I wish I could write like that!

Ernest Buckler (1908 —   )

Ernest Buckler was born in Amherst West, Nova Scotia, and was educated at Dalhousie University and the University of Toronto. Apart from a short time spent working in Toronto, he has lived on the family farm near Annapolis Royal, N.S. His first published novel, *The Mountain and the Valley*, is considered a Canadian classic, and was followed by: *The Cruelest Month* (1963); *Ox Bells and Fireflies* (1968); and *The Rebellion of Young David and Other Stories* (1975). He was awarded the Canada Centennial Medal in 1967 and the Order of Canada in 1974.

Spring

ANTONINE MAILLET

When yer time comes, you gotta give up; you can grumble, 'n kick, 'n get yer back up, but you're gonna go anyway.

This monologue, spoken by an ancient scrubwoman to her husband, Gapi, has been excerpted from Maillet's novel *La Sagouine*.

Ah! well, Holy Mother of Christ! will you look at that this mornin! Gapi! Come 'n see, Gapi! Ain't no less than ten regiments of wild geese in the sky, this mornin. 'n not a speck of snow on the roofs. Makes you feel good to fill up yer lungs with fresh air early in the mornin. April can't be far away now. Gapi! Is the month of March over yet? . . . Should be soon. Mus'be Spring these days, fer sure. If only they hadn' taken my calendars. Had the Arvin's one, 'n the one of l'Aratouère, 'n of the Royal Canadian Mounting Police. But there's always aroun' some kid that takes'em fr'm me, cause of the picture . . . Is the month of March over, Gapi? That's the least of Gapi's worries, what day of the week it is, or what month of the year. He says it ain't cause we got a calendar that we're closer or farther fr'm death; or that we ain't gonna stop the time jus' cause we can give it a name. Maybe we ain't gonna stop it, but we sure can look at it passin by, 'n know that some times is better than others.

Got a sayin of my own, that Spring is the good season fer us. Some say it's summer. But I'm pretty sure that to be happy, a person's gotta hope fer som'n, som'n better. So, durin the whole of Spring, we're hopin fer summer. We wait fer clams 'n quahaugs, fer blueberries 'n warm weather, 'n fer'em picnics at Sainte-Anne's 'n Sainte-Marie's. While in the month of August, we ain't waitin fer not'n anymore. It ain't havin som'n that gets a person feelin good, it's knowin you're gonna have it. That's why Spring is the best of times, I says.

I remember the days when I stayed at my father's, 'n when my mother was still alive. We had us a small piece of land aroun' the house. Ah! not a big farm 'n no lumber land either. Jus' half a field of clover that he'd wanna plough once every five years. In'em years, my mother would hurry 'n plant her gardenin seeds over three or four rows, before my father had time to turn'em into oat fields. 'n then, she'd send us to weed'em. 'n all the time we was weedin, we was thinkin of the month of July with its turnips 'n its carrots, 'n the month of August with'em corn-cobs. We wasn' thinkin 'bout flies 'n mosquitoes, right then, or 'bout crows 'n hail. In Spring, you never think of mosquitoes 'n crows. But you watch the wild geese go by 'n you fill yer lungs with fresh air. 'n you wait.

Gapi says, makes a person moody to keep on hopin like that. We're better off not gettin any ideas, he says, if we don't wanna be disappointed. Says that a person 'd never feel hurt if he hadn' started believin in dreams. All right, all right, I says. Musn' build dreams. Musn' build castles, I says to him. But we can always wait fer the month of July, cause we're pretty sure 'bout that ... Ain't we sure 'bout that? I says to him. We ain't never sure 'bout not'n, he says, 'n you can't believe in'em dreams. So, you know you can't count on Gapi to change yer tune cause yer changin seasons. He don't put his trust in Spring anymore than he puts it in priests, in oysters, or in the gov'ment. Says he don't trust nobody to live his life for him. Fer that matter, couldn' of trust 'mself either, cause his life, well ... Ain't easy when you ain't got a trade, an education, or nobody to get you out of the hole. Gapi says he don't want nobody's help; well, that's cause he knows even if he wanned some, he wouldn' get none ... Ain't easy.

'n yet, he ain't lazy, Gapi. In any case, when he's workin, he's on his feet. 'n the day he came by, his hatchet on his shoulder, lookin fer me at my father's place, − that was more than fifty years ago − well, he wasn' sittin on his butt, I'm tellin you. Young 'n sturdy, he was. 'n his shoulders was stronger than a moose, that's right! He stood straight, in those days, with his hair real black 'n his eyes like the blue sea. 'n he had all his teeth, 'n hair on his chest. It was Spring, like today. The wild geese was comin'in fr'm the South; 'n the seagulls was so crazy they'd throw 'mselves against the masts 'n get caught in the sails. They was already some pine-cones on the trees, almost as big as that, 'n the sap was drippin fr'm the branches. The air 'n the earth that day was smellin so good, that even if Gapi had stunk, I think I wouldn' of noticed, I'm tellin you.

Well, summer passed; 'n autumn came with its rottin soil, 'n winter with ice over the bay 'n wind through the cracks of the house. Those days, I couldn' do my washin no more, without the clothes freezin hard on the line; 'n Gapi started stinkin, like the

André Bieler, Les Patates, Argentenay, *1929*

others. But when Spring started to wake up fr'm its winterin, we all decided to come out, 'n we got back our strength. 'n the air started smellin like perfume, 'n Gapi too, I'm tellin you! ... Well, almost. Almost as much as the year before. But the followin year, Spring came late, 'n we had to bury a newborn child. So, that season, I figured summer had hooked on to winter, 'n they hadn' been any month of April. Even the wild geese wasn' flyin over no more, 'n they was no May flowers to be found. You could of said it was a Spring squeezed in between ice-packs 'n fire-flies. No wild geese, that year, 'n no musk in the woods, 'n Gapi didn' smell too good either.

Well, it went away, like the rest. Bad times always end up passin. They pass like rancid butter when you spread it between two slices of bread. Best thing is to close yer eyes 'n wait fer better times. You can stay with yer eyes shut fer a long while; but every now 'n then, there comes a Spring with wild geese 'n pine-cones. 'n it's jus' like I says to Gapi: after you fasted all through Lent, you find that baloney 'n hard boiled eggs sure taste good on Easter mornin.

... You see, maybe Spring is a gift the Good Lord gives to poor folks alone, since you must of been shiverin jus' about all winter to be wishin so hard fer April's sun; 'n you must of been buried in snow to go out with yer hatchet 'n dig yerself some water furrows; 'n you must of been eatin warmed-up beans fer months in a row, to come out 'n smell the fresh air 'n think 'bout 'em small early carrots still asleep underground. Spring is made fer those folks that had a tough time gettin through winter. That's how come I says it's the season of the ol' folks or of the poor folks.

I says like this, that a person's got a season of his own, like he's got his destiny 'n his final hour. When yer time comes, you gotta give up; you can grumble, 'n kick, 'n get yer back up, but you're gonna go anyway. You also gotta live through yer fate; that's in writin 'n you can't erase it. Well, same thing with the seasons 'n the months of the year. You can't help it. It's cause of the water, 'n the sun, 'n the smell of the woods that gets under yer skin. Ain't only a question of findin som'n to eat. I try to tell Gapi 'bout it. Why is it the salmons come back swimmin up-stream? Why is it the wild geese fly home against the wind? Makes you think, don't it? It means there's som'n in this life-givin earth that looks like you or ties you down.

Yet, that's gotta be why you stay on this earth, cause it looks like you. A person is a little bit like a tree or an animal: he ends up wearin the colour of the earth that fed him. Take the rabbits in the woods, they is white in winter, 'n grey in summer; that's how come they

90

manage not to get caught: they look too much like the green 'r the snow. I think that's why we too end up lookin pretty much like the earth.

Our skin is kind of brown 'n a little bit cracked; 'n as we grow ol', the wrinkles of the face look like furrows in a garden; 'n bones get crooked at the joints like branches of a birch tree; 'n feet sink into the earth like they wanned to take root. We look like this land, I'm tellin you.

This land, 'n the sea. She's the one that fed us most 'n saved us fr'm distress. When the land happens to fail you, you still got the sea, with its clams 'n its smelts. Shouldn' speak ill of the sea, I says to the others, she saved us so many many times. Even if high tides in fall come 'n get you right up to yer kitchen floor; 'n the ice in Spring takes yer boat at sea; 'n storms on the other side of the sand dunes drown fishermen every year. Even then, she's the one that made us, 'n looks like us the most.

Usin her as a mirror, our eyes turned deep 'n blue. 'n havin watched so long fer fish deep in the water, our cheeks rose high 'n our brows grew close. That's why we end up lookin like the sea that surrounds the country. Yep, that's what they says. They says we got a low 'n raspy voice. Maybe true. 'n that we don't talk fast. Well, we ain't use' to talkin a lot cause we don't know too much what to say to people. So, when strangers come around, we hold our tongue. Not that we ain't got not'n to say, we'd like to tell'em 'bout the sea, 'n the country, 'n us . . . But usually, we only ask'em 'bout their folks 'n their jobs. 'n at the end, well . . . Ain't easy talkin to people, with a raspy voice.

Well, I think we've been breathin too long the salt of the water, 'n it stayed stuck in the throat; 'n the nor'easter widened our foreheads; 'n the pebbles hardened the soles of our feet; 'n the cry of the gulls in the sou'wester 'n the wail of the wave that comes crashin on the sand-banks at night got entangled in our ears, 'n that's why we don't talk fast 'n why our voice kind of drawls, like they say.

Well, a person's gotta take 'mself for what he is, 'n not try to talk 'n walk like other folks. When you 'n yer forefathers have been walkin fer two centuries on rows of red soil, or on pebbles 'n shells, you can't have wobbly legs 'n springs in yer feet; 'n when you've been forced to face the winds of the open sea, you jus' can't have skin that's white 'n soft; 'n how can you talk fancy with all that sea salt in yer lungs 'n throat? . . . Nope, a person's gotta look like the land that made him 'n fed him, 'n that's what ties him up at home 'n makes him ache. 'n wakes up in Spring, it does. 'n it makes you remember . . .

Funny, but me, Spring, it makes me wanna go out 'n whistle, 'n walk faster than usual; but it also makes me ache. Hard to explain. Like if I had a cork jammed between the heart 'n the tonsils, or cotton-wool where the lungs is. It ain't a heart-ache, not'n like that. Nope... It's like an achin, but not an achin 'bout som'one or som'n ...more like an achin fer the sun ... way back then.

... The snow would start meltin in March, half through Lent. The other kids, to keep Lent, they wouldn' eat no sugar 'n no chocolate. So us, to try 'n do the same, we'd save the orange we had fer Christmas, 'n we'd leave it there on top of the cupboard till Easter, as penance. 'n on Easter Saturday, on the stroke of the Angelus, we'd jump on the orange: well, it was rotten. We'd lost an orange, but we'd saved our Lent, 'n we was happy. 'n durin the whole month of April, we'd gather small tadpoles fr'm the brooks 'n we'd watch'em turn into frogs inside the bottles; then, we'd let'em go. 'n in the month of May, we'd walk three miles every night to do our prayers fer the *mois de Marie*. It ain't that we had to do it, but it made us go across the baseball field; so we'd stop there fer a while to watch'em play. 'n already in the month of June, they was rhubarb at our neighbour's, 'n all the women was plantin, 'n weedin, 'n callin 'mselves names fr'm one fence to the other. Funny, but each Spring, it all comes back to me, 'n it makes me ache.

...Makes me ache, but it ain't a sad ache. Nope. More like if... All right, just imagine you're out on yer door-step, one Spring mornin, 'n you see wild geese passin over 'n goin inland, behind yer father's place, right where you was born 'n where you was raised. 'n you see a drop of water clingin to the tip of a branch, 'n then you hear it fall on the snow, 'n run in the furrow, 'n rush to the shore, into the sea. 'n you can jus' feel the clover that 'd like to come out of the earth, 'n the ice goin down the river. 'n the seagulls cryin after the wild geese, 'n the wild geese still flying north ... 'n you don't know where you are no more. You start hearin the cries of the tadpoles, the songs of the *mois de Marie*, 'n the crackin of the ice all along the bay. It's like yer life is all bunched up in yer veins 'n you can no longer tell the difference between sunny days of the past 'n the ones of today, or between the gulls' cryin 'n yer neighbours' name-callin. Like all yer memories come rushin back, while Spring closes in, 'n you look at the passin of the wild geese. All yer memories, all yer hopes, 'n all yer achin. You feel like whistlin, 'n diddlin...but you can't cause you got that cork right here 'n cotton-wool where the lungs is...

But one day, maybe we'll find a Spring season, a real one, drippin all over 'n reekin of musk, with endless processions of wild geese in

the sky, 'n no more achin, just a nice easy feelin in yer throat 'n all
over the skin, a real Spring that'll never end, but that'll last, 'n last,
'n ... well, that'll be heaven, 'n that day, gotta feelin we'll all be dead
and in Paradise. Gonna go 'n see if *la Sainte's* got a calendar.

Author's Commentary

Having acquired the ability to write through the spoken word,
mingling these two skills came to me quite naturally.

First, I learned to narrate — a gift which was passed on to me
through my colorful storytelling ancestors. Later, under the
influence of literary masters, I gradually developed a very personal
style, learned to choose my words, phrases and punctuation
effectively, but especially to express my own feelings and perception
of the world around me.

Like most authors or artists, I have an outrageous ambition: that
of making time stand still just long enough to capture and create a
character, a story, a monologue, a novel ... no doubt in order to
make them live on forever. But despite all our efforts, Destiny
prevails and stories must also die. Perhaps that is why even
comedies are basically tragic and why one cannot write about
Spring without hinting at the coming winter.

Antonine Maillet (1929 —   )

An Acadian, born in Buctouche, New Brunswick, Antonine
Maillet was educated at the Université de Montréal and at the
Université de Laval, where she now teaches. She is noted for *La
Sagouine* (1971), sixteen monologues in Acadian French. These
have been dramatized and successfully performed across Canada by
Viola Leger. Maillet's novel *Pelagie-la-Charrette* won the prestigious
Prix Goncourt, one of the world's most coveted literary prizes.

The Butterfly Ward

MARGARET GIBSON

Blink. Stop. Deep breath. Stop. Fast shallow breathing. Stop. Deep, slow breathing. Stop. Blink rapidly. Stop. How used to all this I have become.

Sometimes it can be beautiful inside this space. Most people, people who can ride on buses and streetcars and eat doughnuts for breakfast if and when they want and don't have to dial O on their phones to make a call would think that statement crazy. Maybe it is a bit crazy. Even phone calls cannot be simple here, everything twisted into complications but I am getting used to it now.

I have been here a month now on the neurological ward of a big hospital in Toronto. The biggest, I am told, with new wings that gleam and old ones that make me feel like a nun hiding in a bombed-out convent. I come from Kitchener, that is my home, but they sent me here. They, whoever *they* may be, said that the doctor working here on my case, Dr. Carter, is the best neurologist in Ontario, maybe even all of Canada. The mysterious and secret *they* who have so neatly pigeon-holed my life. I wonder if I was supposed to be impressed with this news as my mother packed my suitcase and told me of all the wonderful little boutiques in Toronto, slipping in the famous name among the dried coloured flowers of the boutiques. My father stood in the doorway with his pipe in a reassuring mouth. I was not impressed. I had seen so many doctors for the secrets that dwelt inside my nebula that I was not. If a year or two ago they had told me of the famous Dr. Carter in this huge city hospital in Toronto — then, then I might have been impressed. Not now. I am a cynic, old and tangled in the opal of my mind. I was 21 last April, it is the end of May now. I came to this place — NEUROLOGICAL WARD, it was like that in bold letters, on the 28th of April and it is now May 30th. Yes, sometimes it is quite beautiful. I lie in my bed at night and creep into my nebula and watch fire and white matter like fine mists drifting past, I float with the clouds. There is no fire in there, my imagination has placed it thus so it can drift with the white mists. I have always loved beautiful things.

They have come to poke and pin Mrs. Watson. She moans, no, no she cannot drink another quart of water and no more needles. Now, now they murmur softly. I am supposed to be asleep but I watch from the fine mists of my nebula, so beautiful and secret in there. I know this game and how to grit your teeth and pretend it doesn't matter that ten times in one night you are pinned with needles like a butterfly to a board or that you must drink a quart of water each time until it is like a poisonous liquid, a gas bloating up your stomach. Now, now the two nurses murmur softly, only two more to go, with their pins and poisonous liquid. One jabs her in the hip with the long, slender needle, pinned again, the other holds out the quart of water to her in a plastic jug. No, Mrs. Watson whimpers, I feel sick to my stomach. Now, now they murmur. The pinned butterfly drinks the poisonous liquid, the two collectors of butterfly wings stand beside her board to make sure she drinks it all. They go. The pinned butterfly flutters and gasps and is free for another two hours. I know this game and how to play it. I have been the butterfly three times. The injections keep the liquid from pouring out, from escaping the body otherwise the doctors could not get a clear picture of the bloated nebula. Brain, to strangers to this place. I know this game.

Mrs. Watson flutters and gasps trying her twisted wings. "It's all right, Mrs. Watson," I murmur now from outside my nebula. I am lying in bed on the neuorological ward and I must say to this woman that it is all right. She is 40 but looks nearly 60. I am 21 but look eighteen. I must say to this woman that it is all right. She has never been pinned on the butterfly board before nor drenched inside with the poisonous liquid bloating her stomach. She has only been here five days.

"Is that you, Kira?"

"Yes," I answer softly. My mother is fond of Russian books and her greatest desire is to go to Russia someday and see the Kremlin and its turrets gleaming in the sun in white snow, thus the name Kira, which is Russian. At my conception visions of Russia and bells and snow going on forever and ever and the Kremlin shining in the sun were mingled with the sperm that made me, Kira. They lay in her womb ready for the sperm that would make me a Russian. Waiting, simply waiting unbeknownst to my father. The sperm came and the womb filled with Russia mingled with the sperm and received its new comrade, Kira. I have forgotten what it means but something very lovely I am sure. Mrs. Watson whispers in the darkness, "You are such a nice girl, Kira, so young. What are you doing here? Are you crazy?"

"No," I say.

"They sent me here from a mental hospital. An O.H. I don't belong here, I didn't belong in that other place either. They said I cried all the time and got angry and threw things but I didn't! Liars, all of them! I don't do those things, you can see that for yourself. I thought the mental hospital was bad but this is worse. I'd rather have a shock treatment any time − zzz − burns out the brain. Does that scare you that I'm from a crazy joint?"

I can see her grey hair frizzled in the darkness like the zzz sound. "No," I answer because it doesn't, nothing much does anymore.

"Then why are you here?" Her voice is curious, grasping for a reason she can borrow.

"I have fits sometimes and no-one knows why. The pills for epilepsy don't work for me. Maybe I'm a new breed of epileptic, I don't know."

"They said I had fits and threw things and hurt people but I never did. Everyone lies, don't you forget it ever, everyone lies so they can get just what they want from you. They lie." Her teeth look purple in the dark and tiny night lights.

"What do they want from you?" I ask.

Mrs. Watson leans toward me from her bed, turning her head closer to me, her breath smells of the poisonous liquid. "Money," she whispers fiercely, "money! I've written my lawyers over and over again to let me out of the crazy house, to tell them how it is all a lie and a sham to get my money, but I know my lawyers never got those letters, never saw the truth. Otherwise I'd be out of there, out of here. The doctors at the crazy house opened them all and laughed and took more money from my estate, ripping my letters to bits, destroying vital information. Just take, take from my estate, laughing while they do it." Mrs. Watson's fierce whispers are filled with hate. I say nothing. I have never known a crazy person before, I am not sure of her map. "I heard you been here a month, right?"

"Yes."

"They ... the staff, do they do this thing with needles and water often? I feel like I could throw up all over this bed but I can't."

"That's because of the needles."

"Well, do they do this often?"

What can I say? I have been pinned on the butterfly board three times and tomorrow comes the bigger board, the worst one. I do not want to tell her about what will happen tomorrow morning.

They have pinned me to the butterfly board so often because the famous Dr. Carter can find nothing. Maybe she will be lucky and they will find something in her nebula. "No," I finally answer, "not often."

"How often?"

A nurse with a flashlight beams it into our corner of the small ward. "Kira, let Mrs. Watson get some sleep, her next injection is in less than two hours. You know we like our patients to rest, sleep between injections." The flashlight beam is gone and she with it. For a moment we do not speak. In fact I don't want to talk to Mrs. Watson and her secret estate any longer. I have decided that I do not like her with her fierce whisper and teeth showing purple in the dark and her breath and her frizzy-zzz grey hair.

"How often?" she repeats.

Now I am mechanical in my answer but I will not tell her about tomorrow, I have decided that, I will not tell her. If she were my friend I would tell her but she is not. "If they find what they're looking for in the picture of your brain maybe just once, maybe you will be lucky. If they don't find it they will do it again. Maybe three times."

"Ahh God, you had it done three times?"

"Yes."

"Ahhh God!" she moans. "What happens in the morning, they told me I can't have any breakfast, what happens in the morning Kira?"

"They weigh you..." I say and let my voice trail off into a pretend sleep. Maybe I will really fall asleep.

"And then?" I do not answer, I breathe deeply as one does in sleep. "And then?" Her hand, thin and veined and wretched-looking is pulling at the sleeve of my nightgown like an old bird's talon. I do not move or speak. "And then?" Her voice is frantic, demanding. I say nothing, I am breathing deeply. She releases the sleeve of my blue cotton nightgown. I hear her whisper hatefully, "Bitch! You little bitch! Let me tell you something, sleeping brat, sleeping little brat, I am the only sane person left in this whole damn world, little brat!" I am glad that I did not tell her what will happen in the morning, she is no friend of mine, she hates me because my veins do not bulge and I have never been to a crazy hospital. I belong to no private club. I am awake for her next injection, I hear the butterfly gasp and flutter and then I am asleep. The pill they gave me at 9 o'clock has finally worked, my nebula turned dark with sleep. Drifting in the mists until morning.

It is a quarter to eight in the morning. Everyone in the small ward is awake, there are six beds in this room counting mine. Three on one side, three on the other. I am lying on my side waiting for my breakfast, pretending I do not hear Mrs. Watson's demand and question over and over, "And then?" I eat my milky scrambled eggs and cold toast and drink the coffee which is good and hot this morning. I brush my long hair then lean back against the two pillows with a lighted cigarette in one hand, my coffee cup in the other. Today I have no tests, I can smoke and drink coffee and watch the television my parents rented for me. The third day I was here a girl from some other part of the neurological wing in a wheelchair came into this small ward and screamed at me, "Where did you get the TV! Who from?"

"From my parents," I answered.

"Christ are you stupid!"

A nurse called her by her name, Linda, I think, and she wheeled herself out of the room giving me a hateful glance. I didn't know what she was talking about and I hated Toronto with its huge hospitals and the famous Dr. Carter. I felt like crying. I asked a nurse to tell Dr. Carter that I wanted to go home. The Cogitator came. "This is just because you are unused to hospital routine. You've never been hospitalized before have you, Kira?"

"Only for a day and a night occasionally."

The Cogitator, a woman called Dr. Wells, patted my hand and told me that I would get used to it. She told me to call her Karen. Dr. Karen Wells. She is in her late thirties and has nice legs and wears eyeshadow. She patted my hand that day and said, "You'll get used to it." She is chief Cogitator for Dr. Carter. One sees Dr. Carter only during the great pinning day or as he flies through the ward, white coat flapping, nodding to his charges, a group of new Dr. Carters trailing behind him from bed to bed. He talks about you at your bedside as if you had merged with the pillow and the new Dr. Carters fumble and ask and answer questions with reddening faces. Perhaps they sense their smallness, know already that they will never be a great and famous Dr. Carter, only small Dr. Carters. There is room for Greatness in only one on this ward.

They have weighed Mrs. Watson. "Gained nine pounds," she says aloud to everyone in the small ward. "Feel like I could burst open," she says to Miss Smith who has Parkinson's disease. "What do you think of that? After my money, all of them." Miss Smith does not answer, only the tremors in her arms seem to weigh the related message and respond to it. Her face frozen in rigidity reveals nothing. "Nine pounds on their vile water in one night," she says again. The first time I gained ten pounds. Oh, how my nebula must have showed up clear and bright and bloated on their pictures! I ignore her. She pulls at my sleeve, I will not talk to her. "Brat! Bitch!" she whispers even in daylight to me. I drink my coffee. If she were my friend. . . . She is not. At ten o'clock The Pinners with a touch of mania to them come and take Mrs. Watson away. She is going to the big butterfly board but she does not know it. Not yet. "I don't get angry or cry, ask that brat Kira! She knows. Thinks she's too good to talk to me. Ask her, that brat knows the truth!" Truth? She is asking The Pinners as they walk her from the small ward, "What's going to happen? What's going to happen?" Her voice is plaintive. The Pinners do not answer, saying only, "There, there," and they are gone.

She said I knew the truth. I used to think I knew all there was to know about truth. I am slender and pleasant looking with long auburn hair and I graduated from high school with honours, in the top fifteen. That was a truth, the diploma and the cleverness. I went to the graduation dance with Adam, who was tall with husky shoulders and sky-blue eyes and soft brown hair, who had been telling me for the last year how much he loved me and that we should consummate our love. He wore a navy blue suit and a pale blue tie and I wore a long pink gown with a scoop neck and we danced all night together and drank a tepid fruit punch from a huge crystal bowl. Our love was never consummated. That was another truth. Adam finally gave up telling me how much he loved me, mouth aching from the word and left me. I didn't care too much.

I went to work in The Home for Retarded Children, that was a different kind of truth. There were mongoloids there and waterhead babies and the simply retarded, retarded beyond grasp or pain. Flies buzzed in the spring and summer in the playground where the children who were mobile went out to play. They constantly fell and cut and bruised themselves, the flies knew this and followed them, a dark buzzing cloud ready to light on the open wounds. The buzzing cloud followed them back into the Home when play period was over. Even after their wounds had been cleaned and bandaged a few flies still hovered with tenacity near the children's beds. Limbs of rubber, the waterheads. Some of them were quite beautiful, limbs of rubber, toes touching forehead. I felt no disgust or pity. I did feel compassion but more than that I felt necessary. That was another truth. "Why do you work in a place that's so depressing and pays so poorly? You're so smart, get a better job," everyone said to me. "Go to university with your fine brain," my mother said. They didn't know that I would simply be a numeral at university, perhaps a clever numeral but a numeral all

Claude Breeze, Head # 5, *1965*

the same. I could think of no other job that would make me feel as necessary. I tried to discuss this with my mother, this truth. I thought that she of all people having held Russia in her womb would understand. I was being a good proletarian working for the collective for a small amount of money per week. My mother had pointed out to me again and again since childhood the Mennonites when they came into town in their horse-drawn wagons, travelling with ease among cars and buses and pedestrians. "Look how selfless they are." She said it over and over again as we bought fruit and vegetables from the somberly dressed Mennonites. Mother, who should have understood but did not said, "You should go to university. It's a very fine thing you are doing working at the Home but Kira you can't go on like that forever. Save your money and then you and I and your father, if he wants to, will go and see Russia next year and the next year you will go to university. It would be a shame to waste such a good brain. Study — study child psychology if you want. But don't waste that brain of yours Kira."

"Russia?"

Yes, the most beautiful country in the world. People for the people, green forests, all that snow, the Kremlin in the winter..." She did not understand that there in Kitchener, Ontario, I was being a good proletarian. But I was doing it out of selfish reasons like a spy. It made me feel necessary.

I got a small apartment with a girl who was a beautician when I was nineteen. I filled the apartment with plants and flowers of all colours and sizes and watered them carefully and put plant pills in their soil before going to work at the Home. The beautician sat under the hairdryer each night for at least two hours, filing and polishing her nails as she sat there. Her hair was as brittle as dried twigs and the colour of straw in the sun. I was happy. That was a truth. It was when I was just twenty that I moved into the nebula, or that is to say it moved in on me. I would have a seizure and remember nothing afterward. "A convulsion, kind of," my roommate with the twig hair told the doctor. I had never thought about the brain, at least not my brain, despite my working in the Home — much less the nebula that had moved in on me. But that realization was only to come later, of the nebula. That was the newest truth, the next truth. I had e.e.g. after e.e.g. and still nothing, minor tests and finally this huge hospital in Toronto with the famous Dr. Carter. "The best in Ontario, maybe in Canada," my mother had said. I was not impressed. My nebula. As I said, it can be beautiful inside this space.

I am dressed in pale blue brushed denim jeans and a blue cotton top. I sit propped up on my bed watching television and drinking coffee, no tests for me today. They came for Mrs. Watson at 10 o'clock, it is now 10:20, I know that for certain because the Phil Donahue Show is just beginning. Mrs. Watson with her secret fortune is now pinned on the biggest butterfly board of them all. There is no anaesthesia for the dying butterfly. Yes, she will feel that this is dying. No anaesthesia, nothing can interfere with the test. She lies on the sterile table, hands clenched by her sides. Dr. Carter will tell her to unclench her hands. Two long needles, one on either side of her face have been driven through her jawbone. Pinned. Dr. Carter will tell her to lie perfectly still, the butterfly will lie pinned like that, still and dead for half an hour. Dr. Carter and others will peer into her bloated brain but only Dr. Carter will matter.

The first time I was the butterfly on the giant board, the pain of it – the sheer, smooth glass covering the butterfly board, from wing tip to wing tip, that first time it took The Pinners three tries before the giant pins settled properly into my jawbone. I thought perhaps my jawbone like my fits was different and unexplainable. The last two times however I was pinned in a neater fashion. I did not move, not the first, second or third time. I did not cry. I threw up afterward each time, ten pounds of poisonous liquid down the toilet. The first time I sat beside the toilet after, sweating and holding my head in my hands, my long hair stank of vomit and my mother waited for me anxiously outside the washroom. We had been sitting in the cafeteria after the pinned butterfly had risen from the board and suddenly I knew I was going to be violently ill. Mother, kind and gentle, wanted to come with me. "No, alone," I managed to say.

"Kira, please." I made it just in time to the washroom. It was there, I think, in that tidy, stinking cubicle that I perceived my brain as a nebula and it was then too that I knew what was in it and what they would never find. At first it was just an idea, a play toy in the long hours of white boredom, but as the tests went on and on, thrice the butterfly, my pain the smooth glass shield, it was no longer a toy. It is my escape. I am not a Mrs. Watson, but when the night comes or I think I cannot bear another commercial for Brillo Pads or Mr. Clean or when I have another e.e.g, I crouch in the mists of my nebula where it is beautiful and everything is calm, safer somehow in that beautiful misty space. "You'll get used to it," and Dr. Karen Wells had patted my hand. It seems so very long ago now. This hospital in the big, shining car city, so many cars here, with streets of sparkling light at night, this city of Toronto where there are no Mennonites, just the famous Dr. Carter who has become the next truth and with him the nebula. Is it the final truth? I am something of a novelty. They probe and pin and stick and pill and nothing changes, nothing works. I was always so ordinary before, simply Kira, a bright comrade born in an alien land but I adjusted, and my life read like a dull book, a simple map.

I think of my mother at home. Is she standing in front of the somberly dressed Mennonites buying their fruit and vegetables and marvelling at their selflessness? Soon I will get a letter from my father and he will write an amusing piece of poetry in it and tell me the latest news of everyone I have known and everyone he knows. He never runs out of words to fill sheets of paper with for my letters, the words brim over the pages like the tears in his eyes when I left. Tall, quiet Father, pipe in his reassuring mouth, gentle, tears in his eyes when I left for this huge monument to science and flesh. Mother finds it difficult to fill a single sheet of paper with words and yet it is she who comes here when I am pinned to the giant board, three times she has come; it is Father who cannot force himself to be witness. To what, I wonder? The Pinning, the aftermath of The Pinning of course. Tears brimmed up in his eyes when I left. Is it because of Russia, the land of the worker, the harsh land, the proletarian land, that my mother can come and bear witness like a good and sturdy comrade and my father cannot?

It is 11 o'clock, the Phil Donahue Show takes a commercial break. The Pinning has been over for ten minutes for Mrs. Watson. Is she vomiting now? Weeping? Cursing the laughing doctors who opened her letters to her lawyers? I only vomited. Dr. Carter himself said I was a very stoic person. Dr. Karen Wells, chief Cogitator, beamed at me and so did the lesser Cogitators at these words for me, all for me, from the famous Dr. Carter. Three times on the butterfly board and I have yet to weep. Is it that I am stoic or simply that I have the secret of my nebula and tell no-one. You see I have deduced what is wrong with my brain. Why don't I tell them? It would all be so simple. Would they think me high-strung giving in to stress? I'm not though, I am a sturdy comrade. I crouch in the mists of the nebula.

Mrs. Watson has to be helped back to her bed, she is weeping and moaning, fingers tentatively exploring her aching, burning jawbone without actually touching it, sketching the pain of it in the air. "I want all my personal belongings! I'm leaving your Dachau!" she screams. The nurses try to calm her down. "There, there," they say. It is their code word. "Nazis!" she screams and begins to tear apart her bed. Pillows fall to the floor, a sheet tears, the night table topples over with a crash and the splinter of the glass ashtray. Pinned again. The slender, efficient needle plunges into her leg muscle. She sleeps. One nurse sighs and then turns to me smiling, "How are you today, Kira?"

"I'm all right, a little bored I guess."

"You can go down to the cafeteria or to the gift shop and buy some magazines, there's nothing scheduled for you today." She means to be kind to this novelty, Kira-stoic.

"I probably will after lunch," I reply. Two aides are straightening up the mess of Mrs. Watson's bombed-out bed, removing the ripped sheet. Mrs. Watson rolls like a piece of clay as they pull it out from under her, oblivious, her mind in a place of Not. Not anything, darkness is not even there. What strength in those thin bird-claw hands!

The next day is simple. I have another electroencephalograph. The needles are placed all over my scalp, little pin pricks, no pain. Blink. Stop. Deep breath. Stop. Fast shallow breathing. Stop. Deep, slow breathing. Stop. Blink rapidly. Stop. How used to all this I have become. Dr. Wells patted my hand, "You will get used to it." Later after the e.e.g. is over I take a brief walk around the hospital block. It is now June. The June air is sweet and cool, a slight breeze caresses my hair and scalp where minutes ago it was covered with the little pin pricks of needles. I do not stay outside long. Soon I am back in the small ward watching the Mike Douglas Show. I drink a ginger ale and smoke. There is a comedian on and everyone in the TV audience laughs, even I laugh a little. It is June second, the beginning of my second month here. The nurse comes and gives Miss Smith a new pill to try, as if anything on earth could stop the small volcano in her arms and fingertips or smooth out the rigidity of her shoulder and face. I am given new pills to try out, grey with black little dots on them. I swallow the three round pills and soon my mind begins to feel heavy. My nebula fills with fat rain clouds. I sleep.

It is June the fifth. I received a long letter from my father today with an amusing poem in it and he ends by saying that he knows that what the doctors are doing is right and that soon his Kira will be healthy and home.

I am to be pinned to the giant butterfly board again this morning, hands flat on the board, no flutter of wings. I could tell them quite simply that the thing that causes my fits is not a thing that a pill can cure. The amoeba. Yes, that is what it is. I knew that after my first pinning to the great board. It is nourishing itself on what they call my brain, enveloping the minute organisms held there. It floats in my nebula. It does not matter how many quarts of water or needles they give me at night to bloat my brain, everyone knows that an amoeba changes shape and because it is so changeable the famous Dr. Carter will never catch it on his bloated-brain scans. Why do I not tell them this? They would not put me in a crazy house like Mrs. Watson, who now wanders in a daze on a new drug, sometimes bumping into walls and furniture. No, not good stoic Comrade Kira. High strung and nervous under all the strain of it they would say kindly. Dr. Karen Wells would simply pat my hand as she did on my third day here when she first told me I'd get used to it. Why don't I tell them that it is the amoeba eating away that is causing me to faint, have fits and forget? Why not?

I am walking to the elevators with The Pinners now, in a few more minutes I will be the butterfly, wing tip to wing tip pinned on the giant board. They will look and find nothing, the famous Dr. Carter will shake his head in confusion. I feel no shiver in the pit of my stomach as I have on other Pinning Days — this will be my fourth time on the giant board. Yes, I am getting used to it. I will lie pinned there as still as the dead butterflies in a collector's box, lovingly, carefully pinned. I will lie like that for half an hour and then my wing tips will flutter faintly and I will rise, the secret of the amoeba held within my lovely, fluttering wing tips, fluttering softly in the large Pinning Room. Everyone will smile. Poor butterfly. Yes, I am getting used to it. Perhaps that is the final truth of them all, the last.

Author's Commentary

Margaret Gibson made these comments on her writing in an interview with Katheryn MacLean Broughton:

Interviewer: You have stated that you begin with a title when you write. How do you move from title to story?

Gibson: I think hard about the title. Some come by themselves and I just think about what the story is going to be without having any facts of the story. Most of my titles come easily — they just do — I don't know how.

Interviewer: Would you say this part of the process is not explainable; is a mystery?

Gibson: Yes, indeed I would. I have to have the first line before I can write the story. Sometimes it comes in dreams; other times I am wide awake. I rarely re-write the first line although I may re-write the rest of the story.

Interviewer: You have stated: "I base my characters on people I've known but it is not journalism; they serve simply as a prototype to the character they will be." How does this process work? Would your friends recognize themselves in a story?

Gibson: I myself am in my books; little bits and pieces of myself. The same is true for people I know. Sometimes they see themselves and sometimes they are offended. Names are important to me. For example, Kira in "Butterfly Ward" was chosen because it has a strong sound. It suits the character since she is a strong girl, able to take the physical punishment of all those pinnings.

Interviewer: Referring to the writing process, you have said: "I have to have a vague idea of how the ending is going to turn out." Since some writers say that the ending came to them in the process of writing, could you explain why you have to know the ending?

Gibson: It gives me a point to move towards. I would not be able to fill in the empty spaces if I did not know the ending. It also speeds up the process — it makes the words come a mile a minute.

Interviewer: Since you work from a title and have to have an ending in mind, both obviously control the plot. Referring to "The Butterfly Ward", can you explain how these two elements affected its plot?

Gibson: I lived through "The Butterfly Ward" — the pinning and all that. It was from first-hand experience. The ending was already in my head — "poor butterfly". I thought about the ward I was on. My mother came to visit me (my father did not) and so a strong mother image developed.

The ending was the only possible one for Kira, who was a strong person. She would go through that for the rest of her life.

Margaret Gibson (1948 —   )

Born in Toronto, Margaret Gibson began writing in her teens. Her first published story appeared in *74: New Canadian Stories.* In 1976 her collection of short stories, *The Butterfly Ward,* was published and received the City of Toronto Award. The movie *Outrageous* was based on her story, "Making It", from *The Butterfly Ward. Considering Her Condition,* her second short story collection, appeared in 1978.

Forgiveness in Families

ALICE MUNRO

Everywhere that boy hits turns into a disaster area, Mother said. If you read it in a book you wouldn't believe it, she said.

I've often thought, suppose I had to go to a psychiatrist, and he would want to know about my family background, naturally, so I would have to start telling him about my brother, and he wouldn't even wait till I was finished, would he, the psychiatrist, he'd commit me.

I said that to Mother; she laughed. "You're hard on that boy, Val."

"Boy," I said. *"Man."*

She laughed, she admitted it. "But remember," she said, "the Lord loves a lunatic."

"How do you know," I said, "seeing you're an atheist?"

Some things he couldn't help. Being born, for instance. He was born the week I started school, and how's that for timing? I was scared, it wasn't like now when the kids have been going to play-school and kindergarten for years. I was going to school for the first time and all the other kids had their mothers with them and where was mine? In the hospital having a baby. The embarrassment to me. There was a lot of shame about those things then.

It wasn't his fault getting born and it wasn't his fault throwing up at my wedding. Think of it. The floor, the table, he even managed to hit the cake. He was not drunk, as some people thought, he really did have some violent kind of flu, which Haro and I came down with, in fact, on our honeymoon. I never heard of anybody else with any kind of flu throwing up over a table with a lace cloth and silver candlesticks and wedding cake on it, but you could say it was bad luck; maybe everybody else when the need came on them was closer to a toilet. And everybody else might try a little harder to hold back, they just might, because nobody else is quite so special, quite so centre-of-the-universe, as my baby brother. Just call him a child of nature. That was what he called himself, later on.

I will skip over what he did between getting born and throwing up at my wedding except to say that he had asthma and got to stay home from school weeks on end, listening to soap operas. Sometimes there was a truce between us, and I would get him to tell me what happened every day on "Big Sister" and "Road of Life" and the one with Gee-Gee and Papa David. He was very good at remembering all the characters and getting all the complications straight, I'll say that, and he did read a lot in *Gateways to Bookland,* that lovely set Mother bought for us and that he later sneaked out of the house and sold, for ten dollars, to a secondhand book dealer. Mother said he could have been brilliant at school if he wanted to be. That's a deep one, your brother, she used to say, he's got some surprises in store for us. She was right, he had.

He started staying home permanently in Grade Ten after a little problem of being caught in a cheating-ring that was getting math tests from some teacher's desk. One of the janitors was letting him back in the classroom after school because he said he was working on a special project. So he was, in his own way. Mother said he did it to make himself popular, because he had asthma and couldn't take part in sports.

Now. Jobs. The question comes up, what is such a person as my brother — and I ought to give him a name at least, his name is Cam, for Cameron, Mother thought that would be a suitable name for a university president or honest tycoon (which was the sort of thing she planned for him to be) — what is he going to do, how is he going to make a living? Until recently the country did not pay you to sit on your uppers and announce that you had adopted a creative life-style. He got a job first as a movie usher. Mother got it for him, she knew the manager, it was the old International Theatre over on Blake Street. He had to quit, though, because he got this darkness-phobia. All the people sitting in the dark he said gave him a crawly feeling, very peculiar. It only interfered with him working as an usher, it didn't interfere with him going to the movies on his own. He got very fond of movies. In fact, he spent whole days sitting in movie houses, sitting through every show twice then going to another theatre and sitting through what was there. He had to do something with his time, because Mother and all of us believed he was working then in the office of the Greyhound Bus Depot. He went off to work at the right time every morning and came home at the right time every night, and he told all about the cranky old man in charge of the office and the woman with curvature of the spine who had been there since 1919 and how mad

Alex Colville, Family and Rainstorm, *1955*
The National Gallery of Canada, Ottawa

she got at the young girls chewing gum, oh, a lively story, it would have worked up to something as good as the soap operas if Mother hadn't phoned up to complain about the way they were withholding his pay check — due to a technical error in the spelling of his name, he said — and found out he'd quit in the middle of his second day.

Well. Sitting in movies was better than sitting in beer parlors, Mother said. At least he wasn't on the street getting in with criminal gangs. She asked him what his favourite movie was and he said *Seven Brides for Seven Brothers*. See, she said, he is interested in an outdoor life, he is not suited to office work. So she sent him to work for some cousins of hers who have a farm in the Fraser Valley. I should explain that my father, Cam's and mine, was dead by this time, he died away back when Cam was having asthma and listening to soap operas. It didn't make much difference, his dying, because he worked as a conductor on the P.G.E. when it started at Squamish, and he lived part of the time in Lillooet. Nothing changed, Mother went on working at Eaton's as she always had, going across on the ferry and then on the bus; I got supper, she came trudging up the hill in the winter dark.

Cam took off from the farm, he complained that the cousins were religious and always after his soul. Mother could see his problem, she had after all brought him up to be a freethinker. He hitchhiked east. From time to time a letter came. A request for funds. He had been offered a job in northern Quebec if he could get the money together to get up there. Mother sent it. He sent word the job had folded, but he didn't send back the money. He and two friends were going to start a turkey farm. They sent us plans, estimates. They were supposed to be working on contract for the Purina Company, nothing could go wrong. The turkeys were drowned in a flood, after Mother had sent him money and we had too against our better judgment. Everywhere that boy hits turns into a disaster area, Mother said. If you read it in a book you wouldn't believe it, she said. It's so terrible it's funny.

She knew. I used to go over to see her on Wednesday afternoon — her day off — pushing the stroller with Karen in it, and later Tommy in it and Karen walking beside, up Lonsdale and down King's Road, and what would we always end up talking about? That boy and I, we are getting a divorce, she said. I am definitely going to write him off. What good will he ever be until he stops relying on me, she asked. I kept my mouth shut, more or less. She knew my opinion. But she ended up every time saying, "He was a nice fellow to have around the house, though. Good company. That boy could always make me laugh."

110

Or, "He had a lot to contend with, his asthma and no dad. He never did intentionally hurt a soul."

"One good thing he did," she said, "you could really call it a good turn. That girl."

Referring to the girl who came and told us she had been engaged to him, in Hamilton, Ontario, until he told her he could never get married because he had just found out there was hereditary fatal kidney disease in his family. He wrote her a letter. And she came looking for him to tell him it didn't matter. Not at all a bad-looking girl. She worked for the Bell Telephone. Mother said it was a lie told out of kindness, to spare her feelings when he didn't want to marry her. I said it was a kindness, anyway, because she would have been supporting him for the rest of his life.

Though it might have eased things up a bit on the rest of us.

But that was then and now is now and as we all know times have changed. Cam is finding it easier. He lives at home, off and on, has for a year and a half. His hair is thin in front, not surprising in a man thirty-four years of age, but shoulder length behind, straggly, graying. He wears a sort of rough brown robe that looks as if it might be made out of a sack (is that what sackcloth is supposed to be, I said to Haro, I wouldn't mind supplying the ashes), and hanging down on his chest he has all sorts of chains, medallions, crosses, elk's teeth or whatnot. Rope sandals on his feet. Some friend of his makes them. He collects welfare. Nobody asks him to work. Who could be so crude? If he has to write down his occupation he writes priest.

It's true. There is a whole school of them, calling themselves priests, and they have a house over in Kitsilano, Cam stays there too sometimes. They're in competition with the Hare Krishna bunch, only these ones don't chant, they just walk around smiling. He has developed this voice I can't stand, a very thin, sweet voice, all on one level. It makes me want to stand in front of him and say, "There's an earthquake in Chile, two hundred thousand people just died, they've burned up another village in Vietnam, famine as usual in India." Just to see if he'd keep saying, "Ve-ery ni-ice, ve-ery ni-ice," that sweet way. He won't eat meat, of course, he eats whole-grain cereals and leafy vegetables. He came into the kitchen where I was slicing beets — beets being forbidden, a root vegetable — and, "I hope you understand that you're committing murder," he said.

"No," I said, "but I'll give you sixty seconds to get out of here or I may be."

So as I say he's home part of the time now and he was there on the Monday night when Mother got sick. She was vomiting. A couple of days before this he had started her on a vegetarian diet — she was always promising him she'd try it — and he told her she was vomiting up all the old poisons stored up in her body from eating meat and sugar and so on. He said it was a good sign, and when she had it all vomited out she'd feel better. She kept vomiting, and she didn't feel better, but he had to go out. Monday nights is when they have the weekly meeting at the priests' house, where they chant and burn incense or celebrate the black mass, for all I know. He stayed out most of the night, and when he got home he found Mother unconscious on the bathroom floor. He got on the phone and phoned *me*.

"I think you better come over here and see if you can help Mom, Val."

"What's the matter with her?"

"She's not feeling very well."

"What's the matter with her? Put her on the phone."

"I can't."

"Why can't you?"

I swear he tittered. "Well I'm afraid she's passed out."

I called the ambulance and sent them for her, that was how she got to the hospital, five o'clock in the morning. I called her family doctor, he got over there, and he got Dr. Ellis Bell, one of the best-known heart men in the city, because that was what they had decided it was, her heart. I got dressed and woke Haro and told him and then I drove myself over to the Lions Gate Hospital. They wouldn't let me in till ten o'clock. They had her in Intensive Care. I sat outside Intensive Care in their slick little awful waiting room. They had red slippery chairs, cheap covering, and a stand full of pebbles with green plastic leaves growing up. I sat there hour after hour and read *The Reader's Digest*. The jokes. Thinking this is how it is, this is it, really, she's dying. Now, this moment, behind those doors, dying. Nothing stops or holds off for it the way you somehow and against all your sense believe it will. I thought about Mother's life, the part of it I knew. Going to work every day, first on the ferry then on the bus. Shopping at the old Red-and-White then at the new Safeway — new, fifteen years old! Going down to the Library one night a week, taking me with her, and we would come home on the bus with our load of books and a bag of grapes we bought at the Chinese place, for a treat. Wednesday afternoons too when my kids were small and I went over there to drink coffee and she rolled us cigarettes on that contraption she had. And I thought, all these things don't seem that much like life, when you're doing them, they're just what you do, how you fill up your days, and you think all the time something is going to crack open, and you'll find yourself, *then* you'll find yourself, in life. It's not even that you particularly want this to happen, this cracking open, you're comfortable enough the way things are, but you do expect it. Then you're dying, Mother is dying, and it's just the same plastic chairs and plastic plants and ordinary day outside with people getting groceries and what you've had is all there is, and going to the Library, just a thing like that, coming back up the hill on the bus with books and a bag of grapes seems now worth wanting, O God doesn't it, you'd break your heart wanting back there.

When they let me in to see her she was bluish-gray in the face and her eyes were not all-the-way closed, but they had rolled up, the slit that was open showed the whites. She always looked terrible with her teeth out, anyway, wouldn't let us see her. Cam teased her vanity. They were out now. So all the time, I thought, all the time even when she was young it was in her that she was going to look like this.

They didn't hold out hope. Haro came and took a look at her and put his arm around my shoulders and said, "Val, you'll have to be prepared." He meant well but I couldn't talk to him. It wasn't his mother and he couldn't remember anything. That wasn't his fault but I didn't want to talk to him, I didn't want to listen to him telling me I better be prepared. We went and ate something in the hospital cafeteria.

"You better phone Cam," Haro said.

"Why?"

"He'll want to know."

"Why do you think he'll want to know? He left her alone last night and he didn't know enough to get an ambulance when he came in and found her this morning."

"Just the same. He has a right. Maybe you ought to tell him to get over here."

"He is probably busy this moment preparing to give her a hippie funeral."

But Haro persuaded me as he always can and I went and phoned. No answer. I felt better because I had phoned, and justified in what I had said because of Cam not being in. I went back and waited, by myself.

About seven o'clock that night Cam turned up. He was not alone. He had brought along a tribe of co-priests, I suppose they were, from that house. They all wore the same kind of outfit he did, the brown sacking nightgown and the chains and crosses and holy hardware, they all had long hair, they were all a good many years younger than Cam, except for one old man, really old, with a curly gray beard and bare feet — in March, bare feet — and no teeth. I swear this old man didn't have a clue what was going on. I think they picked him up down by the Salvation Army and put that outfit on him because they needed an old man for a kind of mascot, or extra holiness, or something.

Cam said, "This is my sister Valerie. This is Brother Michael. This is Brother John, this is Brother Louis." Etc., etc.

"They haven't said anything to give me hope, Cam. She is dying."

"We hope not," said Cam with his secret smile. "We spent the day working for her."

"Do you mean praying?" I said.

"Work is a better word to describe it than praying, if you don't understand what it is."

Well of course, I never understand.

"Real praying is work, believe me," says Cam and they all smile at me, his way. They can't keep still, like children who have to go to the bathroom they're weaving and jiggling and doing little steps.

"Now where's her room?" says Cam in a practical tone of voice.

I thought of Mother dying and through that slit between her lids — who knows, maybe she can see from time to time — seeing this crowd of dervishes celebrating around her bed. Mother who lost her religion when she was thirteen and went to the Unitarian Church and quit when they had the split about crossing God out of the hymns (she was for it), Mother having to spend her last conscious minutes wondering what had happened, if she was transported back in history to where loonies cavorted around in their crazy ceremonies, trying to sort her last reasonable thoughts out in the middle of their business.

Thank God the nurse said no. The intern was brought and he said no. Cam didn't insist, he smiled and nodded at them as if they were granting permission and then he brought the troupe back into the waiting room and there, right before my eyes, they started. They put the old man in the centre, sitting down with his head bowed and his eyes shut — they had to tap him and remind him how to do that — and they squatted in a rough sort of circle round him, facing in and out, alternately. Then, eyes closed, they started swaying back and forth moaning some words very softly, only not the same words, it sounded as if each one of them had got different words, and not in English of course but Swahili or Sanskrit or something. It got louder, gradually it got louder, a pounding singsong, and as it did they rose to their feet, all except the old man who stayed where

114

he was and looked as if he might have gone to sleep, sitting, and they began a shuffling kind of dance where they stood, clapping, not very well in time. They did this for a long while, and the noise they were making, though it was not terribly loud, attracted the nurses from their station and nurses' aides and orderlies and a few people like me who were waiting, and nobody seemed to know what to do, because it was so unbelievable, so crazy in that ordinary little waiting room. Everybody just stared as if they were asleep and dreaming and expecting to wake up. Then a nurse came out of Intensive Care and said, "We can't have this disturbance. What do you think you're doing here?"

She took hold of one of the young ones and shook him by the shoulder, else she couldn't have got anybody to stop and pay attention.

"We're working to help a woman who's very sick," he told her.

"I don't know what you call working, but you're not helping anybody. Now I'm asking you to clear out of here. Excuse me. I'm not asking. I'm telling."

"You're very mistaken if you think the tones of our voices are hurting or disturbing any sick person. This whole ceremony is pitched at a level which will reach and comfort the unconscious mind and draw the demonic influences out of the body. It's a ceremony that goes back five thousand years."

"Good Lord," said the nurse, looking stupefied as well she might. "Who are these people?"

I had to go and enlighten her, telling her that it was my brother and what you might call his friends, and I was not in on their ceremony. I asked about Mother, was there any change.

"No change," she said. "What do we have to do to get them out of here?

"Turn the hose on them," one of the orderlies said, and all this time, the dance, or ceremony, never stopped, and the one who had stopped and done the explaining went back to dancing too, and I said to the nurse, "I'll phone in to see how she is, I'm going home for a little while." I walked out of the hospital and found to my surprise that it was dark. The whole day in there, dark to dark. In the parking lot I started to cry. Cam has turned this into a circus for his own benefit, I said to myself, and said it out loud when I got home.

Haro made me a drink.

"It'll probably get into the papers," I said. "Cam's chance for fame."

Haro phoned the hospital to see if there was any news and they said there wasn't. "Did they have — was there any difficulty with some young people in the waiting room this evening? Did they leave quietly?" Haro is ten years older than I am, a cautious man, too patient with everybody. I used to think he was sometimes giving Cam money I didn't know about.

"They left quietly," he said. "Don't worry about the papers. Get some sleep."

I didn't mean to but I fell asleep on the couch, after the drink and the long day. I woke up with the phone ringing and day lightening the room. I stumbled into the kitchen dragging the blanket Haro had put over me and saw by the clock on the wall it was a quarter to six. She's gone, I thought.

It was her own doctor.

He said he had encouraging news. He said she was much better this morning.

I dragged over a chair and collapsed in it, both arms and my head too down on the kitchen counter. I came back on the phone to hear him saying she was still in a critical phase and the next forty-eight hours would tell the story, but without raising my hopes too high he wanted me to know she was responding to treatment. He said that this was especially surprising in view of the fact that she had been late getting to hospital and the things they did to her at first did not seem to have much effect, though of course the fact that she survived the first few hours at all was a good sign. Nobody had made much of this good sign to me yesterday, I thought.

I sat there for an hour at least after I had hung up the phone. I made a cup of instant coffee and my hands were shaking so I could hardly get the water into the cup, then couldn't get the cup to my mouth. I let it go cold. Haro came out in his pyjamas at last. He gave me one look and said, "Easy, Val. Has she gone?"

"She's some better. She's responding to treatment."

"The look of you I thought the other."

"I'm so amazed."

"I wouldn't 've given five cents for her chances yesterday noon."

"I know. I can't believe it."

"It's the tension," Haro said. "I know. You build yourself up ready for something bad to happen and then when it doesn't, it's a queer feeling, you can't feel good right away, it's almost like a disappointment."

Disappointment. That was the word that stayed with me. I was so glad, really, grateful, but underneath I was thinking, so Cam didn't kill her after all, with his carelessness and craziness and going out and neglecting her he didn't kill her, and I was, yes, I was, sorry in some part of me to find out that was true. And I knew Haro knew this but wouldn't speak of it to me, ever. That was the real shock to me, why I kept shaking. Not whether Mother lived or died. It was what was so plain about myself.

Mother got well, she pulled through beautifully. After she rallied she never sank back. She was in the hospital three weeks and then she came home, and rested another three weeks, and after that went back to work, cutting down a bit and working ten to four instead of full days, what they call the housewives' shift. She told everybody about Cam and his friends coming to the hospital. She began to say things like, "Well, that boy of mine may not be much of a success at anything else but you have to admit he has a knack of saving lives." Or, "Maybe Cam should go into the miracle business, he certainly pulled it off with me." By this time Cam was saying, he is saying now, that he's not sure about that religion, he's getting tired of the other priests and all that not eating meat or root vegetables. It's a stage, he says now, he's glad he went through it, self-discovery. One day I went over there and found he was trying on an old suit and tie. He says he might take advantage of some of the adult education courses, he is thinking of becoming an accountant.

I was thinking myself about changing into a different sort of person from the one I am. I do think about that. I read a book called *The Art of Loving*. A lot of things seemed clear while I was reading it but afterwards I went back to being more or less the same. What has Cam ever done that actually hurt me, anyway, as Haro once said. And how am I better than he is after the way I felt the night Mother lived instead of died? I made a promise to myself I would try. I went over there one day taking them a bakery cake — which Cam eats now as happily as anybody else — and I heard their voices out in the yard — now it's summer, they love to sit in the sun — Mother saying to some visitor, "Oh yes I was, I was all set to take off into the wild blue yonder, and Cam here, this *idiot*, came and danced outside my door with a bunch of his hippie friends —"

"My God, woman," roared Cam, but you could tell he didn't care now, "members of an ancient holy discipline."

I had a strange feeling, like I was walking on coals and trying a spell so I wouldn't get burnt.

Forgiveness in families is a mystery to me, how it comes or how it lasts.

Author's Commentary

Alice Munro made these remarks in an interview with Graeme Gibson.

I'm not a writer who is very concerned with ideas. I'm not an intellectual writer. I'm very, very excited by what you might call the surface of life, and it must be that this seems to me meaningful in a way I can't analyze or describe.

It seems to me very important to be able to get at the exact tone or texture of how things are. I can't really claim that it is linked to any kind of a religious feeling about the world, and yet that might come closest to describing it.

It's there in my head, this story, if you want to call it that, the characters, the relationship, the lives of these people. I can now see it in my mind, not very well, rather dimly, and things will change as I work it out, but something is there that I'm probably going to have to deal with. (Though other things are also there that I have failed to deal with.) Often I fail to deal with things several times before I work them out successfully. But it's all there, and of course it comes from the external world: Where else would it come from? But I'm not the kind of writer that says: Now I've got to do something, I've got to write something about this existing problem or this relationship or this experience I've had. I don't work that directly.

With me writing has something to do with the fight against death, the feeling that we lose everything every day, and writing is a way of convincing yourself perhaps that you're doing something about this. You're not really, because the writing itself does not last much longer than you do; but I would say it's partly the feeling that I can't stand to have things go. There's that feeling about the — I was talking about the external world, the sights and sounds and smells — I can't stand to let go without some effort at this, at capturing them in words, and of course I don't see why one has to do that. You can experience things directly without feeling that you have to do that, but I suppose I just experience things finally when I do get them into words. So writing is a part of my experience.

I can't imagine living without writing. I think possibly that I could attain some level where I would have done enough and where I — maybe as you say, I would know, and then I wouldn't write anymore.

118

Alice Munro (1931 –   )

Born in Wingham, Ontario, and educated at the University of Western Ontario, Alice Munro lived for many years in Vancouver and Victoria, where she raised her three daughters. She now resides in Clinton, Ontario.

She won the Governor General's Award for her first collection of short stories, *Dance of the Happy Shades* (1968). In 1971, *Lives of Girls and Women* appeared; it consists of linked short stories involving the adolescence of a girl living in a small town. *Something I've Been Meaning to Tell You*, another collection of stories, was published in 1974. *Who Do You Think You Are?* – also linked stories – followed in 1978, winning for the author a second Governor General's Award. In the autumn of 1982, *The Moons of Jupiter* was published.

John Redbird, Old Woman, *c. 1971*

Akua Nuten (The South Wind)

YVES THERIAULT

"The cities," he finally said, "they have really been destroyed?"
"Yes," said the pilot.
"Nothing is left any more," said the woman. "Nothing at all."

Kakatso, the Montagnais Indian, felt the gentle flow of the air and noticed that the wind came from the south. Then he touched the moving water in the stream to determine the temperature in the highlands. Since everything pointed to nice June weather, with mild sunshine and light winds, he decided to go to the highest peak of the reserve, as he had been planning to do for the past week. There the Montagnais lands bordered those of the Waswanipis.

There was no urgent reason for the trip. Nothing really pulled him there except the fact that he hadn't been for a long time; and he liked steep mountains and frothy, roaring streams.

Three days before he had explained his plan to his son, the thin Grand-Louis, who was well known to the white men of the North Shore. His son had guided many whites in the regions surrounding the Manicouagan and Bersimis rivers.

He had told him: "I plan to go way out, near the limits of the reserve."

This was clear enough, and Grand-Louis had simply nodded his head. Now he wouldn't worry, even if Kakatso disappeared for two months. He would know that his father was high in the hills, breathing clean air and soaking up beautiful scenes to remember in future days.

Just past the main branch of the Manicouagan there is an enormous rock crowned by two pines and a fir tree which stand side by side like the fingers of a hand, the smallest on the left and the others reaching higher.

This point, which Kakatso could never forget, served as his sign-post for every trail in the area; and other points would guide him north, west, or in any other direction. Kakatso, until his final breath, would easily find his way about there, guided only by the memory of a certain tree, the silhouette of the mountain outlined against the clear skies, the twisting of a river bed, or the slope of a hill.

In strange territory Kakatso would spend entire days precisely organizing his memories so that if he ever returned no trail there would be unknown to him.

Thus, knowing every winding path and every animal's accustomed lair, he could set out on his journey carrying only some salt, tea, and shells for his rifle. He could live by finding his subsistence in the earth itself and in nature's plenty.

Kakatso knew well what a man needed for total independence: a fish-hook wrapped in paper, a length of supple cord, a strong knife, waterproof boots, and a well-oiled rifle. With these things a man could know the great joy of not having to depend on anyone but himself, of wandering as he pleased one day after another, proud and superior, the owner of eternal lands that stretched beyond the horizon.

(To despise the reserve and those who belonged there. Not to have any allegiance except a respect for the water, the sky, and the winds. To be a man, but a man according to the Indian image and not that of the whites. The Indian image of a real man was ageless and changeless, a true image of man in the bosom of a wild and immense nature.)

Kakatso had a wife and a house and grown-up children whom he rarely saw. He really knew little about them. One daughter was a nurse in a white man's city, another had married a turncoat Montagnais who lived in Baie-Comeau and worked in the factories. A son studied far away, in Montreal, and Kakatso would probably never see him again. A son who would repudiate everything, would forget the proud Montagnais language and change his name to be accepted by the whites in spite of his dark skin and slitty eyes.

The other son, Grand-Louis ... but this one was an exception. He had inherited Montagnais instincts. He often came down to the coast, at Godbout or Sept-Iles, or sometimes at Natashquan, because he was ambitious and wanted to earn money. But this did not cause him to scorn or detest the forest. He found a good life there. For Kakatso, it was enough that this child, unlike so many others, did not turn into a phony white man.

As for Kakatso's wife, she was still at home, receiving Kakatso on his many returns without emotion or gratitude. She had a roof over her head, warmth, and food. With skilled fingers she made caribou skin jackets for the white man avid for the exotic. This small sideline liberated Kakatso from other obligations towards her. Soon after returning home, Kakatso always wanted to get away again. He was uncomfortable in these white men's houses that were too high, too solid, and too neatly organized for his taste.

So Kakatso lived his life in direct contact with the forest, and he nurtured life itself from the forest's plenty. Ten months of the year he roamed the forest trails, ten months he earned his subsistence from hunting, trapping, fishing, and smoking the caribou meat that he placed in caches for later use. With the fur pelts he met his own needs and those of the house on the reserve near the forest, although these needs were minimal because his wife was a good earner.

He climbed, then, towards the northern limits of the Montagnais lands on this June day, which was to bring calamity of which he was completely unaware.

Kakatso had heard of the terrible bomb. For twenty years he had heard talk of it, and the very existence of these horrendous machines was not unknown to him. But how was he to know the complex fabric of events happening in the world just then? He never read the newspapers and never really listened to the radio when he happened to spend some hours in a warm house. How could he conceive of total annihilation threatening the whole world? How could he feel all the world's people trembling?

In the forest's vast peace, Kakatso, knowing nature's strength, could easily believe that nothing and nobody could prevail against the mountains, the rivers, and the forest itself stretching out all across the land. Nothing could prevail against the earth, the unchangeable soil that regenerated itself year after year.

He travelled for five days. On the fifth evening it took Kakatso longer to fall asleep. Something was wrong. A silent anguish he did not understand was disturbing him.

He had lit his evening fire on a bluff covered with soft moss, one hundred feet above the lake. He slept there, rolled in his blanket in a deeply dark country interrupted only by the rays of the new moon.

Sleep was slow and when it came it did not bring peace. A jumble of snarling creatures and swarming, roaring masses invaded Kakatso's sleep. He turned over time and again, groaning restlessly. Suddenly he awoke and was surprised to see that the moon had gone down and the night's blackness was lit only by stars. Here, on the bluff, there was a bleak reflection from the sky, but the long valley and the lake remained dark. Exhausted by his throbbing dreams, Kakatso got up, stretched his legs and lit his pipe. On those rare occasions when his sleep was bad he had always managed to recover his tranquillity by smoking a bit, motionless in the night, listening to the forest sounds.

Suddenly the light came. For a single moment the southern and western horizons were illuminated by this immense bluish gleam that loomed up, lingered a moment, and then went out. The dark became even blacker and Kakatso muttered to himself. He wasn't afraid because fear had always been totally foreign to him. But what did this strange event mean? Was it the anger of some old mountain spirit?

All at once the gleam reappeared, this time even more westerly. Weaker this time and less evident. Then the shadows again enveloped the land.

Kakatso no longer tried to sleep that night. He squatted, smoking his pipe and trying to find some explanation for these bluish gleams with his simple ideas, his straightforward logic and vivid memory.

When the dawn came the old Montagnais, the last of his people, the great Abenakis, carefully prepared his fire and boiled some water for his tea.

For some hours he didn't feel like moving. He no longer heard the inner voices calling him to the higher lands. He felt stuck there, incapable of going further until the tumult within him died down. What was /there that he didn't know about his skies, he who had spent his whole life wandering in the woods and sleeping under the stars? The sky over his head was as familiar to him as the soil of the underbrush, the animal trails and the games of the trout in their streams. But never before had he seen such gleams and they disturbed him.

At eight o'clock the sun was slowly climbing into the sky, and Kakatso was still there.

At ten he moved to the shore to look at the water in the lake. He saw a minnow run and concluded that the lake had many fish. He then attached his fire cord to the hook tied with partridge feathers he had found in the branches of a wild hawthorn bush. He cast the fly with a deliberate, almost solemn movement and it jumped on the smooth water. After Kakatso cast three more times a fat trout swallowed the hook and he pulled him in gently, quite slowly, letting him fight as much as he wanted. The midday meal was in hand. The Montagnais, still in no great hurry to continue his trip, began to prepare his fish.

He was finishing when the far-away buzz of a plane shook him out of his reveries. Down there, over the mountains around the end of the lake, a plane was moving through the sky. This was a familiar sight to Kakatso because all this far country was visited only by planes that landed on the lakes. In this way the Indian had come to know the white man. This was the most frequent place of contact between the two: a large body of quiet water where a plane would land, where the whites would ask for help and find nothing better than an Indian to help them.

Even from a distance Kakatso recognized the type of plane. It was a single-engine, deluxe Bonanza, a type often used by the Americans who came to fish for their salmon in our rivers.

The plane circled the lake and flew over the bluff where Kakatso's fire was still burning. Then it landed gently, almost tenderly. The still waters were only lightly ruffled and quickly returned to their mirror smoothness. The plane slowed down, the motor coughed once or twice, then the craft made a complete turn and headed for the beach.

Kakatso, with one hand shading his eyes, watched the landing, motionless.

When the plane was finally still and the tips of its pontoons were pulled up on the sandy beach, two men, a young woman, and a twelve-year-old boy got out.

One of the men was massive. He towered a head over Kakatso although the Montagnais himself was rather tall.

"Are you an Indian?" the man asked suddenly.

Kakatso nodded slowly and blinked his eyes once.

"Good, I'm glad, you can save us," said the man.

"Save you?" said Kakatso. "Save you from what?"

"Never mind," said the woman, "that's our business."

Standing some distance away, she gestured to the big man who had first spoken to Kakatso.

"If you're trying to escape the police," said Kakatso, "I can't do anything for you."

"It has nothing to do with the police," said the other man who had not spoken previously.

He moved towards Kakatso and proffered a handshake. Now that he was close the Montagnais recognized a veteran bush pilot. His experience could be seen in his eyes, in the squint of his eyelids, and in the way he treated an Indian as an equal.

"I am Bob Ledoux," the man said. "I am a pilot. Do you know what nuclear war is?"

"Yes," answered Kakatso, "I know."

"All the cities in the south have been destroyed," said Ledoux. "We were able to escape."

"Is that a real one?" asked the boy, who had been closely scrutinizing Kakatso. "Eh, Mom, is it really one of those savages?"

"Yes," answered the woman, "certainly." And to Kakatso she said, "Please excuse him. He has never been on the North Shore."

Naturally Kakatso did not like to be considered a savage. But he didn't show anything and he swallowed his bitterness.

"So," said the pilot, "here we are without resources."

"I have money," said the man.

"This is Mr. Perron," said the pilot, "Mrs. Perron, and their son ... "

"My name is Roger," said the boy. "I know how to swim."

The Montagnais was still undecided. He did not trust intruders. He preferred, in his simple soul, to choose his own objectives and decide his day's activities. And here were outsiders who had fallen from the sky, almost demanding his help ... but what help?

"I can't do much for you," he said after a while.

"I have money," the man repeated.

Kakatso shrugged. Money? Why money? What would it buy up here?

Without flinching he had heard how all the southern cities had been destroyed. Now he understood the meaning of those sudden gleams that lit the horizon during the night. And because this event had been the work of whites, Kakatso completely lost interest in it.

So his problem remained these four people he considered spoilers.

"Without you," said the woman, "we are going to perish."

And because Kakatso looked at her in surprise, she added, in a somewhat different tone: "We have no supplies at all and we are almost out of fuel."

"That's true," said the pilot.

"So," continued the woman, "if you don't help us find food, we will die."

Kakatso, with a sweeping gesture, indicated the forests and the lake: "There is wild game there and fish in the waters ... "

"I don't have a gun or fishhooks," said the pilot. "And it's been a very long time since I came so far north."

He said this with a slightly abashed air and Kakatso saw clearly that the man's hands were too white; the skin had become too soft and smooth.

"I'll pay you whatever is necessary," said Mr. Perron.

"Can't you see," said his wife, "that money doesn't interest him?"

Kakatso stood there, looking at them with his shining impassive eyes, his face unsmiling and his arms dangling at his sides.

"Say something," cried the woman. "Will you agree to help us?"

126

"We got away as best we could," said the pilot. "We gathered the attack on Montreal was coming and we were already at the airport when the warning sirens went off. But I couldn't take on enough fuel. There were other planes leaving too. I can't even take off again from this lake. Do you know if there is a supply cache near here?"

Throughout the northern forests pilots left emergency fuel caches for use when necessary. But if Kakatso knew of several such places he wasn't letting on in front of the intruders.

"I don't know," he said.

There was silence.

The whites looked at the Indian and desperately sought words to persuade him. But Kakatso did not move and said nothing. He had always fled the society of whites and dealt with them only when it was unavoidable. Why should he treat those who surfaced here now any differently? They were without food; the forest nourishes those who know how to take their share. This knowledge was such an instinctive part of an Indian's being that he couldn't realize how some people could lack it. He was sure that these people wanted to impose their needs on him and enslave him. All his Montagnais pride revolted against this thought. And yet, he could help them. Less than one hour away there was one of those meat caches of a thousand pounds of smoked moose, enough to see them through a winter. And the fish in the lake could be caught without much effort. Weaving a simple net of fine branches would do it, or a trap of bullrushes.

But he didn't move a muscle.

Only a single fixed thought possessed Kakatso, and it fascinated him. Down there, in the south, the whites had been destroyed. Never again would they reign over these forests. In killing each other, they had rid the land of their kind. Would the Indians be free again? All the Indians, even those on the reserves? Free to retake the forests?

And these four whites: could they be the last survivors?

Brothers, thought Kakatso, all my brothers: it is up to me to protect your new freedom.

"The cities," he finally said, "they have really been destroyed?"

"Yes," said the pilot.

"Nothing is left any more," said the woman. "Nothing at all. We saw the explosion from the plane. It was terrible. And the wind pushed us for a quarter of an hour. I thought we were going to crash."

"Nothing left," said the boy, "nobody left. Boom! One bomb did it."

He was delighted to feel himself the hero — a safe and sound hero — of such an adventure. He didn't seem able to imagine the destruction and death, only the spectacular explosion.

But the man called Perron had understood it well. He had been able to estimate the real power of the bomb.

"The whole city is destroyed," he said. "A little earlier, on the radio, we heard of the destruction of New York, then Toronto and Ottawa..."

"Many other cities too," added the pilot. "As far as I'm concerned, nothing is left of Canada, except perhaps the North Shore..."

"And it won't be for long," said Perron. "If we could get further up, further north. If we only had food and gasoline."

This time he took a roll of money out of his pocket and unfolded five bills, a sum Kakatso had never handled at one time. Perron offered them to the Indian.

"Here. The only thing we ask you for is a little food and gas if you can get some. Then we could leave."

"When such a bomb explodes," said Kakatso without taking the bills, "does it kill all the whites?"

"Yes," said the pilot. "In any case, nearly all."

"One fell on Ottawa?"

"Yes."

"Everybody is dead there?"

"Yes. The city is small and the bomb was a big one. The reports indicate there were no survivors."

Kakatso nodded his head two or three times approvingly. Then he turned away and took his rifle which had been leaning on a rock. Slowly, aiming at the whites, he began to retreat into the forest.

"Where are you going?" cried the woman.

"Here," said the man. "Here's all my money. Come back!"

Only the pilot remained silent. With his sharp eyes he watched Kakatso.

When the Indian reached the edge of the forest it was the boy's turn. He began to sob pitifully, and the woman also began to cry.

"Don't leave," she cried. "Please, help us..."

For all of my people who cried, thought Kakatso, all who begged, who wanted to defend their rights for the past two hundred years: I take revenge for them all.

But he didn't utter another word.

And when the two men wanted to run after him to stop him, he put his rifle to his shoulder. The bullet nicked the pilot's ear. Then the men understood that it would be futile to insist, and Kakatso disappeared into the forest which enclosed him. Bent low, he skimmed the ground, using every bush for cover, losing himself in the undergrowth, melting into the forest where he belonged.

Later, having circled the lake, he rested on a promontory hidden behind many spreading cedars. He saw that the pilot was trying to take off to find food elsewhere.

But the tanks were nearly empty and when the plane reached an altitude of a thousand feet the motor sputtered a bit, backfired and stopped.

The plane went into a nosedive.

When it hit the trees it caught fire.

In the morning Kakatso continued on his trip towards the highlands.

He felt his first nausea the next day and vomited blood two days later. He vomited once at first, then twice, then a third time, and finally one last time.

The wind kept on blowing from the south, warm and mild.

Author's Commentary

I've written well over five hundred short stories of all lengths, and well over a thousand dramatic radio and television scripts, of all types and formats. Yet I'd be at a loss to delineate a general, universal creative process or method. I guess what matters essentially is the basic subject, which is chosen by a process of elimination. As for the initial spark, what triggers the telling of the story, its form and structure, let's say that a good deal depends on my familiarity with all aspects of the particular subject. I'd know its geography, its general factors, the various emotions it can provoke, and the kind of people it is inhabited by. As an example: if a story is told of, say, jealousy among cod fishermen, I would have to know the mechanics of cod fishing, its locale, the type of people the fishermen are, their life as a community once off the boats. I must know about the boats themselves, maybe about the economics of fishing, surely a lot about the sea. I must also know the language of the fishermen, their way of expressing themselves, and how and to what extent they will reveal or transmit their emotions.

In other words, storytelling is using a sum of acquired and accumulated knowledge, the result of a constant, perpetual curiosity about everything, about everyone, everywhere, anytime.

A curiosity about past events, present social behaviour, projected future existence. Then is it easy to create a story, and to give it a plausible locale and identifiable characters speaking the language that befits them.

How to acquire such knowledge? Observe keenly, read avidly, seek answers perpetually.

Yves Thériault (1916 —   )

Of French and Montagnais descent, Yves Thériault was born in Quebec City, left school at the age of fifteen, worked at a variety of jobs and later became a writer for the National Film Board and Radio-Canada. He is the most prolific contemporary writer in French Canada; his works include radio and TV scripts, novels, short stories, and essays. Translated novels include *Agaguk* (1967), *Ashini* (1972), and *N'Tush* (1972). *Agaguk* won the Prix de la Provence de Québec and the Prix France-Canada. *Ashini* won the Governor General's Award and the Prix France-Canada.

The Lost Salt Gift of Blood

ALISTAIR MACLEOD

Her eyes contain only mild surprise as she first regards me. Then with recognition they glow in open hostility which in turn subsides and yields to self-control.

Now in the early evening the sun is flashing everything in gold. It bathes the blunt grey rocks that loom yearningly out toward Europe and it touches upon the stunted spruce and the low-lying lichens and the delicate hardy ferns and the ganglia-rooted moss and the tiny tough rock cranberries. The grey and slanting rain squalls have swept in from the sea and then departed with all the suddenness of surprise marauders. Everything before them and beneath them has been rapidly, briefly, and thoroughly drenched and now the clear droplets catch and hold the sun's infusion in a myriad of rainbow colours. Far beyond the harbour's mouth more tiny squalls seem to be forming, moving rapidly across the surface of the sea out there beyond land's end where the blue ocean turns to grey in rain and distance and the strain of eyes. Even farther out, somewhere beyond Cape Spear, lies Dublin and the Irish coast; far away but still the nearest land and closer now than is Toronto or Detroit to say nothing of North America's more western cities; seeming almost hazily visible now in imagination's mist.

Overhead the ivory white gulls wheel and cry, flashing also in the purity of the sun and the clean, freshly washed air. Sometimes they glide to the blue-green surface of the harbour, squawking and garbling; at times almost standing on their pink webbed feet as if they would walk on water, flapping their wings pompously against their breasts like over-conditioned he-men who have successfully passed their body-building courses. At other times they gather in lazy groups on the rocks above the harbour's entrance murmuring softly to themselves or looking also quietly out toward what must be Ireland and the vastness of the sea.

The harbour itself is very small and softly curving, seeming like a tiny, peaceful womb nurturing the life that now lies within it but which originated from without; came from without and through the narrow, rock-tight channel that admits the entering and withdrawing sea. That sea is entering again now, forcing itself gently but inevitably through the tightness of the opening and laving the rocky walls and rising and rolling into the harbour's inner cove. The dories rise at their moorings and the tide laps higher on the piles and advances upward toward the high-water marks upon the land; the running moon-drawn tides of spring.

Around the edges of the harbour brightly coloured houses dot the wet and glistening rocks. In some ways they seem almost like defiantly optimistic horseshoe nails: yellow and scarlet and green and pink; buoyantly yet firmly permanent in the grey unsundered rock.

At the harbour's entrance the small boys are jigging for the beautifully speckled salmon-pink sea trout. Barefootedly they stand on the tide-wet rocks flicking their wrists and sending their glistening lines in shimmering golden arcs out into the rising tide. Their voices mount excitedly as they shout to one another encouragement, advice, consolation. The trout fleck dazzlingly on their sides as they are drawn toward the rocks, turning to seeming silver as they flash within the sea.

It is all of this that I see now, standing at the final road's end of my twenty-five-hundred-mile journey. The road ends here—quite literally ends at the door of a now abandoned fishing shanty some six brief yards in front of where I stand. The shanty is grey and weatherbeaten with two boarded-up windows, vanishing wind-whipped shingles and a heavy rusted padlock chained fast to a twisted door. Piled before the twisted door and its equally twisted frame are some marker buoys, a small pile of rotted rope, a broken oar and an old and rust-flaked anchor.

The option of driving my small rented Volkswagen the remaining six yards and then negotiating a tight many-twists-of-the-steering-wheel turn still exists. I would be then facing toward the west and could simply retrace the manner of my coming. I could easily drive away before anything might begin.

Instead I walk beyond the road's end and the fishing shanty and begin to descend the rocky path that winds tortuously and narrowly along and down the cliff's edge to the sea. The small stones roll and turn and scrape beside and beneath my shoes and after only a few steps the leather is nicked and scratched. My toes press hard against its straining surface.

As I approach the actual water's edge four small boys are jumping excitedly upon the glistening rocks. One of them has made a strike and is attempting to reel in his silver-turning prize. The other three have laid down their rods in their enthusiasm and are shouting encouragement and giving almost physical moral support: "Don't let him get away, John," they say. "Keep the line steady." "Hold the end of the rod up." "Reel in the slack." "Good." "What a dandy!"

Across the harbour's clear water another six or seven shout the same delirious messages. The silver-turning fish is drawn toward the rock. In the shallows he flips and arcs, his flashing body breaking the water's surface as he walks upon his tail. The small fisherman has now his rod almost completely vertical. Its tip sings and vibrates high above his head while at his feet the trout spins and curves. Both of his hands are clenched around the rod and his knuckles strain white through the water-roughened redness of small-boy hands. He does not know whether he should relinquish the rod and grasp at the lurching trout or merely heave the rod backward and flip the fish behind him. Suddenly he decides upon the latter but even as he heaves his bare feet slide out from beneath him on the smooth wetness of the rock and he slips down into the water. With a pirouetting leap the trout turns glisteningly and tears itself free. In a darting flash of darkened greenness it rights itself within the regained water and is gone. "Oh damn!" says the small fisherman, struggling upright onto his rock. He bites his lower lip to hold back the tears welling within his eyes. There is a small trickle of blood coursing down from a tiny scratch on the inside of his wrist and he is wet up to his knees. I reach down to retrieve the rod and return it to him.

Suddenly a shout rises from the opposite shore. Another line zings tautly through the water throwing off fine showers of iridescent droplets. The shouts and contagious excitement spread anew. "Don't let him get away!" "Good for you." "Hang on!" "Hang on!"

I am caught up in it myself and wish also to shout some enthusiastic advice but I do not know what to say. The trout curves up from the water in a wriggling arch and lands behind the boys in the moss and lichen that grow down to the seawashed rocks. They race to free it from the line and proclaim about its size.

On our side of the harbour the boys begin to talk. "Where do you live?" they ask and is it far away and is it bigger than St. John's? Awkwardly I try to tell them the nature of the North

American midwest. In turn I ask them if they go to school. "Yes," they say. Some of them go to St. Bonaventure's which is the Catholic school and others go to Twilling Memorial. They are all in either grade four or grade five. All of them say that they like school and that they like their teachers.

The fishing is good they say and they come here almost every evening. "Yesterday I caught me a nine-pounder," says John. Eagerly they show me all of their simple equipment. The rods are of all varieties as are the lines. At the lines' ends the leaders are thin transparencies terminating in grotesque three-clustered hooks. A foot or so from each hook there is a silver spike knotted into the leader. Some of the boys say the trout are attracted by the flashing of the spike; others say that it acts only as a weight or sinker. No line is without one.

"Here, sir," says John, "have a go. Don't get your shoes wet." Standing on the slippery rocks in my smooth-soled shoes I twice attempt awkward casts. Both times the line loops up too high and the spike splashes down far short of the running, rising life of the channel.

"Just a flick of the wrist, sir," he says, "just a flick of the wrist. You'll soon get the hang of it." His hair is red and curly and his face is splashed with freckles and his eyes are clear and blue. I attempt three or four more casts and then pass the rod back to the hands where it belongs.

And now it is time for supper. The calls float down from the women standing in the doorways of the multicoloured houses and obediently the small fishermen gather up their equipment and their catches and prepare to ascend the narrow upward-winding paths. The sun has descended deeper into the sea and the evening has become quite cool. I recognize this with surprise and a slight shiver. In spite of the advice given to me and my own precautions my feet are wet and chilled within my shoes. No place to be unless barefooted or in rubber boots. Perhaps for me no place at all.

As we lean into the steepness of the path my young companions continue to talk, their accents broad and Irish. One of them used to have a tame sea gull at his house, had it for seven years. His older brother found it on the rocks and brought it home. His grandfather called it Joey. "Because it talked so much," explains John. It died last week and they held a funeral about a mile away from the shore where there was enough soil to dig a grave. Along the shore itself it is almost solid rock and there is no ground for a grave. It's the same with people they say. All week they have been hopefully looking along the base of the cliffs for another sea gull but have not found one. You cannot kill a sea gull they say, the government protects them because they are scavengers and keep the harbours clean.

The path is narrow and we walk in single file. By the time we reach the shanty and my rented car I am wheezing and badly out of breath. So badly out of shape for a man of thirty-three; sauna baths do nothing for your wind. The boys walk easily, laughing and talking beside me. With polite enthusiasm they comment upon my car. Again there exists the possibility of restarting the car's engine and driving back the road that I have come. After all, I have not seen a single adult except for the women calling down the news of supper. I stand and fiddle with my keys.

The appearance of the man and the dog is sudden and unexpected. We have been so casual and unaware in front of the small automobile that we have neither seen nor heard their approach along the rock-worn road. The dog is short, stocky and black and white. White hair floats and feathers freely from his sturdy legs and paws as he trots along the rock looking expectantly out into the harbour. He takes no notice of me. The man is short and stocky as well and he also appears as black and white. His rubber boots are black and his dark heavy worsted trousers are supported by a broadly scarred and blackened belt. The buckle is shaped like a dory with a fisherman standing in the bow. Above the belt there is a dark navy woollen jersey and upon his head a toque of the same material. His hair beneath the toque is white as is the three-or-four-day stubble on his face. His eyes are blue and his hands heavy, gnarled, and misshapen. It is hard to tell from looking at him whether he is in his sixties, seventies or eighties.

"Well, it is a nice evening tonight," he says, looking first at John and then to me. "The barometer has not dropped so perhaps fair weather will continue for a day or two. It will be good for the fishing."

He picks a piece of gnarled grey driftwood from the roadside and swings it slowly back and forth in his right hand. With desperate anticipation the dog dances back and forth before him, his intense eyes glittering at the stick. When it is thrown into the harbour he barks joyously and disappears, hurling himself down the bank in a scrambling avalanche of small stones. In seconds he reappears with only his head visible, cutting a silent but rapidly advancing *V* through the quiet serenity of the harbour. The boys run to the bank's edge and shout encouragement to him — much as they had been doing earlier for one another. "It's farther out," they cry, "to the right, to the right." Almost totally submerged, he cannot see the stick he swims to find. The boys toss stones in its general direction and he raises himself out of the water to see their landing splashdowns and to change his wide-waked course.

"How have you been?" asks the old man, reaching for a pipe and a pouch of tobacco and then without waiting for an answer, "perhaps you'll stay for supper. There are just the three of us now."

We begin to walk along the road in the direction that he has come. Before long the boys rejoin us accompanied by the dripping dog with the recovered stick. He waits for the old man to take it from him and then showers us all with a spray of water from his shaggy coat. The man pats and scratches the damp head and the dripping ears. He keeps the returned stick and thwacks it against his rubber boots as we continue to walk along the rocky road I have so recently travelled in my Volkswagen.

Within a few yards the houses begin to appear upon our left. Frame and flat-roofed, they cling to the rocks looking down into the harbour. In storms their windows are splashed by the seas but now their bright colours are buoyantly brave in the shadows of the descending dusk. At the third gate, John, the man, and the dog turn in. I follow them. The remaining boys continue on; they wave and say, "So long."

The path that leads through the narrow whitewashed gate has had its stone worn smooth by the passing of countless feet. On either side there is a row of small, smooth stones, also neatly whitewashed, and seeming like a procession of large white eggs or tiny unbaked loaves of bread. Beyond these stones and also on either side, there are some cast-off tires also whitewashed and serving as flower beds. Within each whitened circumference the colourful low-lying flowers nod; some hardy strain of pansies or perhaps marigolds. The path leads on to the square green house, with its white borders and shutters. On one side of the wooden doorstep a skate blade has been nailed, for the wiping off of feet, and beyond the swinging screen door there is a porch which smells saltily of the sea. A variety of sou'westers and rubber boots and mitts and caps hang from the driven nails or lie at the base of the wooden walls.

Beyond the porch there is the kitchen where the woman is at work. All of us enter. The dog walks across the linoleum-covered floor, his nails clacking, and flings himself with a contented sigh beneath the wooden table. Almost instantly he is asleep, his coat still wet from his swim within the sea.

The kitchen is small. It has an iron cookstove, a table against one wall and three or four handmade chairs of wood. There is also a wooden rocking-chair covered by a cushion. The rockers are so thin from years of use that it is hard to believe they still function. Close by the table there is a wash-stand with two pails of water upon it. A wash-basin hangs from a driven nail in its side and above it is an old-fashioned mirrored medicine cabinet. There is also a large cupboard, a low-lying couch, and a window facing upon the sea. On the walls a barometer hangs as well as two pictures, one of a rather jaunty young couple taken many years ago. It is yellowed and rather indistinct; the woman in a long dress with her hair done up in ringlets, the man in a serge suit that is slightly too large for him and with a tweed cap pulled rakishly over his right eye. He has an accordion strapped over his shoulders and his hands are fanned out on the buttons and keys. The other picture is of the Christ-child. Beneath it is written, "Sweet Heart of Jesus Pray for Us."

The woman at the stove is tall and fine featured. Her grey hair is combed briskly back from her forehead and neatly coiled with a large pin at the base of her neck. Her eyes are as grey as the storm scud of the sea. Her age, like her husband's, is difficult to guess. She wears a blue print dress, a plain blue apron and low-heeled brown shoes. She is turning fish within a frying pan when we enter.

Her eyes contain only mild surprise as she first regards me. Then with recognition they glow in open hostility which in turn subsides and yields to self-control. She continues at the stove while the rest of us sit upon the chairs.

During the meal that follows we are reserved and shy in our lonely adult ways; groping for and protecting what perhaps may be the only awful dignity we possess. John, unheedingly, talks on and on. He is in the fifth grade and is doing well. They are learning percentages and the mysteries of decimals; to change a percent to a decimal fraction you move the decimal point two places to the left and drop the percent sign. You always, always do so. They are learning the different breeds of domestic animals: the four main breeds of dairy cattle are Holstein, Ayrshire, Guernsey, and Jersey. He can play the mouth organ and will demonstrate after supper. He has twelve lobster traps of his own. They were originally broken ones thrown up on the rocky shore by storms. Ira, he says nodding toward the old man, helped him fix them, nailing on new lathes and knitting new headings. Now they are set along the rocks near the harbour's entrance. He is averaging a pound a trap and the "big" fishermen say that that is better than some of them are doing. He is saving his money in a little imitation keg that was also washed up on the shore. He would like to buy an outboard motor for the small reconditioned skiff he now uses to visit his traps. At present he has only oars.

"John here has the makings of a good fisherman," says the old man. "He's up at five most every morning when I am putting on the fire. He and the dog are already out along the shore and back before I've made tea."

"When I was in Toronto," says John, "no one was ever up before seven. I would make my own tea and wait. It was wonderful sad. There were gulls there though, flying over Toronto harbour. We went to see them on two Sundays."

After the supper we move the chairs back from the table. The woman clears away the dishes and the old man turns on the radio. First he listens to the weather forecast and then turns to short wave where he picks up the conversations from the offshore fishing boats. They are conversations of catches and winds and tides and of the women left behind on the rocky shores. John appears with his mouth organ, standing at a respectful distance. The old man notices him, nods, and shuts off the radio. Rising, he goes upstairs, the sound of his feet echoing down to us. Returning he carries an old and battered accordion. "My fingers have so much rheumatism," he says, "that I find it hard to play anymore."

Seated, he slips his arms through the straps and begins the squeezing accordion motions. His wife takes off her apron and stands behind him with one hand upon his shoulder. For a moment they take on the essence of the once young people in the photograph. They begin to sing:

> Come all ye fair and tender ladies
> Take warning how you court your men
> They're like the stars on a summer's morning
> First they'll appear and then they're gone
>
> I wish I were a tiny sparrow
> And I had wings and I could fly
> I'd fly away to my own true lover
> And all he'd ask I would deny.
>
> Alas I'm not a tiny sparrow
> I have not wings nor can I fly
> And on this earth in grief and sorrow
> I am bound until I die.

John sits on one of the home-made chairs playing his mouth organ. He seems as all mouth-organ players the world over: his right foot tapping out the measures and his small shoulders now round and hunched above the cupped hand instrument.

"Come now and sing with us, John," says the old man.

Obediently he takes the mouth organ from his mouth and shakes the moisture drops upon his sleeve. All three of them begin to sing, spanning easily the half century of time that touches their extremes. The old and the young singing now their songs of loss in different comprehensions. Stranded here, alien of my middle generation, I tap my leather foot self-consciously upon the linoleum. The words sweep up and swirl about my head. Fog does not touch like snow yet it is more heavy and more dense. Oh moisture comes in many forms!

> All alone as I strayed by the banks of the river
> Watching the moonbeams at evening of day
> All alone as I wandered I spied a young stranger
> Weeping and wailing with many a sigh.
>
> Weeping for one who is now lying lonely
> Weeping for one who no mortal can save
> As the foaming dark waters flow silently past him
> Onward they flow over young Jenny's grave.
>
> Oh Jenny my darling come tarry here with me
> Don't leave me alone, love, distracted in pain
> For as death is the dagger that plied us asunder
> Wide is the gulf, love, between you and I.

After the singing stops we all sit rather uncomfortably for a moment. The mood seeming to hang heavily upon our shoulders. Then with my single exception all come suddenly to action. John gets up and takes his battered school books to the kitchen table. The dog jumps up on a chair beside him and watches solemnly in a supervisory manner. The woman takes some navy yarn the colour of her husband's jersey and begins to knit. She is making another jersey and is working on the sleeve. The old man rises and beckons me to follow him into the tiny parlour. The stuffed furniture is old and worn. There is a tiny wood-burning heater in the centre of the room. It stands on a square of galvanized metal which protects the floor from falling, burning coals. The stovepipe rises and vanishes into the wall on its way to the upstairs. There is an old-fashioned mantelpiece on the wall behind the stove. It is covered with odd shapes of driftwood from the shore and a variety of exotically shaped bottles, blue and green and red, which are from the shore as well. There are pictures here too: of the couple in the other picture; and one of them with their five daughters; and one of the five daughters by themselves. In that far-off picture time all of the daughters seem roughly between the ages of ten and eighteen. The youngest has the reddest hair of all. So red that it seems to triumph over the non-photographic colours of lonely black and white. The pictures are in standard wooden frames.

From behind the ancient chesterfield the old man pulls a collapsible card table and pulls down its warped and shaky legs. Also from behind the chesterfield he takes a faded checkerboard and a large old-fashioned matchbox of rattling wooden checkers. The spine of the board is almost cracked through and is strengthened by layers of adhesive tape. The checkers are circumferences of wood sawed from a length of broom handle. They are about three quarters of an inch thick. Half of them are painted a very bright blue and the other half an equally eye-catching red. "John made these," says the old man, "all of them are not really the same thickness but they are good enough. He gave it a good try."

We begin to play checkers. He takes the blue and I the red. The house is silent with only the click-clack of the knitting needles sounding through the quiet rooms. From time to time the old man lights his pipe, digging out the old ashes with a flattened nail and tamping in the fresh tobacco with the same nail's head. The blue smoke winds lazily and haphazardly toward the low-beamed ceiling.The game is solemn as is the next and then the next. Neither of us loses all of the time.

"It is time for some of us to be in bed," says the old woman after a while. She gathers up her knitting and rises from her chair. In the kitchen John neatly stacks his school books on one corner of the table in anticipation of the morning. He goes outside for a moment and then returns. Saying good-night very formally he goes up the stairs to bed. In a short while the old woman follows, her footsteps travelling the same route.

We continue to play our checkers, wreathed in smoke and only partially aware of the muffled footfalls sounding softly above our heads.

When the old man gets up to go outside I am not really surprised, any more than I am when he returns with the brown, ostensible vinegar jug. Poking at the declining kitchen fire, he moves the kettle about seeking the warmest spot on the cooling stove. He takes two glasses from the cupboard, a sugar bowl and two spoons. The kettle begins to boil.

Even before tasting it, I know the rum to be strong and overproof. It comes at night and in fog from the French islands of St. Pierre and Miquelon. Coming over in the low-throttled fishing boats, riding in imitation gas cans. He mixes the rum and the sugar first, watching them marry and dissolve. Then to prevent the breakage of the glasses he places a teaspoon in each and adds the boiling water. The odour rises richly, its sweetness hung in steam. He brings the glasses to the table, holding them by their tops so that his fingers will not burn.

We do not say anything for some time, sitting upon the chairs, while the sweetened, heated richness moves warmly through and from our stomachs and spreads upwards to our brains. Outside the wind begins to blow, moaning and faintly rattling the window's whitened shutters. He rises and brings refills. We are warm within the dark and still within the wind. A clock strikes regularly the strokes of ten.

It is difficult to talk at times with or without liquor; difficult to achieve the actual act of saying. Sitting still we listen further to the rattle of the wind; not knowing where nor how we should begin. Again the glasses are refilled.

"When she married in Toronto," he says at last, "we figured that maybe John should be with her and her husband. That maybe he would be having more of a chance there in the city. But we would be putting it off and it weren't until nigh on two years ago that he went. Went with a woman from down the cove going to visit her daughter. Well, what was wrong was that we missed him wonderful awful. More fearful than we ever thought. Even the dog. Just pacing the floor and looking out the window and walking along the rocks of the shore. Like us had no moorings, lost in the fog or on the ice-floes in a snow squall. Nigh sick unto our hearts we was. Even the grandmother who before that was maybe thinking small to herself that he was trouble in her old age. Ourselves having never had no sons only daughters."

He pauses, then rising goes upstairs and returns with an envelope. From it he takes a picture which shows two young people standing self-consciously before a half-ton pickup with a wooden extension ladder fastened to its side. They appear to be in their middle twenties. The door of the truck has the information: "Jim Farrell, Toronto: Housepainting, Eavestroughing, Aluminum Siding, Phone 535-3484," lettered on its surface.

"This was in the last letter," he says. "That Farrell I guess was a nice enough fellow, from Heartsick Bay he was.

"Anyway they could have no more peace with John than we could without him. Like I says he was here too long before his going and it all took ahold of us the way it will. They sent word that he was coming on the plane to St. John's with a woman they'd met through a Newfoundland club. I was to go to St. John's to meet him. Well, it was all wrong the night before the going. The signs all bad; the grandmother knocked off the lampshade and it broke in a hunnerd pieces — the sign of death; and the window blind fell and clattered there on the floor and then lied still. And the dog runned around like he was crazy, moanen and cryen worse than the swiles does out on the ice, and throwen hisself against the walls and jumpen on the table and at the window where the blind fell until we would have to be letten him out. But it be no better for he runned and throwed hisself in the sea and then come back and howled outside the same window and jumped against the wall, splashen the water from his coat all over it. Then he be runnen back to the sea again. All the neighbours heard him and said I should bide at home and not go to St. John's at all. We be all wonderful scared and not know what to do and the next mornen, first thing I drops me knife.

"But still I feels I has to go. It be foggy all the day and everyone be thinken the plane won't come or be able to land. And I says, small to myself, now here in the fog be the bad luck and the death but then there the plane be, almost like a ghost ship comen out the fog with all its lights shinen. I think maybe he won't be on it but soon he comen through the fog, first with the woman and then see'n me and starten to run, closer and closer till I can feel him in me arms and the tears on both our cheeks. Powerful strange how things will take one. That night they be killed."

From the envelope that contained the picture he draws forth a tattered clipping:

Jennifer Farrell of Roncesvalles Avenue was instantly killed early this morning and her husband James died later in emergency at St. Joseph's Hospital. The accident occurred about 2 A.M. when the pickup truck in which they were travelling went out of control on Queen St. W. and struck a utility pole. It is thought that bad visibility caused by a heavy fog may have contributed to the accident. The Farrells were originally from Newfoundland.

Again he moves to refill the glasses. "We be all alone," he says. "All our other daughters married and far away in Montreal, Toronto, or the States. Hard for them to come back here, even to visit; they comes only every three years or so for perhaps a week. So we be hav'n only him.''

And now my head begins to reel even as I move to the filling of my own glass. Not waiting this time for the courtesy of his offer. Making myself perhaps too much at home with this man's glass and this man's rum and this man's house and all the feelings of his love. Even as I did before. Still locked again for words.

Outside we stand and urinate, turning our backs to the seeming gale so as not to splash our wind-snapped trousers. We are almost driven forward to rock upon our toes and settle on our heels, so blow the gusts. Yet in spite of all, the stars shine clearly down. It will indeed be a good day for the fishing and this wind eventually will calm. The salt hangs heavy in the air and the water booms against the rugged rocks. I take a stone and throw it against the wind into the sea.

Going up the stairs we clutch the wooden bannister unsteadily and say good-night.

The room has changed very little. The window rattles in the wind and the unfinished beams sway and creak. The room is full of sound. Like a foolish Lockwood I approach the window although I hear no voice. There is no Catherine who cries to be let in. Standing unsteadily on one foot when required I manage to undress, draping my trousers across the wooden chair. The bed is clean. It makes no sound. It is plain and wooden, its mattress stuffed with hay or kelp. I feel it with my hand and pull back the heavy patchwork quilts. Still I do not go into it. Instead I go back to the door which has no knob but only an ingenious latch formed from a twisted nail. Turning it, I go out into the hallway. All is dark and the house seems even more inclined to creak where there is no window. Feeling along the wall with my outstretched hand I find the door quite easily. It is closed with the same kind of latch and not difficult to open. But no one waits on the other side. I stand and bend my ear to hear the even sound of my one son's sleeping. He does not beckon any more than the nonexistent voice in the outside wind. I hesitate to touch the latch for fear that I may waken him and disturb his dreams. And if I did what would I say? Yet I would like to see him in his sleep this once and see the room with the quiet bed once more and the wooden chair beside it from off an old wrecked trawler. There is no boiled egg or shaker of salt or glass of water waiting on the chair within this closed room's darkness.

Once though there was a belief held in the outports, that if a girl would see her own true lover she should boil an egg and scoop out half the shell and fill it with salt. Then she should take it to bed

David Blackwood, The Flora F. Nickerson Coming Home From The Labrador, *1979*

with her and eat it, leaving a glass of water by her bedside. In the night her future husband or a vision of him would appear and offer her the glass. But she must only do it once.

It is the type of belief that bright young graduate students were collecting eleven years ago for the theses and archives of North America and also, they hoped, for their own fame. Even as they sought the near–Elizabethan songs and ballads that had sailed from County Kerry and from Devon and Cornwall. All about the wild, wide sea and the flashing silver dagger and the lost and faithless lover. Echoes to and from the lovely, lonely hills and glens of West Virginia and the standing stones of Tennessee.

Across the hall the old people are asleep. The old man's snoring rattles as do the windows; except that now and then there are catching gasps within his breath. In three or four short hours he will be awake and will go down to light his fire. I turn and walk back softly to my room.

Within the bed the warm sweetness of the rum is heavy and intense. The darkness presses down upon me but still it brings no sleep. There are no voices and no shadows that are real. There are only walls of memory touched restlessly by flickers of imagination.

Oh I would like to see my way more clearly. I, who have never understood the mystery of fog. I would perhaps like to capture it in a jar like the beautiful childhood butterflies that always die in spite of the airholes punched with nails in the covers of their captivity — leaving behind the vapours of their lives and deaths; or perhaps as the unknowing child who collects the grey moist condoms from the lovers' lanes only to have them taken from him and to be told to wash his hands. Oh I have collected many things I did not understand.

And perhaps I should go and say, oh son of my *summa cum laude* loins, come away from the lonely gulls and the silver trout and I will take you to the land of the Tastee Freeze where you may sleep till ten or nine. And I will show you the elevator to the apartment on the sixteenth floor and introduce you to the buzzer system and the yards of the wrought-iron fences where the Doberman pinscher runs silently at night. Or may I offer you the money that is the fruit of my collecting and my most successful life? Or shall I wait to meet you in some known or unknown bitterness like Yeats's Cuchulain by the wind-whipped sea or as Sohrab and Rustum by the future flowing river?

Again I collect dreams. For I do not know enough of the fog on Toronto's Queen St. West and the grinding crash of the pickup and of lost and misplaced love.

I am up early in the morning as the man kindles the fire from the driftwood splinters. The outside light is breaking and the wind is calm. John tumbles down the stairs. Scarcely stopping to splash his face and pull on his jacket, he is gone, accompanied by the dog. The old man smokes his pipe and waits for the water to boil. When it does he pours some into the teapot then passes the kettle to me. I take it to the wash-stand and fill the small tin basin in readiness for my shaving. My face looks back from the mirrored cabinet. The woman softly descends the stairs.

"I think I will go back today," I say while looking into the mirror at my face and at those in the room behind me. I try to emphasize the "I." "I just thought I would like to make this trip — again. I think I can leave the car in St. John's and fly back directly." The woman begins to move about the table, setting out the round white plates. The man quietly tamps his pipe.

The door opens and John and the dog return. They have been down along the shore to see what has happened throughout the night. "Well, John," says the old man, "what did you find?"

He opens his hand to reveal a smooth round stone. It is of the deepest green inlaid with veins of darkest ebony. It has been worn and polished by the unrelenting restlessness of the sea and buffed and burnished by the gravelled sand. All of its inadequacies have been removed and it glows with the lustre of near perfection.

"It is very beautiful," I say.

"Yes," he says, I like to collect them." Suddenly he looks up into my eyes and thrusts the stone toward me. "Here," he says, "would you like to have it?"

Even as I reach out my hand I turn my head to the others in the room. They are both looking out through the window to the sea.

"Why, thank you," I say. "Thank you very much. Yes, I would. Thank you. Thanks." I take it from his outstretched hand and place it in my pocket.

We eat our breakfast in near silence. After it is finished the boy and dog go out once more. I prepare to leave.

"Well, I must go," I say, hesitating at the door. "It will take me a while to get to St. John's." I offer my hand to the man. He takes it in his strong fingers and shakes it firmly.

"Thank you," says the woman. "I don't know if you know what I mean but thank you."

"I think I do," I say. I stand and fiddle with the keys. "I would somehow like to help or keep in touch but..."

"But there is no phone," he says, "and both of us can hardly write. Perhaps that's why we never told you. John is getting to be a pretty good hand at it though."

"Good-bye," we say again, "good-bye, good-bye."

The sun is shining clearly now and the small boats are putt-putting about the harbour. I enter my unlocked car and start its engine. The gravel turns beneath the wheels. I pass the house and wave to the man and woman standing in the yard.

On a distant cliff the children are shouting. Their voices carol down through the sun-washed air and the dogs are curving and dancing about them in excited circles. They are carrying something that looks like a crippled gull. Perhaps they will make it well. I toot the horn. "Good-bye," they shout and wave, "good-bye, good-bye."

The airport terminal is strangely familiar. A symbol of impermanence, it is itself glisteningly permanent. Its formica surfaces have been designed to stay. At the counter a middle-aged man in mock exasperation is explaining to the girl that it is Newark he wishes to go to, *not* New York.

There are not many of us and soon we are ticketed and lifting through and above the sun-shot fog. The meals are served in tinfoil and in plastic. We eat above the clouds looking at the tips of wings.

The man beside me is a heavy-equipment salesman who has been trying to make a sale to the developers of Labrador's resources. He has been away a week and is returning to his wife and children.

Later in the day we land in the middle of the continent. Because of the changing time zones the distance we have come seems eerily unreal. The heat shimmers in little waves upon the runway. This is the equipment salesman's final destination while for me it is but the place where I must change flights to continue even farther into the heartland. Still we go down the wheeled-up stairs together, donning our sunglasses, and stepping across the heated concrete and through the terminal's electronic doors. The salesman's wife stands waiting along with two small children who are the first to see him. They race toward him with their arms outstretched. "Daddy, Daddy," they cry, "what did you bring me? What did you bring me?

Author's Commentary

For me, most stories begin with an idea, and the idea for this particular story was the concept of "collecting". People collect what they consider to be valuable to them, but often what they seek is viewed differently by others. What is a "treasure" or "antique" to one individual may be merely "garbage" to another. In the same way "beliefs" or "superstitions" vary according to the individual who encounters them. While voodoo may be "quaint" to most North Americans, it may be very serious business to those who live in other regions of the world or of the mind. In the same way, the "causes" which many people are willing to die for, seem irrelevant to those who stand outside such frameworks of belief.

This was intended as a story about a man who, for a while, did not understand the difference between "taking" and "giving." It is also about the impact he had on others and the impact that they eventually had upon him.

It is set in one of the older regions of Canada (and North America). It seems that in such regions the burden or gift of history is more extensive and that seemed to me something to be taken quite seriously.

I thought of the above for some weeks and then I began to write. When I was not actually writing, I thought about the material a great deal; snatches of songs and old half-forgotten superstitions entered my mind quite willingly once I opened the door and made them welcome. I suppose I was also thinking of past generations; of what I had "taken" and what I had been "given" and what I wished sincerely would never become "lost."

Alistair MacLeod

Born in Saskatchewan, Alistair MacLeod was raised in Alberta and Nova Scotia. He studied and taught at the University of New Brunswick before going to Notre Dame University, where he received his doctorate. In addition to his university career, MacLeod has done other work (including stints as a labourer, milkman, logger, miner, public relations person, and teacher at a one room school) in various parts of Canada, including Newfoundland. He now teaches English and creative writing at the University of

Windsor. His first collection of short stories, *The Lost Salt Gift of Blood,* was published in 1976. Other poetry and fiction have been published in books and periodicals in both Canada and the United States.

Esther Warkov, Family Reunion, *c. 1965*

On Wings of Tongue

ADELE WISEMAN

"It's a nice blizzard," said my mother, looking at her. "If only people who have far to go would have the sense to stay home."

The winter my father went to Vancouver to look for a job Joe and I were still too young to go to school. We stayed home and my mother found things for us to do after Belle and Arty left the house. In those days the house was full of roomers. You'd be surprised at how many tenants can be crowded into a five room bungalow, particularly if the landlady and her four children are flexible about shifting around to accommodate the guests. For Mrs. Lemon alone we had moved our belongings in turn to every room in the house. Every time my mother gave in and said, "All right, you can come," we tried to clear out a room other than the one that she had occupied last time, because my mother wanted it to be a fresh start each time. She did not want to remind Mrs. Lemon that last time she had moved out because we were piping poison gas into her room.

Joe was still practically a baby. He missed my father terribly. Everybody said so, and I could prove it any time. All I had to say was, "Where's Daddy? Daddy's gone away." Fat tears would glaze his trusting eyes; his belly would heave into some mysterious preparatory discipline, and from his mouth would burst the foghorn bass bellow that was the pride of our house. You couldn't bear to listen for long. Remorsefully, I would yell into his weeping, "He's coming! He's coming home!" Joe would hesitate uncertainly, the sobs clucking and gurgling. I completed the cure. "What'll he bring? What'll he bring me?" It was a pleasure to see the joy spread over his good-natured face. "What'll he bring Joe?"

"Me! Me!" chuckled Joe. I played nicely with him for a while after that.

Every morning I took a trip. Sometimes I took Joe. We had our route laid out. To a certain listing, brown-shingled house down the street we went, labouring through unshovelled snow. Up icy front steps we climbed on all fours. Finally we stood rattling the doorknob and banging with our fists on the door. If no one came to the door I would stand back and let Joe holler into the sparkling air. That was when it was good to have him with me. "Mrs. Fi...fer!" His powerful roar shattered the air, scattering the billion tiny crystals that darted thick and glittering in the daylight and sending them blinking to hide in the snow. That brought Mrs. Fifer running.

Joe got his voice from an uncle on my father's side. That uncle was born with church bells in his chest. An aesthetic priest had gone mad over his voice and had pressed him into the service of the church choir, because there was no one in all Russia who could intone like he could, "Christ is risen!" Through three successive pogroms his voice had been the salvation of his entire family, and of everyone else who'd had the sense to seek refuge in his house. For when the parishioners ran amok they left his house religiously alone. "They respect me," he used to say, with not a little pride.

We all of us in our house had little characteristics that were passed on to us from relatives, some of whom we had never known, so that we grew up with the feeling that we were part of a much larger family than we actually had. They told me that I took after my aunt Yenta, my mother's sister, who lived only a few blocks away. It was because I talked too much. Yenta herself was always the first, though, to accuse me of spreading family secrets. Nobody ever told me why they weren't secrets until I talked about them. They were just things everybody in the house discussed. But the minute they found out I'd told Mrs. Fifer they became secrets.

Mrs. Fifer was an old lady. She and her husband lived in one of the ground-floor apartments in the ramshackle house right next door to the apartment of my aunt Yenta's best friend, Dvosieh Krotz. She was always wonderfully pleased to see me, and Joe too, though he wasn't much to talk to yet. She loosed our clothing, unwound our scarves, and gave us cookies from a shredded-wheat box.

As we ate Mrs. Fifer would ask me all kinds of questions, and I would answer her while my index finger kept the turning crumbs poked back safely in my mouth. Mrs. Fifer liked talking to me. She used to tell my mother what a nice little girl I was to come and visit, and how polite I was to spend time talking to an old lady. My mother always smiled in an apprehensive kind of way.

They were not only family things Mrs. Fifer asked about, with her intensely interested, kind old face bent forward to hear what I said. She took an interest in our roomers too, what they said, what they did, what my mother thought of them, did they pay their rent on time, which ones were on relief, did any of them have secret jobs the relief didn't know about, was it true this one had fought with that one over a pot on the stove, and so on. I loved to listen to the talk in our house, so I was particularly good at correcting Mrs. Fifer when she said, for instance, "And did your Daddy say so and so?"

"No, he said such and such," I would reply, proud to be able to set an adult straight.

How did my auntie always know what I'd been saying to Mrs. Fifer? I could tell by her preliminary stamping on the ice outside and by the way she slammed into our house, rattling the frosted windows, how serious her visit was going to be in its consequences for me. She would always call out before she was fully over the threshold, "I'm not staying. Don't make tea." She kicked off my uncle's old galoshes and came up the five hall steps, bringing the chill of the outdoors into the room with her. Joe, who sat with his flannel kimono loose, shuddered up and down his rolls of baby fat, accompanying his shudders with resonant, self-comforting growls.

"What?" cried my aunt, readily indignant, "is the child doing naked?"

"Don't come near him, auntie," I said, "Mama's fixing his combinations. We got the other ones wet outside."

"You," said my aunt, "Leubitchka with the active lips, does Mrs. Fifer know that too already? It hurts me for you Rivka," she turned to my mother. "This child has a faceful of mouth, a mouthful of tongue, a tongueful of every little thing that goes on in this house, so Mrs. Fifer can run and spread it like fire all over the prairie."

"Mrs. Fifer's sick," I said, "in an armchair, covered over. I was there with Joe."

"Not too sick to ask questions," said my aunt bitterly. "It hurts me, Rivka...."

"It hurts me," like "I'm not staying, don't make tea," was one of those baffling statements that Yenta made. She always stayed. She always drank tea. And she never told you where she hurt. She always changed the subject in mid-sentence. "It hurts me your name should be dragged through the mud."

There was no mud any more. "Through the snow." I offered.

"What?" said my aunt.

"Nothing," I said. Maybe she meant "It hurts me your name

should be dug to the mud." But why did it hurt? And how did a name get dragged or dug? Anyway, with her dark, flashing eyes and glowing skin, she never looked as though anything was hurting her.

"It's not Mrs. Fifer spreads the stories," said my mother quietly.

"Don't be foolish," said my aunt heatedly. "They fly by themselves, all over town." She looked at me. "On wings of tongue they fly."

I laughed. I liked the way my aunt talked. She laughed too. In spite of the things she called me we got along, and it sounded as though it might go easy with me and Mrs. Fifer today, though you never could tell. They laughed and laughed and suddenly they jumped you.

"Mama says Mrs. Fifer doesn't tell anything," I said, before I could stop myself.

"Oh she doesn't?" said my aunt. "So if your mother says she doesn't then she doesn't. Should I argue? When your mother gets stubborn I might as well talk to the walls." My aunt stopped talking.

My mother, smiling, looked up from her stitching. "How's your friend Dvosieh?"

My aunt ignored the question and addressed me directly. "Why do you talk so much? Where do you get your tongue? Why do you tell her everything?"

"She asks me," I faltered. "I take after you," I added quickly.

"Don't be disrespectful," said my mother.

"But you say so," I said.

"It's not what you say but when," explained my aunt, "that makes respect. Is it true then?" she continued, "what she told Mrs. Fifer? Are you taking Mrs. Lemon in again? As if you haven't got enough to worry about. Don't do it Rivka. What do you need her for? Tell her no for a change. Let her find somewhere else."

"She's here already," said my mother.

"In the house?" my aunt's voice disappeared suddenly in her lips.

"No, she had to report to the relief," said my mother. "But she moved in this morning."

My aunt frowned. Her eyes seemed to light on me.

"That's what I told Mrs. Fifer," I said.

My aunt shook her head. "She's getting worse, not better. One day she's fine, talks like anybody else; the next day suddenly, out of nowhere, an accusation you can't make sense of; then locks herself in her room, not a word; then starts to run around to the neighbours. Did you hear what happened? Yesterday she went to her husband's people again and made a scandal. She said they're keeping her husband locked up a prisoner in the TB hospital. She said they're paying the government to put germs in his X-rays to kill him. They wouldn't let her into the house so she went shouting up and down their fancy street."

"It must be very embarrassing for them," my mother said. "The rich are so sensitive."

"It hurts me for them," said my aunt in a surprisingly satisfied voice for one in pain. "They didn't even offer her a glass of tea, not a bite. They tried to give her money to go away, five dollars to ease her pain. She threw it at them. And they from behind closed doors, afraid to let her in, a human being like themselves. She didn't have a mouthful of saliva to chew on all day. She walked from their place to the Hudson's Bay Company in the snow, and fainted twice, once in the notions and the second time when they took her to the restroom. So strangers called an ambulance and took her to the hospital. It's all over town."

"I know," said my mother. "An ambulance brought her this morning."

My aunt laughed. "She certainly gets free public transportation. It's always ambulances and police cars." My aunt could never overcome the suspicion that it was somehow useful to Mrs. Lemon to be sick. In spite of her hard talk Yenta had taken Mrs. Lemon into her own house three disastrous times already. Things always started off well enough, with my aunt proud of how well she could handle a problem that had once again vanquished my mother, and Mrs. Lemon temporarily tranquil because she had once again fought-off some obscure threat. Then my auntie's crony, Dvosieh Krotz, would come over to sit in and give advice, the same crony who lived behind the wall of Mrs. Fifer's flat.

Dvosieh advised friendship and reason, and the sane discussion of past delusions in the calm of present clarity. My aunt showed her friendship through the simple means of frequent reiteration. "I say to her," she would explain to my mother, "You see, I'm your friend, Mrs. Krotz is your friend. We're all your friends." And Yenta was not one to be stingy with her sympathy. "Your poor husband, where is this 'san'? Up north? What's up north? The Eskimos! Why would they put a TB san up north? So they can cure him of consumption and kill him with pneumonia?"

Under the stress of reason, advice and friendship, Mrs. Lemon's suspicions were rapidly forced, like monstrous bulbs, in her mind's darkness. By some inspired stroke of malignancy her fits always crystallized around Yenta's most sensitive spot. My aunt is a wonderful cook and a proud one, justly famed in our neighbourhood. Mrs. Lemon always ended up by accusing her of poisoning her food. My aunt could not resist taking it personally. She would become incensed and run among the neighbours herself. When my mother tried to reason with her she grew even more irate, "See here Rivka, listen here. You say it's madness, so let it be an equal madness for everybody. Has she ever told you you poison her food? No!"

"But I've gassed her and drugged her and I whisper in her room at night," my mother defended herself.

"That doesn't make any difference. Three times she's lived in my house and three times I've poisoned her. It's too much. If at least once I'd gassed her I wouldn't feel so much she was deliberately needling me. She means something by it."

"She's sick," sighed my mother.

"You always find something good to say for everybody," sniffed Yenta.

This time, however, my aunt had a more serious threat to disclose against Mrs. Lemon than her own erratic ire. After this last scandal in the south end the in-laws had sworn, in front of witnesses, that if it happened once more, if once more she made trouble, they would have her put away.

"They wouldn't," said my mother after a silence. "She's harmless."

"Oh yes they would," said my aunt. "They're out of all patience. Once more and they'll put her away for good. They don't like scandals on the south side."

"You make money you lose patience," said my mother.

"Where will they put her away?" I asked.

My mother and aunt looked at each other. "Nowhere," said my mother hastily.

"Mrs. Fifer has her radio on," said my aunt, pursing her lips.

"Mrs. Fifer hasn't got a radio," I was happy to contribute.

My mother sighed. "Just don't repeat everything we've said to Mrs. Lemon."

"All right," I said. "I like Mrs. Lemon," I added. "Joe and I don't want them to put her away. Nor Belle nor Arty neither."

"Just don't talk," said Yenta quickly, "and they won't."

"She's like you, Yenta," my mother remarked.

"Like me? How like me? I'm no child. A child shouldn't sell your teeth every time you open your mouth."

This was not the first time I had heard that "they" could do something dreadful to Mrs. Lemon. No wonder she had fits. I could not separate the idea of Mrs. Lemon's being "put away for good" from the memory of the time our dog Rhubarb had to be put away, and the man had come with a closed wagon with a grilled door in back to take her away, and she had stood still behind the grille, and had left us all standing and watching and stained forever with her mute, despairing eyes. Just let them try to come and get Mrs. Lemon.

Mrs. Lemon played with us, not the way most adults do, always with the end of the game in sight, as though telling themselves approvingly over their impatience, "now we are playing with the children for a little while." Rather, she let us play with her. Quietly she sat or stood or turned as we directed her, never imitating us and never rushing us through her time. We usually played in the kitchen those winter afternoons. Sometimes we played in her room, but my mother didn't like that. She said that if Mrs. Lemon saw that we kept strictly away from her room there would be less chance of upsetting her. So it was mostly in the kitchen that we had our games, the warm white kitchen with its frost-fuzzed windows, its big grey electric stove, its knife-scarred wooden table covered by a knife-scarred printed oilcloth, and its wooden rung chairs, behind which Mrs. Lemon allowed herself to be barricaded while Joe and I pretended we had captured her and had her in our power. She stood quietly, occasionally saying something nice in reply to my mother, like "No, they're not bothering me."

I liked the way Mrs. Lemon looked. She made me think. She didn't look like a lemon. She was thin and brown. Her hair was black and rolled round and round at the back of her head. Her eyes were big and bugged out a little, with dark brown middles and yellowish white parts. And she was extra brown all around the eyes.

In spite of my mother's instructions Joe and I were not strangers in Mrs. Lemon's room. We knew her few belongings well, especially the raddled orange fur collar with the fox's head and its loosely snapping jaw. On her bureau sat a little brown old-country picture of her mother, her father, and two sturdy boys, with a little, big-eyed girl between them I knew was Mrs. Lemon long ago. I always wanted to ask her which one was the brother who had dropped dead when they were burying her father; right into the grave he dropped. I knew all about what a sad life she had had that made her go funny sometimes. But I never did. There was another picture, in a small frame, of Mr. Lemon. He wore a white collar and looked bristly, and I said like my mother did when she mentioned him sometimes, "He'll get well soon," in the same confident voice that pleased Mrs. Lemon. The candy was in an almost empty top right-hand drawer, in a box with a gypsy on it.

Sometimes she would say, "Do you want to take a walk with me?" And my mother would say, "Mrs. Lemon, you shouldn't, they're too wild." And she would beg and make promises along with us until my mother said, "All right, but you mustn't buy them anything," And Mrs. Lemon wouldn't say anything and my mother would bite her lip, for fear she had hurt Mrs. Lemon's feelings by implying she couldn't afford to spend her relief tickets on us.

They would truss us up and we would move stiffly off between the snowbanks. I slithered around on Arty's old moccasins and screamed into Joe, knocking him over like a kewpie doll, sideways, into the piled-up snow, where he lay, one arm standing straight out, the other buried. His cries shattered the still, needle-charged air. Mrs. Lemon dug him out, soothed him, called him "little snowman," and I magnanimously let him push me back, which he did, chuckling his deep bass chuckle. I flung myself, screaming, into the bank, and waited for a panting Mrs. Lemon to right me before I flung myself on Joe again. We were snow-plastered and steaming through every layer by the time we reached the corner grocery. Inside it was hot and dingy and glamorous. We consulted with Mrs. Lemon for a long time and then she bought us each a string of pink and white crystallized sugar and a flat square package of bubble gum with a hockey picture in it that Arty would be nice for.

"I'm not giving Arty my hockey picture," I suggested to Joe. Joe gripped his with his mitt against his chest and shook his head fiercely, eyes shining, cheeks fiery, nose running. But I knew very well he would rush, the minute Arty made his noisy, dishevelled entrance from school, with his hockey picture extended, for the immediate gratification of a big brother's thanks. Arty wouldn't win mine so easily. I knew the subtler pleasures of the drawn-out wooing and the gradual surrender "I have one too, Arty, see? No you can't. What'll you give me? Can I play in your igloo?"

So the winter passed. One day, late in February, my mother was sitting alone in the kitchen, sewing and humming to herself. Mrs. Lemon slipped in so quietly my mother didn't even hear her, till the hissing whisper started her out of her chair. "Do you think I don't know why you're singing? But you won't get me that easily." My mother got up and made some tea, which they drank in utter silence. After that, Mrs. Lemon stopped talking almost entirely. Sometimes she sat in the kitchen without speaking for hours at a time, while my mother did her work, occasionally throwing her an anxious glance. At other times Mrs. Lemon stayed in her room. My mother warned us to leave her alone, then, and I heard her tell my sister that maybe if we just kept still too it would blow over.

One day she left the house very early. She spent the whole day wandering among the neighbours and talking to people about her suspicions. My mother knew what she was doing, as she had often received such confidences when Mrs. Lemon was living elsewhere. "Maybe she'll just talk it out of her system," she told my aunt, who had come rushing over with the news.

"No," My aunt was triumphantly certain. "There'll be trouble."

Mrs. Lemon returned home that evening, thoroughly chilled, blue tints frozen into her swarthy skin, and for the next few days she lay coughing in bed. My mother tended to her, talking gently and soothingly, and pretended she didn't notice that she got no answer.

"Maybe the fever will burn it away," said my mother hopefully.

"No," said my aunt, "I tell you Rivka, you won't avoid a scandal, And this time...."

"I'll try to keep her in the house till it blows over," said my mother.

The coughing ceased and my mother listened anxiously to the silence. She sighed more frequently as she listened, and raised her hand often from her sewing to run it through her softly waving black hair.

Then one day Mrs. Lemon, who must have been waiting behind her door for a long time, took advantage of a moment when my mother had gone into her bedroom to slip out of her room, through the kitchen, down the hall steps and out the side door. Joe and I were playing on the kitchen floor and we called out to her, but she didn't seem to hear our pleased hellos; she was all dug down into her coat. Only the fox winked and snapped at us from her back as she bounded down the steps.

My mother ran out of our bedroom, but too late she scratched at the ice of the window. "What was she wearing? Was she dressed warmly?"

"Her winter coat and her live fox," I said. My mother still looked worried. She looked more worried as the day wore on. She talked to my sister in a low voice when Belle and Arty got home from school, and my sister looked worried too. I hung around them and looked worried too, and asked questions that touched on raw worry and was hushed up.

We were eating supper when Mrs. Lemon returned. She rushed up the stairs and through the kitchen to her room, still hunched in her coat, and I called after her, but again there was no reply, and my mother shushed me up.

We were still around the table when my aunt came stamping in. She came up the stairs with her coat still buttoned and a very excited expression on her face. "Is she in?" she nodded in the direction of Mrs. Lemon's room, and formed the words through almost silent lips.

My mother nodded.

"You'll have visitors tomorrow," said Yenta softly, and nodded toward Mrs. Lemon's room again. "Didn't I warn you?' My aunt undid her coat but remained planted in my uncle's old galoshes in the kitchen doorway. "She went there again, threw herself down into the snow on their lawn, made a big outline, it's still there, for all the neighbours to see, made a scene...." "She'll catch cold again," murmured my mother.

"She'll be well taken care of," said my aunt grimly. She paused and looked anxiously toward Mrs. Lemon's room and we all listened with her. "So...that's it. Maybe it's better this way Rivka, though...you know...somehow...it hurts me..."

"It hurts me too," said my mother softly, staring down at Joe's plate. "It hurts me too."

The next morning I fought against going out of the house, though a part of me wanted to go and talk to Mrs. Fifer. I felt funny-bad all over, and I could tell that my mother felt badly too, though she insisted on sending us out for our fresh air until she realized that there was a blizzard blowing up. I whined about after her all morning, and Joe growled after me. It was out of his range to whine.

By early afternoon the snow was whipping past the windows and piling up against the fences and walls and making spooky sounds all around the house. We had to turn the lights on. Mama began to worry about the children who were at school. I told her not to worry about any little blizzard bothering Arty and Belle.

Suddenly, Mrs. Lemon made her appearance in the kitchen. She looked around quickly and without saying anything went to stand at the kitchen window, looking out to where you could see nothing but swirling snow. My mother was looking at her.

"Joe," I jumped up. "Let's capture Mrs. Lemon!" Delighted, Joe slid off his chair and began to push it toward her, while I began to push my own. "You're our prisoner!" I shouted out, and rushed to pull another chair to her side. "Prisoner!" repeated Joe in organ tones.

"Children!" said my mother.

Mrs. Lemon had turned from the window and stood looking at us from behind the chairs.

"Children," said my mother again. "Come here!" She had risen.

I looked from her to Mrs. Lemon. "She'll be our prisoner," I cried. "Then they can't put her away!"

"Leuba!" cried my mother, in a terrible voice.

I started to cry. "We don't want them to send Mrs. Lemon away!"

At the word "away," Joe cut loose like a trained bullfrog. "Gone away!" he bellowed, eyes closed, mouth enormous, comprehending in its quivering pink cavern the whole reverberating enormity of deprival. Unable to compete with his mighty gust of expression I contented myself with short, breathy, gasping whimpers and siren whines.

"Children!" my mother implored, "children!" We pitched on fervently. "Away!" I prompted as Joe paused for breath. Instantly he exhaled his heartbreak in a fresh gust of shattering sound.

"Children!" my mother's hands were at her ears. "Children! Children!"

"Children," said Mrs. Lemon suddenly, from behind her barricade. "Children," she said in a dazed voice.

I stopped in mid-note, amazed at the first sound I had heard Mrs. Lemon utter in days. Joe, unaware of all else but his art, bellowed on. Confused, I forgot how to turn him off. "Joe," I yelled. He redoubled his efforts. His face had turned a fierce red that extended all down his neck. My mother, alarmed, started to pat him lightly on the back, murmuring, "Yosele, what's the matter? Yosele."

"Shut up!" I yelled, right into Joe's open mouth, so suddenly that he made a gulp and clicking sound and a little "whirrr," as though his spring had snapped, and he remained voiceless, staring at me with the big, wounded, swimming eyes of one utterly betrayed.

"Leuba!" cried Mrs. Lemon, and for the first time ever, other than to help me across the street or to put on my overthings, she laid her hand on me. She had me gently by the shoulder and her voice was dazed and shocked and urgent. "Never say that to your brother. Never, never say that to your brother."

I had an awful feeling inside of me, as though I had swallowed a big stone. I started to cry, this time soft, painful tears that wouldn't make a noise but only little groans inside of me. "I only meant," I said to Joe, who was also streaming big, sighing tears, "I only meant, Daddy's coming, honest Joe, he's coming soon," I bawled. My mother held and rocked us both.

"They miss their father," said Mrs. Lemon. "Poor children, they miss their father."

By the time my aunt arrived, all puffy and snowed over, Mrs. Lemon was sitting with Joe on her lap, playing tickle with him and receiving raucous response. No blizzard has ever prevented my aunt from just dropping by at the crucial moment of a crisis, and from sitting with her lips all pursed up and her eyes fixed on one or other of us, with an accusing or anticipatory stare. Only this time she quickly became aware that something was amiss. Yenta's glance shot questioningly back and forth from my mother to Mrs. Lemon. What had happened? My aunt looked almost indignant. Had Mrs. Lemon gone crazy all of a sudden?

"It's a nice blizzard," said my mother, looking at her. "If only people who have far to go would have the sense to stay home."

"Troublemakers should always stay home," said my aunt, and smiled at Mrs. Lemon in the friendliest way.

Suddenly, three more people were huffing and puffing up the stairs into the kitchen, all in enormous, snowed-over coats, all standing and making cold noises and throwing chills around while my mother and aunt helped them off with their overthings, all apologizing because they were dripping on the kitchen floor, as the hall was too small to hold them. Mrs. Lemon went and got a chair from her room and my aunt brought another from our room and my mother took her sewing off another chair and pretty soon they were all sitting and blowing on their knuckles and talking about how cold it was and my mother had a fresh kettle on.

Joe had offered himself genially back to Mrs. Lemon's arms, and he now sat at princely ease, staring at the visitors from astride her knee. Mrs. Lemon started to demonstrate my brother's extraordinary vocal endowments to the newcomers by tickling his belly. The strangers were struck dumb with admiration.

Then the men started to explain how hard it was to drive in a snowstorm, and how they had started out long ago and had stalled twice along the way. The heavy woman who had come with them sat gingerly on her seat and looked all around and finally up and down over her black beads at my aunt, who wore my uncle's old red woollen socks over her shoes, and pulled right up under her skirt, because my uncle is a tall man, with her bloomers tucked into them. They had big yellow and blue darns on them, beautifully sewn, because my aunt is a perfectionist. The lady coughed as she looked, and my aunt spread her knees further apart to give herself purchase, leaned slightly forward, straight of back, folded her arms across her chest, and stared back, with pursed lips and a coldly ironic eye. My aunt is a handsome woman, with a haughty face and thick, straight black hair. She was not going to be stared down on account of her socks.

One of the men, smallish, with a glistening stone in his tie that looked as though it would melt any minute, leaned from his chair and whispered, hesitantly but loudly enough for me to hear, to the beaded lady, "Er... which one?" The beaded lady then introduced Mrs. Lemon as her sister-in-law, and all kinds of cross-introductions were made. I stared at her. This was the enemy, on whose lawns the scandals were enacted, who never even offered a glass of tea, though my mother even now was pouring hers.

I cannot remember in detail exactly what was said during the next little while, but I do remember that I behaved very badly. The kitchen gradually filled and filled and stretched outward with sound, much of it coming from my lips. Numerous faces all turned toward me, with varying expressions of amazement, distaste, disapproval, despair, as I talked, interrupted, contradicted and mimicked. The rich lady coughed at the smoke from the cigarettes the men had lit, which was mingling with the steam from the kettle to fog up the room. She took noisier and noisier breaths. My aunt told her very kindly that she hoped her brother's ailment didn't run in the family, which made her cough so hard her beads rattled. I started to cough too, and my brother Joe chuckled approvingly at me, adding a stentorian spur to my antics. He thought it was a fine game. My mother pleaded with me in a shocked voice to be quiet, please. I couldn't. I no longer knew how.

Then my aunt and the rich relative got into what seemed to me a traitorously amiable conversation about what an unmanageably talkative child I was, and my aunt told her how I couldn't keep family secrets, and I remember being fiercely hurt that she should sell a family secret of such magnitude to an enemy, and in front of strangers.

Finally, my mother ordered me out of the room and I stood there bawling and insisted that I wouldn't go unless Mrs. Lemon came with me. By this time she was the only true ally I had left in the world and I could not leave her to treachery. My last-ditch tantrum was interrupted by loud noises at the door. My brother Arty and my sister Belle were outside quarrelling about who would get into the house first, Belle, with both arms book-laden, with snowpants under her thick coat, besparkled and dishevelled, and chubby Arty, in breeches and high boots and fur-lined jacket, banging his hockey stick against the wall of the house and lashing icicles from the eaves as he argued. There wasn't room for both to squeeze in at once, so meanwhile they held the door open and the blast whipped up blue around the fogged-up kitchen, and everybody shivered.

"I don't care if you are a lady," challenged Arty, who had wedged his hockey stick in front of Belle so that it suddenly appeared in the kitchen doorway with an ancient pair of razor-sharp skates hanging from knotted yellow laces over its edge.

"Belle! Arty!" boomed Joe joyously, as the skates narrowly grazed his skull. The three strangers exchanged glances as the stick and swinging skates advanced into the kitchen, the blades blinking ferociously and slashing indiscriminately through the air.

"Arty!" cried my mother aghast. "Belle, shut the door for goodness' sake! We have guests!" she added hopefully.

"I can't," wailed my sister. "He won't let me in."

"Arty, take your skates away!" cried my mother, as the wind howled around the kitchen.

The guests broke for the bedroom. They found their coats. There was confusion in the kitchen for the next few moments, with Belle and Arty getting out of their wet clothes and the guests trying to get into theirs, and everybody exchanging polite "good-byes" and "come agains" and the beaded lady saying something about "in good hands," and the small man with the pin saying something about "family atmosphere," as he nodded his way vigorously to the hall. Then they left. Soon afterwards my aunt left, having just remembered she had a word to say to her friend Dvosieh down the street. Mrs. Lemon said she was tired, suddenly, she didn't know why, and retired to the quiet of her room.

"What happened?" asked my sister.

"She feels better," said my mother.

Joe deserted us to go and look at Arty's sled with him in the cellar. Belle and my mother started doing the dishes. My mother said she was afraid supper might be a little late tonight. Everything was flat and quiet suddenly. I picked up the crumbs on the table. "What can I do?" I asked. My mother came to the table and stood looking down at me. She looked lovely, with her long, fine nose, her delicate skin all pink, her deep-set eyes shining golden brown. "Aren't you tired?" she asked, as though she really thought I might be, so early.

"No. Can I help you?"

"You know," said my mother, "the way you behaved..." Suddenly, unaccountably, she grabbed me up, so violently that my curls bounced over my eyes. "You've helped enough," she said into my ear, and it felt, from the way her stomach was shaking and from the muffled sounds she was making in my hair, as though she was laughing.

———————

Author's Commentary

As a reader, I come to a short story with the hope of having a small, satisfying whole put within my grasp. Even the most apparently fragmented kind of short story succeeds with me if I can come away with this underlying sense of some kind of wholeness glimpsed. And one of the most interesting things about the short story as a form is the fact that there are so many ways in which this glimpse of a possible wholeness can be achieved. At the same time, short story writing is one of the most demanding of literary exercises, the most unforgiving of sloppiness of thought or feeling; it requires a precision of expression and absolute attention to appropriate detail which makes it one of the most difficult of the verbal arts.

"On Wings of Tongue" is a pretty straightforward example of the genre. Of all the fiction I have written, it is the story that is pinned most closely to an autobiographical framework. It is a fiction because it never actually happened, and because the people in it never actually existed in precisely the way I describe them in the story. However, the setting is that of the Winnipeg winters of my childhood. I recognise in the story transformed elements from my own life: we were a family of four children, two boys and two girls; my own position in the family is roughly that of the little heroine of the story, third child sandwiched between two brothers. We were poor and lived in a small bungalow through which passed a stream of roomers when I was a child, some of them most extraordinary people toward whom we children developed fierce loyalties and antagonisms. The story tries to recreate something of the feeling of those days. I see it in part as a kind of retroactive wish-fulfillment fiction, in which the child is somehow miraculously given the power to protect, if only briefly, a beloved adult from the partially comprehended injustices of the adult world. The stubborn, indignant little girl responds much as I recall myself responding, and in fact, can sometimes see myself responding still.

Adele Wiseman (1928-   )

Born in Winnipeg and educated at the University of Manitoba, Adele Wiseman travelled extensively before settling down to university teaching. Her novel, *The Sacrifice* (1956) is about a Jewish immigrant family; *Crackpot* (1974) is the story of a girl who is born to handicapped parents, and becomes a prostitute out of ignorance and poverty. Adele Wiseman also writes stories and articles. She now lives in Toronto.

The Roller Rink

ANDREAS SCHROEDER

The jukebox operator gave the sign. Smoothly, as if driven by electricity, I glided off, pulling my assistant supervisor after me.

I will admit at the very outset of the following history that parts of it may be untrue. Unfortunately, I can no longer tell which parts — I have been reworking these notes for such a long time now that my own fabricated sections have become indistinguishably blended with the original facts. I am not even certain precisely how I first stumbled into the environs of the story, though I seem to recall it was while I was stranded in a small village in southern Germany many years ago. I remember nursing a particularly vicious headache at the time and attending to several impressive bruises (unfortunately I have no idea where I might have sustained these knocks) when, for some reason, I noticed a long, oval building standing fairly far back from the street. There was a jagged hole broken through one of its walls.

Normally I wouldn't have paid much attention, but directly below the hole I saw the imprint of a body which presumably had fallen through the hole and lain for some time on the grass below. From the hole itself I could hear the smooth rush of countless ball-bearinged wheels against a background of lilting electric-organ music.

The oval building was a Roller Rink, and a very popular one it appeared, for when I approached the front booth for my ticket I was given a card indicating my application had been noted and instructing me to take a room in one of the nearby hotels until my turn came up. I took a room as directed and settled in for a wait which lasted many months and often threatened to drive me quite mad with boredom, had I not had the company of others who were also waiting to take their turn. I soon discovered that virtually the entire village was comprised of hotels and boarding houses, all of which were constantly filled to capacity with persons waiting to be admitted into the Rink.

After almost three seasons had passed, an errand boy brought the message that I was to present myself the following morning at the front ticket booth to complete certain formalities prerequisite to my entry into the hall. I spent that night with my waiting companions celebrating the good news, accepting the tearful goodbyes and good wishes accorded those about to take their turn. In the morning, after a hurried breakfast, I paid my bill and headed for the Rink.

My excitement was such by this time that I paid scant attention to the "formalities" and am consequently unable to reproduce them here, but I do remember being ushered assiduously into the Dressing-Room, a large, high-ceilinged almost clinical looking chamber with white walls and a bevy of brisk girls in white smocks always available to help newcomers into their skates.

My enquiries about the hole in the wall — my initial reason for seeking entry into the Rink — were politely but firmly ignored, and I was entreated to hurry with the putting on of my skates to make room for others who had waited as long as I and were understandably impatient. I realized there was little I could do for the present and decided therefore to have a closer look at the hole once I was mobile and able to inspect this mystery on my own.

To maintain one's balance in this rink implied learning to skate from scratch, regardless of any former skating experience, and irrespective of the skater's age or native abilities.

At first, people landed on their knees, slid about on their backsides or completely disappeared; others, though not immediately recognizable as themselves, suddenly flickered into view and bounced heavily across my vision. At times, then more and more often, they struggled by, eventually streaked by, pieces of wall stood firmly for a moment, then glanced away hesitantly, soon casually, and I began to lose sight of the individual boards and sections of rail. Later, possibly much later, people receded swiftly in perspective, about-faced, dipped and rolled smoothly away, and the business of maintaining my balance became a matter of personal, not public survival.

By the time I was secure enough on my feet to think about destinations, many more months had passed, and I had almost forgotten what I had entered the Rink to find. Almost as an afterthought, one day, I set course for the far wall where I had seen the hole.

Ivan Eyre, Vertigo, *1971*

The hole was not there. The hole was no longer there. There was no hole. There had never been a hole broken through the wall of this Roller Rink.

Standing against the railing alongside the wall, I couldn't decide which statement was the true explanation for what I couldn't find. A long, smoothly dove-tailed, highly varnished barrier receded unbroken into the distance, where it curved slightly and disappeared. Wherever it might have been, the hole was no longer anywhere in evidence.

Though I was badly disappointed with this conclusion, there seemed to be little I could do to change it. Standing as I was on the edge of the main stream of traffic, I suffered several near-accidents as the skaters, unaccustomed to stopping or circumnavigating others who had stopped, collided with me from behind and nearly pulled me down. I soon realized that stopping virtually anywhere on the course was extremely dangerous, and that the safest thing was to keep moving at a steady, moderate rate, regardless of any irregularities which aroused my curiosity. This way, at least, there tended to be no surprises.

Of the following dozen years there is little to tell. I skated incessantly, round and round the enormous oval hall, gradually losing all sense of time before my entry into the Rink. From the continual circling I developed a mild but perpetual dizziness which dulled the senses in a peculiarly pleasant sort of way, so that I stopped even my formerly habitual jotting down of notes. There seemed little point to it after all; what minor changes occurred in the daily routine were hardly sufficient to warrant mention.

Not that my subsequent life became completely uneventful; there were enough clashes and quarrels with other skaters to provide an often disagreeable overtone to my life in the Rink. Most of the squabbles occurred when I began to tire of the persistently monotonous pace and attempted to skate in reverse or engage in a little racing. Invariably, the ripples of indignation and even fear which passed through the crowd soon forced me to realign myself in the proper manner and subside. The skaters clung to each other timidly, carefully balancing their proprieties before themselves in sober ritual. Confrontations for any reason whatsoever were considered entirely unacceptable. Instead, the singing of hymns and patriotic songs was encouraged, effectively masking the sounds of argument or dispute.

In retrospect, now, I doubt that I would have lasted many more years in that Rink had I not been offered, by the Rink directors, a course in roller rink management. I was informed that, though my rebelliousness had compromised my position to some extent, the directors were willing to consider the past a period of adjustment, and that I would be given this unusual chance to redeem myself.

My studies would encompass the entire area of skate mechanics, the styles and techniques of the skill, the different types of music and their effects on the skating masses, also designs of rinks, the various kinds of flooring, different brands of varnish, paint, leather padding and the variety of layouts available for lobby and rest areas. I was to study the arts of timing and pacing, the various rhythms, the tension of centrifugal and gravitational forces played off against one another for balance; in short, the entire problem of the man on wheels.

Though I balked somewhat at the tone of the offer I decided to accept, realizing that I had been in the Rink too long to remember how to survive elsewhere, and hoping this would make my life in the Rink a little more interesting or at least endurable. Under diligent direction I began to spend hours every day repairing torn buckles and straps, replacing lost bearings, exchanging worn wheels and tightening loose or damaged screws. With my manual in one pocket and a small set of portable tools in the other, I spent whole weeks cruising the skating floor, helping hapless skaters who had run into difficulties. As time passed I worked with increasing desperation, feeling always on the edge of disillusionment, always on the verge of betrayal, hoping somehow that a deeper involvement would result in a more secure commitment to the idea of the Rink itself. For when I stopped to think about it, I could feel it slipping from my grasp like a smooth round elusive stone, the belief in the skaters, the Rink, the skating round and round the interminable oval, the never-ending repairs to equipment which stumbled along for a short while, then collapsed again. It began to make less and less sense to me how I could have abandoned all that I had been before (though I had to admit I could no longer remember with any certainty just what I had been) with little more than a shrug of the shoulders and a vague curiosity about a hole in the wall which I couldn't even locate anymore.

The more I realized this, the more I tried to smother my uneasiness in additional work, driving myself with a fiercely clenched mind, deeper and deeper into the tendrils of a vocation leading to Supervisor of Those Who Skate.

When, ten years later, I had chased myself through the entire course, I took up my post as administrator of the large, well-worn Rink and settled in for a term of helping the skaters through their paces.

The Rink, by this time, had been growing too small for my taste and I made immediate application for permission to undertake major renovations throughout the hall. There was bickering, grumbling and much frustrating pedantry, but the permission eventually materialized and the work was launched. By spring of the following year the renovations were almost complete, with work going on solely in the main rink of the skating complex. This area was, as you might imagine, my special concern.

Through my studies I had begun to realize that the secret to a happy congregation and a long-lasting Rink was to position its walls in such a way as to make the skater believe he is moving constantly in a straight line. With this in mind I laboured long hours over the walls and floor to ensure absolute smoothness and continuity. As I sanded and polished each board again and again, it seemed to me that I was not only smoothing the way for others, but straightening the compromising curvature out of my own life.

When the renovations were entirely completed several weeks later, a great inauguration celebration was proposed.

It was decided we would begin the ceremony by all skating once over the entire area of the Rink. At the signal of the jukebox operator (who had recorded a new piece of music designed especially with the new walls in mind) we would begin, with myself in front and the whole skating pack following in neat, orderly rows behind.

The planned celebration was to last throughout an entire week and drew much attention and excitement among the masses which gathered in the Rink lobby on the first day of the feast. It took much effort to prod the entire crowd into its correct position for the beginning of the journey; confused skaters stumbled about everywhere, falling against railings, losing their balance to crash into already assembled lines which promptly lost their cohesion; there was much quibbling over which rows were the most desirable and who should warrant skating where. When everyone was finally in his place, I raised my hand and waved for silence.

The jukebox operator gave the sign. Smoothly, as if driven by electricity, I glided off, pulling my assistant supervisor after me. Row after row set off, until soon the entire herd was in motion, swaying leisurely, easily, from foot to foot. Old women smiled at old men who grinned and nudged each other playfully; the atmosphere was high-spirited, contented and free.

A little time passed. I began to increase the pace bit by bit; the floor was so smooth and the wall so continuous, there was nothing by which anyone could gauge their speed − so there were no complaints. I tried to count the boards in the wall to keep track of our progress but we were soon skating so fast that the boards blurred as we rolled by and I found it difficult to decide where one board ended and the next began. Someone behind me had begun a hymn; I remember being annoyed for an instant that someone should have started the singing without my prior consent, but there was no sense in making a scene on such a special occasion and, besides, we were now speeding along at such a rate that my turning around would have meant placing the balance of the entire skating assemblage in jeopardy.

Suddenly, I thought I felt myself beginning to edge very slowly toward the right, toward the wall. Surprised, uneasy, I looked down at my skates; everything seemed in order, the wheels were spinning along quietly, the leather straps were tight and the metal clamps for the toes seemed secure. It was when I pushed a little harder with my right leg in an attempt to reposition myself into my former place, that I heard the click. It sounded as if a bearing had chipped.

Puzzled, I looked up to see that I was still moving very slowly toward the wall. Trying to ignore the noise in the bearings (which was becoming more and more pronounced) I strained once again toward the left. My skates resolutely refused to shift — and suddenly it dawned on me that we had reached that section of the wall at which the curve began.

I turned my head, glanced back — nothing but elation, singing, horseplay — no-one noticed the drift of the curve.

A flood of anger, exasperation and resentment poured through my mind as I began to realize the implications of this trap, but there was no longer time for thought; I struggled bitterly now, closer and closer to the speeding wall; my skates making a terrific racket but everyone singing so loudly that no-one could hear. My eyes began to hurt; I saw nothing but smooth continuous boards streaking past my pupils back into my skull — stooped down in a grasping effort to undo my straps, thinking possibly to leap out of them, more image than idea — a split-second later I felt my shoulder brush the wall, my right skate screamed along the varnish, dug in, my body swung around and slammed into the wall, I saw an enormous blackness and then there was nothing. ...

Total silence. Or a gentle hissing sound around the edges of a hole which may not even be an exit, which possibly exists in outline only, in the imagination of a skater just escaped into the confines of a larger surrounding rink. There is room for argument of course, and some evidence that there was, in fact, an actual hole. But it may perhaps be appropriate to point out that it is not as uncommon a thing as it might appear, for a man to construct his past in ramp-like fashion to launch himself into a future he might not otherwise be able to afford. It is possible, for instance, that this gaping story is itself the hole through which the man in question fell, or that it is a substitute for the hole he never found. Another possibility may be arrived at by superimposing the identities of the man at the beginning and the man at the end, placing them on opposite poles of the story's own oval configuration.

Of course it may be that none of these possibilities apply, being suggested, as they are, by the author himself who has admitted from the beginning that an undeterminable part of this fiction may have been fabricated and therefore be untrue. For one thing, it must be pointed out that such feinting is characteristic by persons attempting to make good an escape by confusing their pursuers with false leads and half-true information. But of course this warning, too, is suspect, having been made by the presumed escapee himself. . . .

Author's Commentary

For openers, I'd like to take issue with the notion that today's short story writers and novelists have a great deal in common. Many people still seem to think that a short story is really nothing more than a foreshortened novel, or that a novel is essentially an extended short story. Wrong on all counts. If anything, the writing of a short story has more in common with the writing of a *poem* than with the writing of a novel. Most novels are essentially compressed histories, and we experience them much as we might examine a Brueghel or a Bosch painting: we start in the middle and slowly fan out through the many separate incidents on the canvas until the whole surface has been perused, or we move from top to bottom, or from side to side to side. We don't grasp it all at a single glance. We weren't meant to. The painting (novel) is generally too large or detailed to function as a single simile or metaphor. It's an assemblage, an amalgam of linked events that eventually cohere in our minds to create an entire sample (model) world or cosmology. It tends to be ungainly, unruly, inclusive and apparently real — just like (you might say) reality itself.

The best short stories, on the other hand, like lyric poems or modern paintings *are* graspable "at a single glance." Not (obviously) literally, but in terms of their meaning or effect. Because the heart of most poems and short stories is the metaphor, that powerful magnet around which events and description, like iron filings, arrange themselves (are arranged) with an intense, unique purpose. And that purpose can only be to establish the metaphor quickly, efficiently (create it, evoke it) and then back away, letting it grow and flower however it will in our minds. In this way poems and short stories share the same profound economy, an economy of image and language characterized not only by less quantity but also by a greater directness and sharpness of focus. There's no such thing as a neutral word in a good poem or short story; each word either helps or hinders the metaphor, and in any case, too many words invariably overwhelm a metaphor and weaken it. Imagine the damage that might have been done to Stephen Crane's extraordinary 1500-word (3-page) short story, "The Octpush", if he'd added so much as another paragraph to that jewel of a tale.

By the same token, the best short story writers don't start on a story by *concocting* or *devising* a plot. Novelists (quite rightly) do that. Short story writers, like poets, *recognize* the metaphoric implications of some particularly meaningful incident (plot) that happens or occurs to them, and any subsequent elaboration or alteration to it as they put it to paper (however much fantasized) is carried out strictly in keeping with the requirements of the metaphor they have recognized. (Shirley Jackson's "The Lottery" is a good example.) Novelists, conversely, are explorers; they find or create for themselves an intriguing predicament and then pursue it "to find out what happens." Because of their tendency toward the allegoric or symbolic, short story writers tend not to begin until they already (intuitively) know.

Andreas Schroeder (1946 —   )

Andreas Schroeder was born in Germany and raised in Winnipeg and in Agassiz, British Columbia. A graduate of the University of British Columbia, he lives in Mission, B.C., where he edits *Contemporary Literature in Translation*. His publications include: *The Ozone Minotaur* (1969) — poetry; *The Late Man* (1972) — short stories; and *Shaking It Rough: a Prison Memoir* (1976).

One's a Heifer

SINCLAIR ROSS

His smoky lantern threw great swaying shadows over us; and the deep clefts and triangles of shadow on his face sent a little chill through me, and made me think what a dark and evil face it was.

My uncle was laid up that winter with sciatica, so when the blizzard stopped and still two of the yearlings hadn't come home with the other cattle, Aunt Ellen said I'd better saddle Tim and start out looking for them.

"Then maybe I'll not be back tonight," I told her firmly. "Likely they've drifted as far as the sandhills. There's no use coming home without them."

I was thirteen, and had never been away like that all night before, but, busy with the breakfast, Aunt Ellen said yes, that sounded sensible enough, and while I ate, hunted up a dollar in silver for my meals.

"Most people wouldn't take it from a lad, but they're strangers up towards the hills. Bring it out independent-like, but don't insist too much. They're more likely to grudge you a feed of oats for Tim."

After breakfast I had to undress again, and put on two suits of underwear and two pairs of thick, home-knitted stockings. It was a clear, bitter morning. After the storm the drifts lay clean and unbroken to the horizon. Distant farm-buildings stood out distinct against the prairie as if the thin sharp atmosphere were a magnifying glass. As I started off Aunt Ellen peered cautiously out of the door a moment through a cloud of steam, and waved a red and white checkered dish-towel. I didn't wave back, but conscious of her uneasiness rode erect, as jaunty as the sheepskin and two suits of underwear would permit.

We took the road straight south about three miles. The calves, I reasoned, would have by this time found their way home if the blizzard hadn't carried them at least that far. Then we started catercornering across fields, riding over to straw-stacks where we could see cattle sheltering, calling at farmhouses to ask had they seen any strays. "Yearlings," I said each time politely. "Red with white spots and faces. The same almost except that one's a heifer and the other isn't."

Nobody had seen them. There was a crust on the snow not quite hard enough to carry Tim, and despite the cold his flanks and shoulders soon were steaming. He walked with his head down, and sometimes, taking my sympathy for granted, drew up a minute for breath.

My spirits, too, began to flag. The deadly cold and the flat white silent miles of prairie asserted themselves like a disapproving presence. The cattle round the straw-stacks stared when we rode up as if we were intruders. The fields stared, and the sky stared. People shivered in their doorways, and said they'd seen no strays.

At about one o'clock we stopped at a farmhouse for dinner. It was a single oat sheaf half thistles for Tim, and fried eggs and bread and tea for me. Crops had been poor that year, they apologized, and though they shook their heads when I brought out my money I saw the woman's eyes light greedily a second, as if her instincts of hospitality were struggling hard against some urgent need. We too, I said, had had poor crops lately. That was why it was so important that I find the calves.

We rested an hour, then went on again. "Yearlings," I kept on describing them. "Red with white spots and faces. The same except that one's a heifer and the other isn't."

Still no one had seen them, still it was cold, still Tim protested what a fool I was.

The country began to roll a little. A few miles ahead I could see the first low line of sandhills. "They'll be there for sure," I said aloud, more to encourage myself than Tim. "Keeping straight to the road it won't take a quarter as long to get home again."

But home now seemed a long way off. A thin white sheet of cloud spread across the sky, and though there had been no warmth in the sun the fields looked colder and bleaker without the glitter on the snow. Straw-stacks were fewer here, as if the land were poor, and every house we stopped at seemed more dilapidated than the one before.

A nagging wind rose as the afternoon wore on. Dogs yelped and bayed at us, and sometimes from the hills, like the signal of our approach, there was a thin, wavering howl of a coyote. I began to dread the miles home again almost as much as those still ahead. There were so many cattle straggling across the fields, so many yearlings just like ours. I saw them for sure a dozen times, and as often choked my disappointment down and clicked Tim on again.

And at last I really saw them. It was nearly dusk, and along with fifteen or twenty other cattle they were making their way towards some buildings that lay huddled at the foot of the sandhills. They passed in single file less than fifty yards away, but when I pricked Tim forward to turn them back he floundered in a snowed-in water-cut. By the time we were out they were a little distance ahead, and on account of the drifts it was impossible to put on a spurt of speed and pass them. All we could do was take our place at the end of the file, and proceed at their pace towards the buildings.

It was about half a mile. As we drew near I debated with Tim whether we should ask to spend the night or start off right away for home. We were hungry and tired, but it was a poor, shiftless-looking place. The yard was littered with old wagons and machinery; the house was scarcely distinguishable from the stables. Darkness was beginning to close in, but there was no light in the windows.

Then as we crossed the yard we heard a shout, "Stay where you are," and a man came running towards us from the stable. He was tall and ungainly, and, instead of the short sheepskin that most farmers wear, had on a long black overcoat nearly to his feet. He seized Tim's bridle when he reached us, and glared for a minute as if he were going to pull me out of the saddle. "I told you to stay out," he said in a harsh, excited voice. "You heard me, didn't you? What do you want coming round here anyway?"

I steeled myself and said, "Our two calves."

The muscles of his face were drawn together threateningly, but close to him like this and looking straight into his eyes I felt that for all their fierce look there was something about them wavering and uneasy. "The two red ones with the white faces," I continued. "They've just gone into the shed over there with yours. If you'll give me a hand getting them out again I'll start for home now right away."

He peered at me a minute, let go the bridle, then clutched it again. "They're all mine," he countered. "I was over by the gate. I watched them coming in."

His voice was harsh and thick. The strange wavering look in his eyes steadied itself for a minute to a dare. I forced myself to meet it and insisted, "I saw them back a piece in the field. They're ours all right. Let me go over a minute and I'll show you."

With a crafty tilt of his head he leered, "You didn't see any calves. And now, if you know what's good for you, you'll be on your way."

"You're trying to steal them," I flared rashly. "I'll go home and get my uncle and the police after you — then you'll see whether they're our calves or not."

My threat seemed to impress him a little. With a shifty glance in the direction of the stable he said, "All right, come along and look them over. Then maybe you'll be satisfied." But all the way across the yard he kept his hand on Tim's bridle, and at the shed made me wait a few minutes while he went inside.

The cattle shed was a lean-to on the horse stable. It was plain enough: he was hiding the calves before letting me inside to look around. While waiting for him, however, I had time to realize that he was a lot bigger and stronger than I was, and that it might be prudent just to keep my eyes open, and not give him too much insolence.

He reappeared carrying a smoky lantern. "All right," he said pleasantly enough, "come in and look around. Will your horse stand, or do you want to tie him?"

We put Tim in an empty stall in the horse stable, then went through a narrow doorway with a bar across it to the cattle shed. Just as I expected, our calves weren't there. There were two red ones with white markings that he tried to make me believe were the ones I had seen, but, positive I hadn't been mistaken, I shook my head and glanced at the doorway we had just come through. It was narrow, but not too narrow. He read my expression and said, "You think they're in there. Come on, then, and look around."

The horse stable consisted of two rows of open stalls with a passage down the centre like an aisle. At the far end were two box-stalls, one with a sick colt in it, the other closed. They were both boarded up to the ceiling, so that you could see inside them only through the doors. Again he read my expression, and with a nod towards the closed one said, "It's just a kind of harness room now. Up till a year ago I kept a stallion."

But he spoke furtively, and seemed anxious to get me away from that end of the stable. His smoky lantern threw great swaying shadows over us; and the deep clefts and triangles of shadow on his face sent a little chill through me, and made me think what a dark and evil face it was.

I was afraid, but not too afraid. "If it's just a harness room," I said recklessly, "why not let me see inside? Then I'll be satisfied and believe you."

He wheeled at my question, and sidled over swiftly to the stall. He stood in front of the door, crouched down a little, the lantern in front of him like a shield. There was a sudden stillness through the stable as we faced each other. Behind the light from his lantern the

William Kurelek, Manitoba Barn

darkness hovered vast and sinister. It seemed to hold its breath, to watch and listen. I felt a clutch of fear now at my throat, but I didn't move. My eyes were fixed on him so intently that he seemed to lose substance, to loom up close a moment, then recede. At last he disappeared completely, and there was only the lantern like a hard hypnotic eye.

It held me. It held me rooted, against my will. I wanted to run from the stable, but I wanted even more to see inside the stall. And yet I was afraid to see inside the stall. So afraid that it was a relief when at last he gave a shame-faced laugh and said, "There's a hole in the floor — that's why I keep the door closed. If you didn't know, you might step into it — twist your foot. That's what happened to one of my horses a while ago."

I nodded as if I believed him, and went back tractably to Tim. But regaining control of myself as I tried the saddle girths, beginning to feel that my fear had been unwarranted, I looked up and said, "It's ten miles home, and we've been riding hard all day. If we could stay a while — have something to eat, and then get started —"

The wavering light came into his eyes again. He held the lantern up to see me better, such a long, intent scrutiny that it seemed he must discover my designs. But he gave a nod finally, as if reassured, brought oats and hay for Tim, and suggested, companionably, "After supper we can have a game of checkers."

Then, as if I were a grown-up, he put out his hand and said, "My name is Arthur Vickers."

Inside the house, rid of his hat and coat, he looked less forbidding. He had a white nervous face, thin lips, a large straight nose, and deep uneasy eyes. When the lamp was lit I fancied I could still see the wavering expression in them, and decided it was what you called a guilty look.

"You won't think much of it," he said apologetically, following my glance around the room. "I ought to be getting things cleaned up again. Come over to the stove. Supper won't take long."

It was a large, low-ceilinged room that for the first moment or two struck me more like a shed or granary than a house. The table in the centre was littered with tools and harness. On a rusty cook-stove were two big steaming pots of bran. Next to the stove stood a grindstone, then a white iron bed covered with coats and horse blankets. At the end opposite the bed, weasel and coyote skins were drying. There were guns and traps on the wall, a horse collar, a pair of rubber boots. The floor was bare and grimy. Ashes were littered around the stove. In a corner squatted a live owl with a broken wing.

He walked back and forth a few times looking helplessly at the disorder, then cleared off the table and lifted the pots of bran to the back of the stove. "I've been mending harness," he explained. "You get careless, living alone like this. It takes a woman anyway."

My presence, apparently, was making him take stock of the room. He picked up a broom and swept for a minute, made an ineffective attempt to straighten the blankets on the bed, brought another lamp out of a cupboard and lit it. There was an ungainly haste to all his movements. He started unbuckling my sheepskin for me, then turned away suddenly to take off his own coat. "Now we'll have supper," he said with an effort at self-possession. "Coffee and beans is all I can give you — maybe a little molasses."

I replied diplomatically that that sounded pretty good. It didn't seem right, accepting hospitality this way from a man trying to steal your calves, but theft, I reflected, surely justified deceit. I held my hands out to the warmth and asked if I could help.

There was a kettle of plain navy beans already cooked. He dipped out enough for our supper into a frying pan, and on top laid rashers of fat salt pork. While I watched that they didn't burn he rinsed off a few dishes. Then he set out sugar and canned milk, butter, molasses, and dark heavy biscuits that he had baked himself the day before. He kept glancing at me so apologetically all the while that I leaned over and sniffed the beans, and said at home I ate a lot of them.

"It takes a woman," he repeated as we sat down to the table. "I don't often have anyone here to eat with me. If I'd known, I'd have cleaned things up a little."

I was too intent on my plateful of beans to answer. All through the meal he sat watching me, but made no further attempts at conversation. Hungry as I was, I noticed that the wavering, uneasy look was still in his eyes. A guilty look, I told myself again, and wondered what I was going to do to get the calves away. I finished my coffee and he continued:

"It's worse even than this in the summer. No time for meals — and the heat and flies. Last summer I had a girl cooking for a few weeks, but it didn't last. Just a cow she was — just a big stupid cow — and she wanted to stay on. There's a family of them back in the hills. I had to send her home."

I wondered should I suggest starting now, or ask to spend the night. Maybe when he's asleep, I thought, I can slip out of the house and get away with the calves. He went on, "You don't know how bad it is sometimes. Weeks on end and no one to talk to. You're not yourself — you're not sure what you're going to say or do."

182

I remembered hearing my uncle talk about a man who had gone crazy living alone. And this fellow Vickers had queer eyes all right. And there was the live owl over in the corner, and the grindstone standing right beside the bed. "Maybe I'd better go now," I decided aloud. "Tim'll be rested, and it's ten miles home."

But he said no, it was colder now, with the wind getting stronger, and seemed so kindly and concerned that I half forgot my fears. "Likely he's just starting to go crazy," I told myself, "and it's only by staying that I'll have a chance to get the calves away."

When the table was cleared and the dishes washed he said he would go out and bed down the stable for the night. I picked up my sheepskin to go with him, but he told me sharply to stay inside. Just for a minute he looked crafty and forbidding as when I first rode up on Tim, and to allay his suspicions I nodded compliantly and put my sheepskin down again. It was better like that anyway, I decided. In a few minutes I could follow him, and perhaps, taking advantage of the shadows and his smoky lantern, make my way to the box-stall unobserved.

But when I reached the stable he had closed the door after him and hooked it from the inside. I walked round a while, tried to slip in by way of the cattle shed, and then had to go back to the house. I went with a vague feeling of relief again. There was still time, I told myself, and it would be safer anyway when he was sleeping.

So that it would be easier to keep from falling asleep myself I planned to suggest coffee again just before we went to bed. I knew that the guest didn't ordinarily suggest such things, but it was no time to remember manners when there was someone trying to steal your calves.

When he came in from the stable we played checkers. I was no match for him, but to encourage me he repeatedly let me win. "It's a long time now since I've had a chance to play," he kept on saying, trying to convince me that his short-sighted moves weren't intentional. "Sometimes I used to ask her to play, but I had to tell her every move to make. If she didn't win she'd upset the board and go off and sulk."

"My aunt is a little like that too," I said. "She cheats sometimes when we're playing cribbage — and, when I catch her, says her eyes aren't good."

"Women talk too much ever to make good checker players. It takes concentration. This one, though, couldn't even talk like anybody else."

After my long day in the cold I was starting to yawn already. He noticed it, and spoke in a rapid, earnest voice, as if afraid I might lose interest soon and want to go to bed. It was important for me too to stay awake, so I crowned a king and said, "Why don't you get someone, then, to stay with you?"

"Too many of them want to do that." His face darkened a little, almost as if warning me. "Too many of the kind you'll never get rid of again. She did, last summer when she was here. I had to put her out."

There was silence for a minute, his eyes flashing, and wanting to placate him I suggested, "She liked you, maybe."

He laughed a moment, harshly. "She liked me all right. Just two weeks ago she came back — walked over with an old suitcase and said she was going to stay. It was cold at home, and she had to work too hard, and she didn't mind even if I couldn't pay her wages."

I was getting sleepier. To keep awake I sat on the edge of the chair where it was uncomfortable and said, "Hadn't you asked her to come?"

His eyes narrowed. "I'd had trouble enough getting rid of her the first time. There were six of them at home, and she said her father thought it time that someone married her."

"Then she must be a funny one," I said. "Everyone knows that the man's supposed to ask the girl."

My remark seemed to please him. "I told you didn't I?" he said, straightening a little, jumping two of my men. "She was so stupid that at checkers she'd forget whether she was black or red."

We stopped playing now. I glanced at the owl in the corner and the ashes littered on the floor, and thought that keeping her would maybe have been a good idea after all. He read it in my face and said, "I used to think that too sometimes. I used to look at her and think nobody knew now anyway and that she'd maybe do. You need a woman on a farm all right. And night after night she'd be sitting there where you are — right there where you are, looking at me, not even trying to play —"

The fire was low, and we could hear the wind. "But then I'd go up in the hills, away from her for a while, and start thinking back the way things used to be, and it wasn't right even for the sake of your meals ready and your house kept clean. When she came back I tried to tell her that, but all the family are the same, and I realized it wasn't any use. There's nothing you can do when you're up against that sort of thing. The mother talks just like a child of ten. When she sees you coming she runs and hides. There are six of them, and it's come out in every one."

It was getting cold, but I couldn't bring myself to go over to the stove. There was the same stillness now as when he was standing at the box-stall door. And I felt the same illogical fear, the same powerlessness to move. It was the way his voice lowered, the glassy, cold look in his eyes. The rest of his face disappeared; all I could see were his eyes. And they filled me with a vague and overpowering dread. My voice gone a whisper on me, I asked, "And when you wouldn't marry her — what happened then?"

He remained motionless a moment, as if answering silently; then with an unexpected laugh like a breaking dish said, "Why, nothing happened. I just told her she couldn't stay. I went to town for a few days — and when I came back she was gone."

"Has she been back to bother you since?" I asked.

He made a little silo of checkers. "No — she took her suitcase with her."

To remind him that the fire was going down I went over to the stove and stood warming myself. He raked the coals with the lifter and put in poplar, two split pieces for a base and a thick round log on top. I yawned again. He said maybe I'd like to go to bed now, and I shivered and asked him could I have a drink of coffee first. While it boiled he stood stirring the two big pots of bran. The trouble with coffee, I realized, was that it would keep him from getting sleepy too.

I undressed finally and got into bed, but he blew out only one of the lamps, and sat on playing checkers with himself. I dozed a while, then sat up with a start, afraid it was morning already and that I'd lost my chance to get the calves away. He came over and looked at me a minute, then gently pushed my shoulders back on the pillow. "Why don't you come to bed too?" I asked, and he said, "Later I will — I don't feel sleepy yet."

It was like that all night. I kept dozing on and off, wakening in a fright each time to find him still there sitting at his checker board. He would raise his head sharply when I stirred, then tiptoe over to the bed and stand close to me listening till satisfied again I was asleep. The owl kept wakening too. It was down in the corner still where the lamplight scarcely reached, and I could see its eyes go on and off like yellow bulbs. The wind whistled drearily around the house. The blankets smelled like an old granary. He suspected what I was planning to do, evidently, and was staying awake to make sure I didn't get outside.

Each time I dozed I dreamed I was on Tim again. The calves were in sight, but far ahead of us, and with the drifts so deep we couldn't overtake them. Then instead of Tim it was the grindstone I was straddling, and that was the reason, not the drifts, that we weren't making better progress.

I wondered what would happen to the calves if I didn't get away with them. My uncle had sciatica, and it would be at least a day before I could be home and back again with some of the neighbours. By then Vickers might have butchered the calves, or driven them up to a hiding place in the hills where we'd never find them. There was the possibility, too, that Aunt Ellen and the neighbours wouldn't believe me. I dozed and woke – dozed and woke – always he was sitting at the checker board. I could hear the dry tinny ticking of an alarm clock, but from where I was lying couldn't see it. He seemed to be listening to it too. The wind would sometimes creak the house, and then he would give a start and sit rigid a moment with his eyes fixed on the window. It was always the window, as if there was nothing he was afraid of that could reach him by the door.

Most of the time he played checkers with himself, moving his lips, muttering words I couldn't hear, but once I woke to find him staring fixedly across the table as if he had a partner sitting there. His hands were clenched in front of him, there was a sharp, metallic glitter in his eyes. I lay transfixed, unbreathing. His eyes as I watched seemed to dilate, to brighten, to harden like a bird's. For a long time he sat contracted, motionless, as if gathering himself to strike, then furtively he slid his hand an inch or two along the table towards some checkers that were piled beside the board. It was as if he were reaching for a weapon, as if his invisible partner were an enemy. He clutched the checkers, slipped slowly from his chair and straightened. His movements were sure, stealthy, silent like a cat's. His face had taken on a desperate, contorted look. As he raised his hand the tension was unbearable.

It was a long time – a long time watching him the way you watch a finger tightening slowly in the trigger of a gun – and then suddenly wrenching himself to action he hurled the checkers with such vicious fury that they struck the wall in front of him and clattered back across the room.

And everything was quiet again. I started a little, mumbled to myself as if half-awakened, lay quite still. But he seemed to have forgotten me, and after standing limp and dazed a minute got down on his knees and started looking for the checkers. When he had them all, he put more wood in the stove, then returned quietly to the table and sat down. We were alone again; everything was exactly as before. I relaxed gradually, telling myself that he'd just been seeing things.

The next time I woke he was sitting with his head sunk forward on the table. It looked as if he had fallen asleep at last, and huddling alert among the bed-clothes I decided to watch a minute to make sure, then dress and try to slip out to the stable.

While I watched, I planned exactly every movement I was going to make. Rehearsing it in my mind as carefully as if I were actually doing it, I climbed out of bed, put on my clothes, tiptoed stealthily to the door and slipped outside. By this time, though, I was getting drowsy, and relaxing among the blankets I decided that for safety's sake I should rehearse it still again. I rehearsed it four times altogether, and the fourth time dreamed that I hurried on successfully to the stable.

I fumbled with the door a while, then went inside and felt my way through the darkness to the box-stall. There was a bright light suddenly and the owl was sitting over the door with his yellow eyes like a pair of lanterns. The calves, he told me, were in the other stall with the sick colt. I looked and they were there all right, but Tim came up and said it might be better not to start for home till morning. He reminded me that I hadn't paid for his feed or my own supper yet, and that if I slipped off this way it would mean that I was stealing, too. I agreed, realizing now that it wasn't the calves I was looking for after all, and that I still had to see inside the stall that was guarded by the owl. "Wait here," Tim said, "I'll tell you if he flies away," and without further questioning I lay down in the straw and went to sleep again. ... When I woke coffee and beans were on the stove already, and though the lamp was still lit I could tell by the window that it was nearly morning.

We were silent during breakfast. Two or three times I caught him watching me, and it seemed his eyes were shiftier than before. After his sleepless night he looked tired and haggard. He left the table while I was still eating and fed raw rabbit to the owl, then came back and drank another cup of coffee. He had been friendly and communicative the night before, but now, just as when he first came running out of the stable in his long black coat, his expression was sullen and resentful. I began to feel that he was in a hurry to be rid of me.

I took my time, however, racking my brains to outwit him still and get the calves away. It looked pretty hopeless now, his eyes on me so suspiciously, my imagination at low ebb. Even if I did get inside the box-stall to see the calves — was he going to stand back then and let me start off home with them? Might it not more likely frighten him, make him do something desperate, so that I couldn't reach my uncle or the police? There was the owl over in the corner, the grindstone by the bed. And with such a queer fellow you could never tell. You could never tell, and you had to think about your own skin too. So I said politely, "Thank you, Mr. Vickers, for letting me stay all night," and remembering what Tim had told me took out my dollar's worth of silver.

He gave a short dry laugh and wouldn't take it. "Maybe you'll come back," he said, "and next time stay longer. We'll go shooting up in the hills if you like — and I'll make a trip to town for things so that we can have better meals. You need company sometimes for a change. There's been no one here now quite a while."

His face softened again as he spoke. There was an expression in his eyes as if he wished that I could stay on now. It puzzled me. I wanted to be indignant, and it was impossible. He held my sheepskin for me while I put it on, and tied the scarf around the collar with a solicitude and determination equal to Aunt Ellen's. And then he gave his short dry laugh again, and hoped I'd find my calves all right.

He had been out to the stable before I was awake, and Tim was ready for me, fed and saddled. But I delayed a few minutes, pretending to be interested in his horses and the sick colt. It would be worth something after all, I realized, to get just a glimpse of the calves. Aunt Ellen was going to be sceptical enough of my story as it was. It could only confirm her doubts to hear me say I hadn't seen the calves in the box-stall, and was just pretty sure that they were there.

So I went from stall to stall, stroking the horses and making comparisons with the ones we had at home. The door, I noticed, he had left wide open, ready for me to lead out Tim. He was walking up and down the aisle, telling me which horses were quiet, which to be careful of. I came to a nervous chestnut mare, and realized she was my only chance.

She crushed her hips against the side of the stall as I slipped up to her manger, almost pinning me, then gave her head a toss and pulled back hard on the halter shank. The shank, I noticed, was tied with an easy slip-knot that the right twist and a sharp tug would undo in half a second. And the door was wide open, ready for me to lead out Tim — and standing as she was with her body across the stall diagonally, I was for the moment screened from sight.

It happened quickly. There wasn't time to think of consequences. I just pulled the knot, in the same instant struck the mare across the nose. With a snort she threw herself backwards, almost trampling Vickers, then flung up her head to keep from tripping on the shank and plunged outside.

It worked as I hoped it would. "Quick," Vickers yelled to me, "the gate's open — try and head her off" — but instead I just waited till he himself was gone, then fairly flew to the box-stall.

The door was fastened with two tight-fitting slide-bolts, one so high that I could scarcely reach it standing on my toes. It wouldn't yield. The head of the pin was small and round, and the whiffle-tree kept glancing off. I was too terrified to pause a moment and take careful aim.

Terrified of the stall though, not of Vickers. Terrified of the stall, yet compelled by a frantic need to get inside. For the moment I had forgotten Vickers, forgotten even the danger of his catching me. I worked blindly, helplessly, as if I were confined and smothering. For a moment I yielded to panic, dropped the piece of whiffle-tree and started kicking at the door. Then, collected again, I forced back the lower bolt, and picking up the whiffle-tree tried to pry the door out a little at the bottom. But I had wasted too much time. Just as I dropped to my knees to peer through the opening Vickers seized me. I struggled to my feet and fought a moment, but it was such a hard, strangling clutch at my throat that I felt myself go limp and blind. In desperation then I kicked him, and with a blow like a reflex he sent me staggering to the floor.

But it wasn't the blow that frightened me. It was the fierce, wild light in his eyes.

Stunned as I was, I looked up and saw him watching me, and, sick with terror, made a bolt for Tim. I untied him with hands that moved incredibly, galvanized for escape. I knew now for sure that Vickers was crazy. He followed me outside, and, just as I mounted, seized Tim again by the bridle. For a second or two it made me crazy too. Gathering up the free ends of the rein I lashed him hard across the face. He let go of the bridle, and, frightened and excited too now, Tim made a dash across the yard and out of the gate. Deep as the snow was, I kept him galloping for half a mile, pommelling him with my fists, kicking my heels against his sides. Then of his own accord he drew up short for breath, and I looked around to see whether Vickers was following. He wasn't — there was only the snow and the hills, his buildings a lonely little smudge against the whiteness — and the relief was like a stick pulled out that's been holding up tomato vines or peas. I slumped across the saddle weakly, and till Tim started on again lay there whimpering like a baby.

We were home by noon. We didn't have to cross fields or stop at houses now, and there had been teams on the road packing down the snow so that Tim could trot part of the way and even canter. I put him in the stable without taking time to tie or unbridle him, and ran to the house to tell Aunt Ellen. But I was still frightened, cold and a little hysterical, and it was a while before she could understand how everything had happened. She was silent a minute, indulgent, then helping me off with my sheepskin said kindly, "You'd better forget about it now, and come over and get warm. The calves came home themselves yesterday. Just about an hour after you set out."

I looked up at her. "But the stall, then — just because I wanted to look inside he knocked me down — and if it wasn't the calves in there —"

She didn't answer. She was busy building up the fire and looking at the stew.

Author's Commentary

Sinclair Ross made these remarks in a taped interview with Earle Toppings.

Interviewer: Mr. Ross, why do you write? What do you really want to accomplish? Is it basically something for yourself?

Ross: Well, you know that's another question that I don't know, that I never ask myself. I don't know whether writers do ask themselves. You know when we see something and we're with somebody, we say "look". You're walking along a road and you round a corner and there's a beautiful scene before you or it may be a garden or an animal or something. You say "look". It isn't necessary because the other fellow has good eyes too; he can see it. But we seem to have that urge, and if there's no one to whom we can say it, probably we feel just a little bit disappointed. And I think that's the beginning of all writing. Something impresses you — this sounds a bit pompous — but you feel it so intensely that you must get it said and so you write it. I think probably that's the basic urge behind all writing.

Interviewer: So that someone else can see it as well as you?

Ross: That's right, yes. You have something to communicate and I suppose it's a form of conceit and arrogance — the way I feel it — that that's the right way, and I must communicate the way I feel it. Where you start on a story — it's that needle under the skin where you get the shot of something ... which grows and becomes your story. It's pretty hard to pin it down because you don't take notes at the time and then by the time you do look at it, it's grown considerably. The actual beginning you don't pay any attention to. I've often tried to run down a story. For instance, "One's a Heifer".

All I can remember of that is that I was out on horseback and a woman waved to me, and when I got to the door she said they had lost two calves and she asked me if I'd seen them and she said, "One's a heifer and the other ain't." Well, that's a long way from the story — but that must have been what stayed in my mind.

Interviewer: Do you find that you have many other "givens" that way; either you hear a phrase or you see something memorable and then you *have* to write about it sometime, even if it's much later?

Ross: I don't think it works that way with me. I think probably something happens and then it becomes imbedded in my mind as it were, and then later I come back to it. But at the time, I don't say this is something I must write about. I think it grows and then reaches the stage where it may be somewhat urgent. But that's later on; it may be months later or years later.

Sinclair Ross (1908 — 　)

Born in Saskatchewan, the son of prairie homesteaders, Sinclair Ross worked as a banker in prairie towns during the 1920s and 1930s. During World War II, he was with the Royal Ordnance Corps in London, England. Upon his return, he was transferred by the bank to Montreal where he lived until 1968. Since then he has lived in Greece and Spain. Ross has written many short stories, some of which are collected in *The Lamp at Noon and Other Stories* (1968). His novels are *As for Me and My House* (1941), *The Well* (1958), *Whir of Gold* (1970) and *Sawbones Memorial* (1974).

Tom Forrestal, May's Verandah

I'm Still Here

VERONICA ROSS

"How long do you think you can hold out here?"
"I will stay forever," he said.
"Forever's a long time."
"So I'll stay. Till hell freezes over."

They had sent a woman this time, a young one. She knocked on the back door, and Jake stood against the kitchen wall, peeking at her through the window curtains. He'd thought of nailing up blankets over the window but then he had decided that it would be better if the house looked as normal as possible, like a house where the occupants were at home, but just not answering the door.

She looked young, hopeful, with a great tangle of red hair above a small face made rosy by the cold. She had a grey scarf wrapped around her neck, flung over the shoulder of her duffle coat, and she carried a large shoulder bag, out of which stuck her notebook. She smiled when she knocked. When there was no answer she gazed around, perturbed. Then she knocked again, smiling once more. It was a louder rap this time. The man they'd sent had knocked loudly, had muttered under his breath. The girl looked all around, then moved closer to the window as if to look in. But she didn't; she knew he was in there. There was another faint little tap on the door and then he heard her move away. He went into the front room and looked out the window there. He saw a man waiting in a small car. It was not the same man who'd come before but another man, a younger one. The man and the girl looked at the house and conferred. After a moment, the girl got in and the car moved away.

Maybe they'd thought that being a bachelor, he'd open his door to a pretty young female.

The newspapers overflowed the mailbox; he thought that he'd like to sneak out at night to pick up his mail. Particularly the newspapers. They'd probably written him up.

The Millers had moved away last month; they'd bought a place on the other side of the river. The MacMillans had gone to visit the son in Toronto. When they came back they were going to put up one of those prefabricated jobs on a little strip of land along the highway. But he wasn't moving.

As long as he was in the house, they couldn't tear it down. It was as simple as that. He imagined the outcry. *Man Killed Defending Property,* a headline would read. There would be letters to editors. Letters to MPs. Letters to the Prime Minister. No, they wouldn't tear the house down around his ears. As long as he stayed here, there was nothing they could do.

The thought excited him. He was growing used to excitement. The boredom he'd feared when he'd gone into his house and locked the door behind him hadn't overtaken him. His thoughts were clear; he was finding that he could remember everything, that he was developing rare insights into the state of things.

He had waited until the last minute to close the house up. He hadn't given any interviews, hadn't taken part in the kind of thing where they got people to sit in rocking chairs, to say: *this place is all I've got.* Cameras panning over fields, barn, river, while his voice said: *my grandfather built that barn. All the neighbours came to help when the original one burned down. The men worked and the women cooked and that night they had a big dance.*

He'd heard the story many times. Maybe they'd have filmed the cemetery, the leaning tombstone of Emilia Garson, age 22, Resting In The Lord, with his voice saying: *she was the first wife of my great-great-grandfather. She died in childbirth the first winter here, before the house was built. Only a log cabin they had then.*

He could also have gone into a country bumpkin act. *First bastard sets foot on my land's gonna get his head blown off.* Or played the feisty village philosopher. *Government's into everything these days. The next thing you know, you'll have to get permission to wipe your ass.* They wouldn't edit that out today either, he thought.

But none of that. He'd tacked a small note to the front door: *I'm still here.* Let them see about expropriation and provincial parks then. Let them figure out how to steal land for bathrooms and canteens and paved parking-lots.

It was a wonder they hadn't cut his power off. He had expected it and had filled all the old oil lamps and piled two cords of hardwood in the summer kitchen in preparation. The phone was still working too. Several times reporters had called and he had hung up without a word.

He spent the evenings watching television, only the CBC now

because his aerial had blown off the roof and he couldn't go out of the house to fix it. One night, as he had been expecting, *The National* covered *him*. It was at the end of the news, in the time slot usually devoted to things like polar bears being born in captivity.

"Plans are under way for a new provincial park in the Millbrook area of Nova Scotia," he heard. Several properties have been expropriated with — according to government officials — fair compensation being paid. One man isn't giving up so easily, however. Jake Garson left this note … "

There was a close-up of *I'm still here* and then the camera pulled back to show his house, his yard. It was a woman's voice speaking, the young woman who had been here perhaps.

"Millbrook is a pleasant area of lakes, streams and woods. Not surprisingly, many local residents are cheering Mr. Garson, although local businessmen say that the proposed development will bring badly needed tourist dollars to the area."

There was a quick glimpse of old MacDonald, standing in front of his store, MacDonald's Groceries and Dry Goods. He had a white shirt and tie on, Jake noticed. He had even washed his store windows.

"I thought you were going to take the money." It was his brother, Joe, calling from Montreal. "That's what you said in your last letter."

"I changed my mind."

"I couldn't believe it when I saw it. I just couldn't believe it."

"Well, I'm still here."

"I thought the deal had gone through."

"The theft, you mean. I thought you were against it too."

"I am. But if there's nothing you can do about it … "

"I am doing something about it," Jake said mildly.

"A dumb note nailed to your door," Joe said. "You got rocks in your head? Take my advice and take the money and get yourself some nice little business."

"A chicken take-out maybe?" Jake asked.

"Look, Jake, they're gonna get you. You're just making a fool of yourself." When Jake didn't answer, he added, "You'll run out of food."

"Nope," Jake said. "Got enough to last me a year. Got the cellar stocked up."

"They'll get you out."

"Tell you what," Jake said, smiling. "Next son-of-a-bitch reporter that calls, I'll tell him to call you."

"You want me to sound like a fool too?"

"You can say you disagree with me. You can tell them I'm slightly touched."

"Go to hell," Joe said. "Don't you dare give the reporters my name."

Sitting behind heavy drapes, Jake thought of his family, of Joe in Montreal, of Myrna in Toronto, of Lexy in Ottawa when she was at home. They had all left home right after high school. Joe was the eldest. He hadn't wanted to go. He had wept, getting in the train in his new brown suit and brogues. At first, he had come home every year. The girls had left together. Jake supposed they had done all right.

He, Jake, had stayed. He liked to think it had been a conscious act, staying. His brother and sisters had urged him to leave, both in person and in letters. Later, when he had begun to publish his poems in obscure literary journals, the protests had dwindled. He supposed that they thought that a minor poet living on ancestral lands had something about it, gave them a way of mentioning him to their friends. He did not think that they often mentioned that they had a brother driving a school bus back home, which he also did.

Since he had closed the house up, it seemed to him that he had finally discovered his reason for staying in this place. He was meant to be the observer, the witness, not only to their lives, but to the entire state of things. And this was a thing he could do best on his own land, in his own quiet country.

The young woman was back. She came after lunch. He had set the table carefully for himself, had read a chapter of *Resurrection,* had smoked one hand-rolled cigarette — he had to ration his tobacco — and was washing the dishes when she knocked on the door. He turned around and this time her face appeared above the curtains. She smiled when she saw him, and for a moment they stood looking at each other.

"Please talk to me," he heard her say. "I'd really like to talk to you, Mr. Garson."

He knew he could not let her in. But he moved close to the window and told her, through the glass, "I won't talk to you. I'm not moving out. I'm still here and I'm staying."

"Do you think you will be successful in holding on to your place?

"I'm not going," he said simply. "That's all there is to it."

"I understand the land has been taken."

"How can that be if I'm still here?" He refused to say more, although he felt like talking to her. There were things he wanted to say: how simple life had been, how right, before the government started messing around in people's affairs, before they started making institutions of everything, even nature. How rich they had found the land, how inspiring, how promising, how lives revolved naturally around the seasons. How no-one went hungry. How people weren't glued to the TV then, but actually talked and sometimes even read books.

"Could I come back again?"

"Suit yourself. But I'm not saying anything more." But he did smile at her.

Myrna called.

"Are you all right?" she asked anxiously.

"Fine as can be. Did you see me on TV last night?"

"I thought they didn't actually show you."

"I meant in the spirit. They showed the house."

"I was watching a movie. Too bad I didn't know about it. Joe called me today."

"That's not surprising."

"Are you sure you're okay? What about food?"

"Don't worry. I've got plenty."

"But you can't stay there forever. Dick says ... "

"I'm staying. There's not a thing anyone can do about it. What does Dick say?"

"For me not to talk to reporters."

"Does *he* think I'm nuts too?"

There was a moment's silence. Then, "I'm so worried about you, Jake. What if they *do* something?"

"Do what?"

"They could shoot you."

"Don't be silly. I'll be all right. I'll be fine."

"I'm going to watch the news from now on. In case you're on."

"I won't be. They've already tried to interview me and I refused. But I expect they'll have something about the whole thing on again."

"I'll watch anyway. Joe's really upset."

"I know he is. He called me last night."

"He's worried too."

"Sure. Listen, this is costing you a fortune."

He wasn't on the news. He turned the TV on after supper, half-listening to the programs while he read a Buckler novel. But there was nothing. He waited for that lift in Knowlton Nash's voice at the end, imagined him saying: *and for those of you who are wondering about Jake Garson on his expropriated farm in Nova Scotia, well, he's still there.* And then the next night they might move him ahead to be part of the major news. And then they'd have interviews with politicians. Maybe a politician himself would actually come knocking at his door.

But there was nothing.

And Lexy hadn't called either.

The girl was back the next day. This time she did not knock on the door; she knocked on the window and smiled at him as if he were a true friend.

"I've brought your mail," she said, holding up a bundle. "I thought you might want it."

He did want it; he'd been afraid to go out at night to get it. When he did not answer, she said, brightly, like a schoolgirl, "I'll just leave it on the doorstep then. You can wait till I'm gone to pick it up. Can I talk to you today?"

"No."

"Do you have anything at all to say? Is there anything I can get you?"

Tobacco, he thought. But he shook his head: no.

He was glad she had brought his mail. He felt sorry for her. He didn't like to mess up her assignment.

"I'm sorry," he said

He was surprised that she only nodded and went away. He went to the front-room window. By the time he got there, her car was already leaving.

When he was sure that the car was really gone, he opened the back door quickly. How cold the air was! He looked around furtively and then scooped up his mail. So much of it! There were the newspapers, neatly tied together with white string. Perhaps the girl had done it. An oil bill, a bank statement. A form letter to all bus drivers, setting out the Christmas holiday schedule. This must have been in his box since the day he locked the house up. A letter from a parent complaining that he did not take the bus down their lane. *I don't think it's rite Mr. Grason that the littl ones should have to walke so long a ways.* There was also a letter from Myrna suggesting that he come and stay with them once the land thing was settled. Obviously it had been written before she'd heard what he'd done. A postcard from Lexy, who was in Mexico. That was why he hadn't heard from her. Another postcard postmarked Moncton, showing a puppy and a kitten in a basket. On the back was written, "We'll burn your house down, you fool."

He tacked this one on the cupboard.

He was on the news after all. They showed the house and then, as he watched, he saw the door open, saw himself look around furtively, saw himself bend to pick up the mail. She had tricked him, the bitch. It seemed to him that he looked dazed and frightened on the television. And also very clean-cut. He wished he had grown a beard.

Several local people were interviewed then. The town librarian mentioned his poems, but said that they had none of his work in the town library. Then came a young woman whom he did not know, but he supposed she must be an import, one of those people from the States who were buying up farms. "We're very proud of Mr. Garson," she said. Old Red Fisher, town character, said from between toothless gums, "Well, now, I guess it's his land."

He was part of the main news.

There was no phone call from Joe but Myrna called to say that she had watched him. She had all her friends watching too.

He awoke from a dream of swimming in the river, to the sound of voices. They were yelling his name. "Garson, Garson, Garson!"

He looked out the bedroom window cautiously.

Kids. Maybe twenty of them. Some of them carried placards. "We're with you, Jake." "Down With Government Meddling." Boys and girls. They had come in two vans. They had their faces raised to his windows, expectantly.

A thought crossed his mind: *is this because of the poems?*

Nevertheless he opened his curtains and waved. They cheered. Should he ask them in? He couldn't. If he asked them in he would have to feed them and food was rationed.

He did not quite know what to do about them and so he closed his curtains. He decided for a start not to shave. He took his time with breakfast, frying his one egg, squeezing an orange. (He had bags of Tang for when the oranges were gone.) He could hear them outside, calling for him.

What if they intended to stay? They would pitch tents; they would have bonfires at night and sing. It would be like a party. At the same time, their noise, he thought, would disturb the clarity of his thinking.

He went to the front of the house and opened a window.

"I'm still here," he called.

"We're with you!" they yelled back.

"Thank you."

"We'll picket Government House! Down with government controls!" A cheer, in unison.

He gave a dignified but friendly wave of his arm and closed the window. This seemed to satisfy them. He watched from behind closed curtains. They were setting up a tent. One boy was passing beer out from the back of a van. A girl reached into the van and produced a guitar.

The girl was back after lunch. He had been watching the kids, and he saw her drive up. This time she came in a van. TV cameras to film his supporters, he assumed.

He went to stand by the kitchen window.

She smiled her bright smile, indicating the pile of mail.

"You tricked me," he said.

"People are interested in you, Mr. Garson. There's been quite a reaction to your situation. What do you think of the support you're getting?"

He shrugged. Was this an interview?

"How long do you think you can hold out here?"

"I will stay forever," he said.

"Forever's a long time."

"So I'll stay. Till hell freezes over."

Good. This was what she wanted to hear.

What if he asked her in? He would make tea. She would be sympathetic.

"If you would only talk ... "

But he shook his head.

"Why do you want to hold on to this land?"

He ignored her and went into the front room. Presently he saw that she was holding a mike up to some of the kids.

He couldn't think. He wandered aimlessly around the house, peering out now and then at the kids. Some of the locals were there too, but they kept apart from the kids. Ernie, the bootlegger, arrived with a case of wine; money changed hands. The RCMP came, looked around, left. Several kids were reading what looked like comic books. Their signs were leaning against the vans. Later when he looked, they were cooking on a Coleman stove: hot dogs and beans. From a side window he saw a couple embracing in the hollow by the barn.

A man knocked at the door, the front door this time. He looked to Jake like a reporter. Jake ignored him. It occurred to him that the girl must have been a country girl, to have come to the back door the way she did. A country girl with dreams of making it big on TV, a girl with proud parents who watched the news nightly on TV.

She seemed like a nice girl.

But he would not talk to her. Because ... because ... he knew that everything depended on maintaining a certain mystery. If he talked, everything would change.

There they were, the kids, on *The National*. Several of them were interviewed. They all said the same thing: that Jacob Garson was a hero, a man brave enough to stand up for his freedom. And that they were behind him.

Jacob, not Jake.

And there was Joe. In his office.

"What kind of man is your brother?" he was asked.

"A complicated person. The family intellectual, you might say. He always was a loner, even as a kid. We're all very proud of him."

"Would you do the same thing?"

Joe hesitated. "In the same situation, I suppose I might," he said finally. And then, his voice gaining strength, "It's just not right, the way the government meddles in people's lives."

"Do you think he'll be successful?"

"Knowing my brother, I'd say he stands a pretty good chance."

"What does that land mean to you?"

"I was born on that land," Joe said. "And before me, my father and my grandfather. It's been in the family 180 years. My roots are there. Losing it would be like losing a part of myself."

This time, Jake called Joe.

"Saw you on TV tonight."

"I'm just trying to help," Joe said. "How did I sound?"

Jake had been prepared to say, "Like a Dale Carnegie man." But he didn't. "All right, I guess."

"I'm getting to be pretty popular," Joe said. "I had ten calls today, people wanting to know if we were related. I'm telling you, people think you're really something."

There were lots of letters this time. Someone had added to the pile left by the TV girl. "Glad to see you're standing up for your rights," he read. "We had the same thing happen to us, but we didn't have your courage. Good luck." "Your land could be enjoyed by all, you selfish son of a bitch." "Regards from the Browns." A letter from a national magazine asking for an exclusive interview. A long, tearful letter from Myrna about how good life was back home. She wanted to go on TV herself but Dick wouldn't let her. Someone sent him a $2 bill. Someone wrote that they'd saved his poems and could they please have his autograph.

A kid asked for water. He told him to use the well.
    Each night they had a sing-song.
    Nothing from the government.
    He counted the cans of soup and stew and spaghetti in the cellar.
    There was nothing about him on *The National*.
    He decided to take the old grandfather clock apart and fix it.
    His beard was growing.
    He wondered if it would be different if he had a wife and children. They'd probably send in food and milk, like they did in hostage cases.
    He saw the trucks going down the road. Construction was starting, even though it would surely snow soon.
    Anyway, he was still here.

The kids were gone. One afternoon they just packed up and left. The water tasted funny. He wondered if they had accidentally thrown something into the well. He found that he missed them, despite their noise. He wished that the TV girl would come back. One night he saw her on *The National*, interviewing strikers. Her hair was blowing in the wind and she looked cold but she was smiling.
    The mail was collecting in the mailbox again.
    Why hadn't Myrna called? Because the phone was dead, that was why. Probably the notice was in the mailbox too.
    And then the power was shut off and he had to use the oil lamps and fill the old wood stove with wood. He missed the television.
    If the TV girl came back, he thought, he would ask her in. She would hang her coat and scarf on the back of a chair, and he would make tea and she would sit with her cold, red hands pressed against her cheeks, her elbows on the table. They would talk. He would tell her his ideas about land, about government, about family. She wouldn't have a tape recorder going either. He imagined her just driving up some Sunday afternoon, on her own time, to see how he was doing. Maybe she'd tell him a little bit about herself, like how she was going with this guy who wanted to marry her but she wanted a career too and he wanted children, and anyway she did not

know if she really loved him although she thought so. She'd say that she admired him, Jake. Maybe she'd even be attracted to a man like him, a man who was a bit different, with a bit of mystery about him.

He found himself missing the land. All the leaves were gone now. The trees were fragile grey wisps against a snow-promising sky. In the woods the air would be cold and the leaves underfoot would crunch as he walked. At this time of year you could hear the ocean from the woods, even though it was more than half a mile away.

He could hear the construction crews down the road.

One Friday, it snowed. The trucks did not come back on Monday morning. Maybe they were calling a halt to everything until spring.

But where was everyone else?

Had they all forgotten about him?

He decided to go for a walk.

The world was bright and beautiful and dazzling. He took deep breaths of air and became dizzy. The world expanded around him, grew in front of his eyes. His head cleared and he saw a rabbit scamper away. He saw deer tracks, and what he thought were moose prints. His woods. His land. And his the only human tracks marking the snow.

This would be an appropriate day for them to come. Surely they were watching. They would seize the house while he was out of it. When he turned to go back to the house, he half expected that he would find the sheriff there, and the police, and men in dark overcoats who would be carrying official documents. He would sneak back in by the old side door to the summer kitchen and he would lock the door again. What could they do then?

But there was no-one there. There was grey smoke from the chimney curling into the white sky. There were no new footprints.

Taking a chance, he walked across the road to the mailbox, which appeared to be empty. But when he checked, there was a card in it. It was a note to call at the post office for a parcel. Had they bundled his mail up?

As he crossed the road back to his house, he saw that the note on his door was gone. He would have to make another. He did this, not taking off his wet boots to go into the kitchen. He wrote: *I'm still here*. On impulse, he added: *Can you see me?* He wrote it on cardboard and nailed it to the front door.

As he did this, he wondered how long it would be before anyone came by to see it. He wondered if some decision had been made of which he was not aware.

He took a look around at the skies and the bare branches of late autumn and then he went back into his house and closed the door. And then he locked it behind him.

Author's Commentary

About a dozen years ago, I looked out of my kitchen window and saw a bear routing in the garbage. The "bear" raised its head and turned out to be an old woman in a long black coat. For a moment, we looked at each other. I believe my emotion was fright. Then the old woman left, but not before giving the garbage one final poke. I had never seen the woman before and I have never seen her since. I do not know her name. I know nothing about her.

But she's still in my mind. I've been thinking about her. Perhaps I will do a short story about her sometime. I think I'll have her looking through garbage bins for bones for her dog. Obviously, she does not care what anyone thinks. She'll live in a shack somewhere. I could make her into a sad, sentimental, lonely old woman, but I don't think so. The person who is growing in my mind is tough, humourous, philosophical. Still, she's not completely formed. She has not fully become a person, a person of my creation, a person whose actions are determined by who and what she is. The moment has not yet come when the idea can escape from my mind onto paper.

I write in my head. All the time. A funny hat worn by a person before me at the check-out, a girl trying on cheap lime green earrings at the dime store, a gesture by a man on a bus: glimpses into lives revealed. Unlike the novel, the short story gives only a brief (but telling) look into a life. It is like driving along the highway and seeing a family beside their home. You will never see the people again but perhaps you will have noticed something which will have given you a glimpse into their lives. A glimpse translated by *you*, seen through *your* eyes.

A short story does not have to give answers. Sometimes I think it asks questions. But still, it tells you something.

In any case, writing a short story is a joy, especially when the ideas in my head are ready to be put down on paper. It is then that I find out whether or not the story "works." There is one reminder I keep in mind — Chekhov's statement that if there is a gun hanging on a wall in a short story, someone must sooner or later shoot that gun. Being brief and concise is a skill I am still learning.

Are there *rules* though? I don't know.

Veronica Ross (1946 —   )

Born in Germany, Veronica Ross came to Canada at an early age and grew up in Montreal and Toronto. She has had her work published in magazines in both Canada and the United States, winning the Benson and Hedges Magazine Writing Award in 1977 for "Where are you Susannah Brown?", which appeared in *Axiom*, and the Periodical Distributors of Canada Award for the story "Whistling", which was printed in *Atlantic Insight*. Her collection of stories, *Good-bye Summer*, appeared in 1980. She lives in Liverpool, Nova Scotia.

Acknowledgements

"The Wedding Gift" by Thomas Raddall: reprinted by permission of the author.

"What Language Do Bears Speak?" by Roch Carrier, from *The Hockey Sweater and Other Stories*, translated by Sheila Fischman (Toronto: House of Anansi Press, 1979).

"The Loons" by Margaret Laurence, from *A Bird in the House* by Margaret Laurence, used by permission of The Canadian Publishers, McClelland and Stewart Limited, Toronto.

"Dead to the World" by H.A. Hargreaves, reprinted by permission of the author and Peter Martin Associates Ltd., copyright © H.A. Hargreaves 1976.

"Skald" by W.D. Valgardson is reprinted from *Red Dust* by permission of Oberon Press.

"The First Born Son" by Ernest Buckler from *The Rebellion of Young David* by Ernest Buckler, used by permission of The Canadian Publishers, McClelland and Stewart Limited, Toronto.

"Spring" by Antonine Maillet from *La Sagouine* by Antonine Maillet, reprinted by permission of Les Editions Lemeac, Montreal. Translation by Luis de Céspedes.

"The Butterfly Ward" by Margaret Gibson is reprinted from *The Butterfly Ward* by permission of Oberon Press.

"Forgiveness in Families" by Alice Munro: from *Something I've Been Meaning to Tell You* © Alice Munro, 1974, reprinted by kind permission of the author.

"Akua Nuten" by Yves Theriault from *Stories of the Bomb* by Yves Theriault, by permission of the author. Translation by Howard Roiter.

"The Lost Salt Gift of Blood" by Alistair MacLeod, from *The Lost Salt Gift of Blood* by Alistair MacLeod, used by permission of The Canadian Publishers, McClelland and Stewart Limited, Toronto.

"On Wings of Tongue" by Adele Wiseman: reprinted by permission of the author.

"The Roller Rink" by Andreas Scroeder. From the short story collection *The Late Man & Other Fictions* by Andreas Schroeder, Sono Nis Press, 1972.

"One's a Heifer" by Sinclair Ross from *The Lamp at Noon* by Sinclair Ross, used by permission of The Canadian Publishers, McClelland and Stewart Limited, Toronto.

"I'm Still Here" by Veronica Ross is reprinted from *Goodbye Summer* by permission of Oberon Press.

Author's Commentary by Margaret Laurence from Commentary by Margaret Laurence from *Sixteen By Twelve* edited by John Metcalf. Reprinted by permission of McGraw-Hill Ryerson Limited.

Author's Commentary by Alice Munro excerpted from commentary by Alice Munro from *Eleven Canadian Novelists* ed. Graeme Gibson (Toronto: House of Anansi Press, 1973).

206

Author's Commentary by Sinclair Ross is excerpted from *Canadian Writers on Tape*, produced by Earle Toppings for The Ontario Institute for Studies in Education Press.

Picture Acknowledgements

Page 16   Clarence Gagnon, 1881-1942
François in the Blizzard, 1928-1933
Gouache
18.7 x 21.6 cm
The McMichael Canadian Collection,
Gift of Colonel R.S. McLaughlin

Page 29   William Kurelek, *Grizzly Sliding Down Glacier*, 1974
Reproduced from *Kurelek's Canada* by William Kurelek with permission by
The Pagurian Corporation Limited, Toronto, Canada.

Page 37   Yvonne McKague Housser, 1898-
Margeurite Pilot of Deep River (Girl with Mulleins), c. 1932
Oil on canvas
76.2 x 61.0 cm
The McMichael Canadian Collection,
Anonymous donor

Page 46   Christopher Pratt, *Exit*, 1978-79,
oil on board, 131.8 x 81.28 cm,
(Polysar Collection) Photograph courtesy Mira Godard Gallery, Toronto and
Calgary.

Page 60   D.P. Brown, *Young Canadian*, 1968,
egg tempera on panel, 20,94 x 40.6 cm,
Collection: Dr. H.M. Jolley

Page 79   Thoreau MacDonald, *Hawk at Evening*, 1937,
oil on canvas, 51.1 x 76.5 cm,
Art Gallery of Hamilton, Gift of William Colgate Esq., 1954, Cat. No. 54.87.1

Page 89   André-Charles Bieler, *Les Patates, Argentenay*, 1929,
oil on canvas, 66.0 x 86.4 cm,
Art Gallery of Hamilton, Gift of Mr. and Mrs. Roger Inglis, 1976, Cat. No.
77-4

Page 100   Claude Breeze, *Head #5*, 1965,
ink, 45.7 x 30.5 cm,
Collection: Miss Amy Smith

Page 109   David Alexander Colville, *Family and Rainstorm*, 1955,
tempera on board, 57.1 x 74.9 cm,
The National Gallery of Canada, Ottawa

Page 120   John Redbird, *Old Woman*, c. 1971
Reproduced from *Red on White, The Biography of Duke Redbird* by Marty
Dunn (Toronto: New Press, 1971).

Page 144   David Blackwood, *The Flora F. Nickerson Coming Home From The Labrador*, 1979, etching, 27.9 x 40.6 cm

Page 150   Esther Warkov, *Family Reunion*, c. 1965,
pencil, 58.4 x 73.7 cm,
Mr. David P. Silcox, Toronto

Page 169   Ivan Eyre, *Vertigo*, 1971,
acrylic and oil on canvas, 182.9 x 149.9 cm,
The Canada Council Art Bank,

Page 180   William Kurelek, *Manitoba Barn*,
sepia ink, 54.6 x 33 cm,
Courtesy the Isaacs Gallery, Toronto, Collection: Mr. and Mrs. Christopher Ondaatje

Page 192   Tom Forrestal, *May's Verandah*,
watercolour, 50.8 x 38.1 cm,
Collection: Mr. James Stacey